DEAD MAN RIDING

Young Nell Bray is doing her best to live up to the standards of conduct demanded of an Oxford woman student in 1900. A summer reading party in the company of male undergraduates is frowned upon, but given the opportunity of fresh air and Greek philosophy in the Lake District, she can't refuse. She and her friends discover a house under siege and are met by a shotgun blast from their host. Events take an even more desperate turn when a silver stallion gallops out of the mist with a dead man on his back...

DEAD MAN RIDING

DEAD MAN RIDING

by

Gillian Linscott

Magna Large Print Books
Long Preston, North Yorkshire,
BD23 4ND, England.

British Library Cataloguing in Publication Data.

Linscott, Gillian
    Dead man riding.

        A catalogue record of this book is
        available from the British Library

        ISBN   0-7505-2182-1

First published in Great Britain by Virago in 2002

Published in Large Print 2004 by arrangement with
Time Warner Books UK

Magna Large Print is an imprint of Library Magna Books Ltd.

Printed and bound in Great Britain by
T.J. (International) Ltd., Cornwall, PL28 8RW

Introduction

Other women tend to be asked about their first kiss. In my case it's my first murder. As it happened, kissing came into it as well but then that was inevitable because we were young, confident and pleased with ourselves. Younger in some ways than we had any right to be – considering that we were mostly in our twenties after all. Pleased with ourselves to an extent that, looking back, seems both enviable and infuriating because we were so sure that the world was waiting just for us with our brains, education and advanced opinions to keep it turning. Confident – in that first summer of the twentieth century and what proved to be the last summer of Queen Victoria's reign – that as the world turned our lives and most other things would go on getting better and better. It was that confidence that took a blow early one morning in July in a river meadow to the north of Skiddaw when a horse named Sid came galloping out of the mist with a dead man on his back.

Chapter One

I was in paradise and it was annoying me. The sky was a deep navy blue with the first stars coming out at the end of a long hot day. The scent of gently crushed grass and lake water was all around us, with the occasional waft from the honeysuckle and roses winding themselves lovingly up the college walls. There were two swans on the lake, one with its head tucked under its wing, the other with its head in the water and neck bent into a hoop. A stage had been built on the lawn at the lake edge surrounded by candle lamps and big pale moths were circling round. Altogether Oxford in June was much as I'd dreamed it would be in damp rooms of German cities on foggy November days or wandering on my own around scorching Spanish streets at siesta time. I only wished it would be a little less perfect so that I didn't feel guilty for not appreciating it enough.

There was nothing to complain about in the human landscape either. Two of the best friends I'd made since coming back to England were sitting on the grass beside me, Imogen with her head bent and her fair hair flopping forward, Midge with her hat off and her brown hair untidy as usual, laughing so that her eyes screwed up and the freckles met over the bridge of her nose. She was laughing at something one of the men had just said, Alan probably because he was doing most of the talking. He was sitting cross-legged on the other side of Imogen, his right knee in its grey silk stocking almost touching her dress, no more than a hand's breadth between them. He was at least as easy to look at as everything else in the college garden, only if there was a hint of imperfection it was that the stockings were wrinkling round his calves. He was conscious of that and every now and then he'd smooth them with both hands, up from the ankle then slowly round the knee. I noticed that Imogen's eyes – hidden from him by the screen of her hair – were following the movement until she saw me watching too, blushed and looked away. A waste, because Alan looked good in Elizabethan costume. His hair was only a few shades darker than Imogen's own primrose-pale swathes and his face that seemed too pale and fine-boned by day was sharp and intelligent in the half-light. His friend Kit sitting alongside him was less convincing as a Renaissance grandee. It wasn't a period that suited his small, wiry stature and you could more easily have imagined him as one of Robin Hood's band swinging down from trees or running through the forest. He was a better actor than Alan, especially in comedy, but for this production was condemned to walk on as an attendant lord and make do with what was left in the college's theatrical wardrobe when the leading actors had finished with it. Pink stockings, clumsily darned, sagged round his calves and the black velvet doublet was meant for broader shoulders. In spite of that, he was more to my taste, considered from a purely aesthetic point of view, than the conventionally handsome Alan. Kit had dark eyes and a way of looking at people very directly then looking away, as if his stare might take from them more than they wanted to give. He had a wicked sense of humour, wrote good poetry and played lawn tennis like an avenging demon. We'd been partners once in carefully chaperoned mixed doubles and beat the opposition so thoroughly that nobody would take us on after that. But if I'd hoped – and perhaps I had hoped a little – that the acquaintance might ripen off the tennis court, I'd been disappointed. Perhaps height had something to do with it. I stand at five foot seven in my tennis shoes so overtopped him by a couple of inches and men are sensitive about these things. Alan and Kit had been friends since their schooldays, both went to the same college to read classics and were usually together. They were both competitive with other people but so far not with each other. Alan was hard-working and probably heading for a respectable second-class degree while Kit was brilliant and almost certainly destined for a first.

The five of us had been sitting there on the grass and talking all the long interval while the stage was being prepared for the torchlight masque in the last act of *Love's Labours Lost*. We'd been discussing whether it was Shakespeare's best comedy, general verdict going against. From all around us the murmuring voices of other groups like ours rose gently upwards and mingled with the just-audible screeches of swallows taking their last looping flights of the day, out over the lake and back over the lawn. Perfect surroundings, company of friends, intelligent conversation – what more could I possibly want? The annoying thing was, I didn't know.

I can see now that in that first summer of the twentieth century I was coming, belatedly, to the stage where the endless possibilities of being young narrowed down to the question of what you intend to do with your life. It wasn't entirely my fault that I hadn't got there until the age of twenty-three. My parents had been whole-heartedly in favour of education for women. In fact, they'd been in the vanguard of almost every advanced

14

movement in the last two or three decades of the nineteenth century. Whatever you cared to name – socialism, Ibsenism, mixed bathing or rational dress reform – if it annoyed the majority we were in favour of it. So it had been taken for granted that I'd go up to Oxford when I was eighteen and study for a career.

What went wrong was that my father, a doctor, died in a diphtheria epidemic when I was seventeen and my mother took to travelling. She said it was because living was cheaper on the Continent and since my father had never been attracted to rich patients we had to be careful with money. But the truth was, it was the only way she could cope with missing my father. As soon as the novelty of a place wore off her sense of loss would come back, sharp as ever, so for three years we zigzagged across and up and down Europe in search of the place where the food and the beds were clean, cheap and wholesome and there wasn't a space at the table where my father should have been sitting. In the end, the nearest thing we found to it was in Athens, where my mother met a German professor of archaeology. They did their courting around the Acropolis, married in a Protestant church and set up home in a tent on a site he was excavating.

I wished them joy with all my heart and went back to England to take up the place at

Somerville College that I'd wanted so much through all our wanderings. That had been almost two years ago and things had gone well enough. I'd made friends, managed to smooth the idiomatic French, German and Italian I'd picked up on our travels into something more polished and academic. But my disorderly life had left me with a restlessness that wouldn't go away and nights like this made it worse, because it seemed like ingratitude.

'Oh, you're so lucky.'

That long sigh from Imogen was directed not at me, who deserved it, but at the two men. She now had Alan's plumed hat in her lap. One of the ostrich feathers had got bent and she was trying to straighten it, running her long fingers through the clinging fronds. Both Alan and Kit seemed mesmerised by it.

'Aren't they lucky, Nell?'

'Why?'

'They're going to spend the long vac scholar-gypsying in the Lake District.'

Midge said, more prosaically, 'They're getting up a reading party in July. Healthy open-air life, reading ancient Greek and discussing philosophy.'

Midge is a mathematician, so sceptical. Kit gave her a long look, not liking being teased.

'Not philosophy the way the examiners

mean it. We want to step back from the world for a while and discuss what's wrong with it and what we should be doing about it.'

'Will you be like the men in *Love's Labours Lost?*' Imogen asked. 'You'll swear to eat only one meal a day and sleep three hours a night and have nothing to do with women.'

'Not necessarily,' Alan said. His voice sounded strained. Perhaps it was from having to pitch his lines in the first act against the quacking of mallards on the lake.

'Why not necessarily?'

'We thought you might like to come with us.'

There was a sudden silence among our little group. Imogen stopped stroking the feather.

'We being...?'

'You and Nell and Midge and anybody else you like.'

He tried hard to make it sound light, but he knew he'd probably gone too far. The fact was that even sitting here in the twilight and talking we were at or beyond the outer limits of what our colleges would regard as acceptable behaviour between male and female students. The limits weren't often stretched as far as this because, more than twenty years after women students had first appeared at Oxford, most undergraduates still chose to regard us as freaks of nature that might go away if ignored. The fact that Alan and Kit were sitting here on the grass with us on friendly terms, as if we were something normal and acceptable like other men's sisters, was explained by two things. The first was that Alan and Kit took a pride in being advanced men in politics and social matters, a cut above the mindless sportsmen and natural conservatives who made up the majority of the student population. The second thing was Imogen's beauty. It was a fact of Oxford life that couldn't be ignored even by the most crass of the sporting hearties who pretended that women students were all frights and blue stockings. Those two things might save Alan and Kit from the heavy-footed jokes of their colleagues but they wouldn't have helped us if our college authorities had seen us. Behaviour that was just about acceptable for men would, on our part, give rise to gossip, provide ammunition for people who argued that women at university would only cause trouble and set back the cause of women's education for generations. We'd only been allowed out unchaperoned for the play on the grounds that it was Shakespeare, therefore educational, and I being two years older than the others was a responsible person. We'd been told to be back by ten. Since it was past nine already and the play was running late, that would mean missing most of the last act. I could see that Midge was already fidgeting. In the circumstances, Alan's modest proposal that we should join their reading party was like suggesting a little afternoon outing to storm the Bastille.

'We couldn't,' Midge said.

'Give one logical reason why not.'

Imogen said, 'They'd throw us out, that's why not.'

'Your college? They needn't know.'

'Oh, so we start deceiving people, do we?'

I was pleased with Imogen for being so sharp with Alan. She'd shown signs recently of being altogether too impressed by him – especially since he'd sent her a rather laboured sonnet cycle tucked in a small basket of roses. I worried sometimes that rivalry over Imogen might threaten Alan and Kit's long friendship. As far as Midge and I could tell, Alan was the favoured one but she hadn't taken us into her confidence and it was hard to be sure because there weren't many opportunities for men and women to meet. No question, of course, of Imogen being alone with either of them. Safety in numbers was the motto of various college authorities as far as they tolerated any social contact at all between the sexes. But at any of the occasions where we were allowed to mix, chatting for a few minutes on the pavement after lectures or at plays or concerts like this, you'd usually find Imogen with Kit on one side and Alan on the other, the two men staring at her or each other with that little crackle of electricity in the air that means storms ahead. We'd got through to the last week of Trinity term with no thunder and lightning but I could tell from the way that Kit was glancing from Alan's face to Imogen's and back that this business of the reading party mattered to him as well.

Before Alan could answer, the toe of a brown brogue nudged his grey silk knee and a voice above our heads said, 'You're wanted, both of you.'

Unlike the other two Nathan was in modern dress, in his case flannel trousers that looked crumpled and grass-stained even in the half-light, a tweed jacket with wood shavings clinging to it, a soft collar and a tie worn in a loose loop with a tight knot so that it looked more like a noose. Even by student standards he was not a fussy dresser. He was tall, plump and bear-like. Unfashionably, he wore sideburns and a bushy beard, ginger brown in colour, so that his round face was framed in a mass of hair that seemed a perpetual fire risk in view of his fondness for pipe smoking. He was short-sighted and his thick-lensed glasses were often smeared with paint, as now. His excuse for being even more untidy this evening was that he was scene builder and property master for the play. Nathan had been baptised Nathaniel, but nobody used the name, any more than they expected Midge to answer to Millicent. If there hadn't been storms between Kit and Alan, Nathan was probably the reason, the best-tempered one of their trio, less brilliant than Kit and not as serious-minded as Alan with a love of practical jokes and conjuring tricks. Nathan would go to endless lengths to get a friend out of trouble – then more lengths to climb into his room and sew his pyjama legs together or serve him sausages that squeaked when he dug a fork into them. He'd have rather gone to art college than Oxford but his father had insisted and he was studying theology from – as he put it – a safe distance. The distance was so safe that in two years he claimed not to have learned the way to the lecture halls and the man assigned to be his tutor had bumped into him in The High without recognising him. By his own account the only reason he'd survived so far was that theology dons were the laziest creatures this side of the South Seas and it would have been too much trouble to send him down. That might have been true, or it might simply have been that everybody liked Nathan. Alan twitched his knee away.

'Already?'

'If you don't get a move on it will be pitch-dark before we get to the Masque of the

Worthies and all my lovely work will be wasted.'

Kit was on his feet already, in one supple movement. Alan followed more slowly and Imogen gave him back his plumed hat. The two of them flourished the hats at arms' length then held them over their hearts in a courtly bow to all of us. Imogen watched as they walked away.

'May I join you, ladies?'

We nodded and Nathan sat down on the flattened grass where the other two had been. Midge asked him, 'Are you going on this reading party with them?'

'Wouldn't miss it for the world. I've never met a centaur in the flesh before.'

Imogen, ignoring his nonsense, said, 'He invited us to join them.' I was surprised she'd bothered to mention it.

'Jolly good idea. We can swim in the river and help with the haymaking and have all kinds of larks.'

I pointed out that haymaking would be over by the time they got there but nobody took any notice. Midge was still trying to make sense of his earlier remark.

'Do they have centaurs in Cumberland, then?'

'Not sure about the plural. As far as I know, Alan's uncle is the only one.'

'Alan's uncle?'

'Great uncle, I think. Old as the hills and

as mad as King Lear.'

'And half horse?'

'At least half, from what Alan says. He's got this stud of Arabians. Only thing he cares about. The story Alan heard from his father was that the old boy kicked around the world a lot when he was younger, native wars, piracy on the high seas and goodness knows what. Anyway, at some point he fetches up in the desert, saves the life of some sheik or other high-up and gets presented with a stallion and two mares as a reward. So he ships them back to Southampton and sets up a stud in Hampshire.'

'I thought you were going to the Lake District?'

'Hampshire was about twenty years ago. The Centaur's a migratory beast. Apparently he keeps quarrelling with his neighbours and having to pack up his saddlebags and move on because he's made the place too hot for himself. He's used up most of England now and is within sight of the Scottish border. It's the very last bit of the Lake District he's in, overlooking the Solway Firth.'

'I know where you mean. It's the view when you're looking north from the top of Skiddaw.'

They all looked at me, wondering why I thought that added to the story, and of course it didn't. The fact was I loved the Lake District but hadn't dared set foot in it since I'd come back to England. It was where we'd spent family holidays when my father could tear himself away from whatever city he'd been practising and politicking in at the time. My brother Stuart and I had walked for miles with him over the fells, rowed on Ullswater, learned to climb on the crags at Dungeon Ghyll. Suddenly and sharply, I wanted to be back there on Skiddaw's slatey summit looking out over the Solway to the Scottish hills.

'Did his wife and family migrate with him?' Imogen asked.

'Neither chick nor child. He travels light, does Uncle Centaur. Apart from his mares and stallions, of course.'

Midge said, 'I think you're making this up.'

'Come with us then and see.'

'Perhaps we will.' From Midge of all people. She was teasing him of course.

'You'll come, won't you Nell? You're an adventuress.'

'Nathan.' Midge spluttered with laughter and slapped him lightly on the back of his hand. 'Apologise to Nell. Adventuress means something entirely different.'

'Does it? I'm sorry. All I meant was Nell's been all over the shop and probably done all kinds of things–'

'That's even worse.'

Again, Imogen ignored their nonsense.

She seemed to be following some line of her own.

'I suppose he has a housekeeper or somebody?'

'Suppose so.'

'And he's invited you all?'

'To be honest, he's only actually invited Alan, but all we need is a barn or something for a roof over our heads, hay to sleep on and ale and bread and cheese from the local inn. So Alan's written to ask if he can bring a friend or two.'

'That's you and Kit?'

'Yes, plus Michael Meredith probably.'

'What?' Imogen sat bolt upright. 'Mr Meredith coming with you. But he's a *don*.'

'He's Alan's and Kit's tutor.'

'But I thought he–'

'All right, not officially any more but they still see him. Kit says he's the only man in the university who makes sense of philosophy.'

Imogen said nothing. I sensed that for a moment or two, under the influence of the stars and the swans and the men dressed as Spanish grandees, she'd been playing with the idea of accepting the invitation, the way you do play with things when they're safely impossible. Then the involvement of Michael Meredith had made the thing so far out of the question that she wasn't going to think about it any more. In any case, at that point the play started again.

Candlelit figures came and went across the platform by the lake, drifting into the light and out of it as what they were saying to each other wandered in and out of hearing. '...*which he would call abbominable. It insinuateth me of insanie...*' Time to think of other things like what I was going to do in the long vac. My new stepfather had invited me to join them in Athens and probably meant it but I couldn't afford the fare, even third class. If he'd guessed that he'd probably have paid it for me but though I liked him I didn't want to put myself under any obligation. Beside me, Midge was fidgeting again. When I looked her way she mouthed, 'What time is it?' I looked at my watch. Ten to ten. She started getting up.

'We'll have to run.'

We all motioned to her to sit down. There were still streaks of light in the sky and fluttering home like scared schoolgirls was more than Imogen and I would stand. '...*To congratulate the Princess at her pavilion, in the posteriors of the day; which the rude multitude call the afternoon...*'

I wondered if Michael Meredith really intended to join their reading party. With most dons the question wouldn't need asking because you couldn't imagine them sleeping in barns and living on bread and cheese. Meredith was different. For one

26

thing, he wasn't so very much older than we were, probably under thirty. For another, he was quite capable of doing it just to annoy the university authorities. In the small world of Oxford Meredith was famous or, more accurately, notorious. He was such a brilliant classicist that his college had very little choice except to award him a fellowship. Once installed – and college fellows are notoriously difficult to shift – he'd set about trampling under foot most of the conventions that had kept Oxford snug for the past six hundred years or so. Stories grew round him. For instance, it was a condition of his fellowship that he should read the lesson in chapel once a term, in Latin naturally. He was an agnostic so, according to legend, simply slipped a copy of Apulius's *The Golden Ass* inside the Bible and read a passage about Cupid and Psyche without any of the drowsy congregation noticing. He complained in public about the stupidity of some of the pupils who came to him from the public schools and said he could take a boy at random from any board school in the country and make a better classicist out of him. He proved it, rumour said, by secretly coaching the son of his college scout and entering him for Moderations under an assumed name, with the result that he came out second from top on the list. (His opponents denied the story.

His supporters, mostly undergraduates, said of course the authorities had hushed it up.) There was no telling whether it was one of his real or legendary offences that had led to his removal as Alan's and Kit's tutor but it was no surprise. Though the college could take away his tutorial pupils it couldn't stop him lecturing on philosophy, either as part of the official university course or un-officially to anybody who cared to come along, women included. Among his other eccentricities, he was a leading figure in the campaign to allow women to take degrees, just like the men. It didn't make him any more popular with the die-hard dons that his lectures were always packed out, with people standing at the back. Alan and Imogen had met when he gave up his seat to her.

'I Pompey am, Pompey surnam'd the Big...' We'd got to the masque scene now. The last of the light was gone from the sky but the platform was bright with torch flares, held on long poles by assorted courtiers and rustics. There was a cough from behind us.

'Excuse me sir, do you know where Mr Alan Beston is?'

It was a lad of about fourteen in cap, jacket and heavy boots. He was holding an envelope. Nathan pointed towards the platform where Alan was standing in his plumed hat as the King of Navarre among the courtiers.

'There's a telegram come for him. Been in his pigeon-hole all afternoon and the porter said as I was coming home this way I should look in and give it to him, in case it was urgent.'

'Thanks. I'll give it to him when he comes off.' Nathan held out his hand, but the boy kept hold of the envelope.

'The porter said I was to give it to him directly, nobody else.'

Before we could stop him he was stumping towards the platform, weaving dangerously in his thick boots among the hems of delicate summer dresses spread over the grass.

'Shouldn't worry,' Nathan said. 'They'll think it's part of the play, another messenger come with despatches.'

The play was near its end now. We were only a few minutes from the heart-stopping moment when the jokes, the romance and the rough comedy are cut off in just two lines with the brutality of an express train crashing into buffers. *The King your father – Dead, for my life! Even so; my tale is told.* The messenger of death would come in a punt across the lake. If you strained your eyes you could just see the ripples like black treacle in the torchlight where the punt was already moving.

Meanwhile the porter's boy had managed to push himself to the side of the platform.

We saw him tug at Alan's cloak and shove the envelope into his hand. Luckily the attention was on the masquers at this point, not the King's party, so he was able to thumb the envelope open and glance at the telegram. I'd picked up the opera glasses Midge had brought with her and was watching, more from amusement than anything. When Alan bent his head to read the telegram his face was shaded by his hat so it was only as he looked up that I caught his expression. It was thunderstruck. Not grief at bad news, as the princess was about to get in the play, but shock and incomprehension.

Imogen asked, 'What's up, Nell?'

But by then the dark-cloaked messenger was in sight, standing in the prow of the punt and everybody was concentrating on the play. Alan had one of the first lines to deliver after the messenger's words and Kit had to nudge him to remind him. He managed it and if other people noticed the hesitation and the shakiness in his voice they probably put it down to good acting. After all, he was supposed to be shocked.

The play ended and Midge practically dragged us away to get out before the rest of the crowd. Alan and Kit, still in costume, caught up with us. They wanted to escort us back to Somerville, but we pointed out that if anything were needed to make our delinquency more conspicuous it was being squired to a locked door by the King of Navarre and friend. Even so, Alan managed to get in a few quick words with Imogen before Midge hustled us out to the street.

'Come on. Run.'

I'd been walking fast, but I slowed down deliberately. 'No point. We're late and that's it.'

'Oh Nell, they'll have to unlock the gate for us. We'll be in such trouble.'

The feeling of rebellion that had been with me for most of the term took practical form.

'Then we'll just have to climb in over the back gate like the men do.'

'Men climbing in over our back gate?' Midge was appalled.

'Of course not. Over their own back gates into their own colleges. They've been doing it for centuries so if we want to be equal it's about time we started.'

As the three of us walked side by side up Walton Street I said to Imogen, 'Did you ask Alan what was in the telegram?'

'It was an answer from his uncle. It said he was welcome to come and bring his whole tribe with him.'

So I must have been wrong. Torchlight can be deceptive after all.

Chapter Two

At breakfast next morning I told Imogen I'd decided to go. She dropped her toast.

'Nell, there'll be such a terrible row.'

'Why? What could be more worthy than a pure and simple life discussing philosophy?'

'With a party of men?'

'I've been thinking about that.' (I hadn't been able to sleep much. When I closed my eyes I kept seeing the black messenger rippling across the water.) 'We've been talking about the kind of world we want in the twentieth century – no hypocrisy or silliness between the sexes, men and women meeting and working together on equal terms. So do we mean it or don't we?'

'Of course we do, but discussing it's one thing. Going off and risking your reputation for the sake of...'

'In other words, it's all right having theories as long as you don't do anything about them?'

'No, I don't mean that. But you don't go off and wreck your whole future just to make a debating point.'

'How would I be wrecking my future?'

'If it gets out, they might not allow you

back next term.'

'Would that be such a bad thing?'

It would at least bring to a crisis the question of what to do with my life.

'Of course it would, and you know how people would take advantage of it. Give women a chance of higher education and they throw the whole thing over chasing after men.'

'That's ridiculous. You know that's not true.'

We were getting angry. Other women were turning to look at us.

'I know it's not true about you, but it's what people will say all the same.'

'Well, if people are as stupid as that, maybe that's the best reason for doing it.'

'Just to shock them?'

'No. To refuse to give up a perfectly rational course of action because of other people's irrationality.'

Midge came towards us carrying her coffee cup, obviously intending to act as peacemaker. She was trying to hide a limp, the result of twisting her ankle jumping down from the back gate. As soon as she sat down Imogen hissed, 'Nell says she's going on their reading party.'

'That's good. So am I.'

'What!'

Imogen's one of the few people I know who can still look beautiful with her jaw dropped and her mouth wide open.

'I need somewhere to work in peace and there's precious little chance of that at home with my brothers all over the place.'

'But what will your father say?'

'I shall tell him I'm staying with friends.'

'That's lying by implication.'

Midge is one of the most honest people I know and fair minded as well. I watched her face as she thought about it.

'Then I'll tell him we're a mixed party. I don't think he'll mind.'

That was possible. Midge's father, a widower, was also a mathematician and in spite or because of that seldom seemed to know how many of his large family were in residence at any particular time.

'But the college...'

'In any case, I can say Nell's there as a chaperone.'

'Oh no you can't,' I said. 'I spent months chaperoning my own mother and I'm not going to start doing it for my friends. If you come, it's on your own responsibility, not mine.'

After all those walks trailing tactfully behind two middle-aged lovers in the cool of the Athens evenings I felt I'd already paid a lifetime's subscription to convention. Midge took it calmly.

'Come on Imogen. Admit you want to go with us. You've said your aunt wouldn't miss you.'

Imogen's father was helping the Viceroy rule India with her mother in support, so she was doomed to spend the long vac with an aunt she didn't like much in Eastbourne. The remoteness or lack of our parents was one of the things that had brought the three of us together. Imogen stared down at her plate.

'It's just not possible.'

Two weeks later, sitting in the corner seat of a railway compartment as the train hauled northwards up Shap Fell, she said it again.

'It's just not possible. I don't know why I ever said yes to it.'

Midge said, 'You didn't say yes. You just stopped saying no.'

Steam from the engine was blowing back, half hiding the green fells to our left, on the eastern flank of the Lake District. It was quite cool for early July with cloud shadows flying over the hillsides and shafts of sunlight in between picking out patches of bright green bracken or pink-green bilberry, glinting on small waterfalls. We'd closed our window against the smuts and steam because the engine was having to labour hard to pull us up the gradient, and the smell inside the compartment was of faint soot from the upholstery and ripe strawberries. But my mind was full of memories of musky bracken and moss by little hidden pools. Beyond the hills going past our window were fells I'd known the names of almost as long as I'd known anything, the long ridge of High Street, Helvellyn, Scafell Pikes and, to the northwest, my father's favourite, Great Gable. I decided that if the reading party got tedious I'd go wandering off on my own and see them all again. My walking boots were in the old knapsack in the bulging baggage net overhead, along with the battered case that held enough books for a month, including Plato's *Republic* in Ancient Greek. Learning Greek and reading Plato in the original was one of my aims for the next few weeks. Imogen, Alan and Kit could all read it easily and I was tired of being told that I couldn't understand the subtleties of Plato's arguments in translation. Two more cases, not quite as battered as mine, contained Imogen's and Midge's books.

We'd unpinned our hats and they were lying on the seats beside us. There was plenty of room to spread ourselves and our luggage because we had the whole compartment to ourselves. The four men were in the one ahead of us. That had been agreed at the start of the journey on the grounds that we couldn't be expected to stand the fug of Nathan's pipe at close quarters, but we all knew that there was more to it than that. Now that the decision had been taken we were all – women and men – a little scared.

We knew that we were being rational and blazing a trail, only anticipating the way we hoped all men and women would be able to live in the century ahead: in honesty, in companionship, in respect for each other, not confused or embittered by what Imogen had referred to blushingly one day as 'the sex question'. The sex question was another matter that would have to be dealt with and debated in its place, but that was a different place and a different time. So we were all clear about what we were doing, but when it came to it we were quite happy to put the interval of a long day's rail journey between the decision and its effect. Not that we were completely isolated from each other. We met on platforms when we changed trains and the men kept putting their heads round the compartment door to ask if we were quite comfortable and did we want anything. Alan was the most attentive. At Crewe he'd somehow got hold of a punnet of strawberries for us, and after Preston, it was lemonade in a glass-stoppered bottle. From the way he looked at Imogen you could tell he could hardly contain his wonder at having her there in the same carriage with only the compartment partition between them. He seemed nervous, untypically clumsy and dropped strawberries on Midge without even noticing. Thinking of the weeks ahead of us, I wondered whether the sex question would wait its turn to be dealt with, after 'What is the purpose of life?' and 'Why don't good men go into government?'.

After a while I felt restless from being so near the hills and not walking on them and went into the corridor to stretch my legs. There was somebody outside the men's compartment, smoking a cigarette and looking out at the scenery. When I saw it was Michael Meredith I thought I'd walk the other way. The three of us had been formally introduced to him by Alan on the platform at Oxford station. Apart from that, we'd never exchanged a word in our lives and I knew him only as a presence on the lecture platform. I was still surprised that he'd bothered to come on an undergraduate reading party and was also a little wary of his quick and mocking intelligence. But before I could turn away he smiled at me, an open smile with no visible mockery in it.

'Are you enjoying the journey, Miss Bray?'

'Very much.'

He was satisfactorily taller than I was and slim as a greyhound. Watching him on the platform when we changed trains it had struck me that he stood and moved like a gymnast, in a relaxed way but with an underlying tension, as if he might suddenly turn a back somersault. He was wearing a light grey suit and a soft-collared shirt with a floppy blue tie, unconventional but not eccentric. His clean-shaven face was dark in complexion and his black hair cut very short, curving neatly round his ears. According to Oxford gossip his mother was Jewish, born in Andalucia, 'which explains the complexion', people said. If they didn't like him – and he made enemies in academic society with the carelessness of a puppy scattering flocks of pigeons – there'd be an unspoken addition that it explained a lot of other things as well.

'Cigarette?'

He was offering me one from a silver case. I said no thank you, but was pleased he thought I was a woman unconventional enough to smoke in public.

'They tell me you're a great traveller.'

'Hardly that.'

As the train picked up speed and went down towards Penrith I told him about our wanderings, Athens and even my father's death and my mother's remarriage. It surprised me that he was easy to talk to. I'd expected sharp questions, even attack for some sloppiness of thought or phrasing. He just listened and nodded occasionally, wafting his clouds of cigarette smoke away from me.

'Don't you find Oxford a little constricting after all that?'

'It's not Oxford's fault.'

'Meaning yes.' Still not sharply, but he was smiling.

'If I'd come to Oxford when I was just out of school it would have been everything I'd hoped for. Now I can't help thinking that I'm wasting time. I shouldn't be sitting in libraries reading French classical drama. I should be out in the world doing something.'

'Such as what?'

'Doing something about injustice.'

That was deliberately putting myself in danger of being intellectually squashed. 'What is Justice?' had been the title of his popular lecture series on Plato. He raised his eyebrows. Very elegant eyebrows they were too, like the inside sweep of a bird's wing. I plunged on, like the train rushing downhill.

'Social injustice, I mean. My father worked deliberately in some of the worst slums in England because most other doctors wouldn't. Money the rich wouldn't miss could transform those places.'

'The rich are defined by their money. Would you politely request a pig to abdicate its piggy nature?'

'I might give it a smaller trough.'

He laughed. He was on holiday after all, and this wasn't a tutorial in logic.

'So what are you going to do about it?'

'I thought for a while that I might be a lawyer.' The eyebrows went up again. 'I know. I sat in at the back of lectures on Roman law for three whole terms. It cured me.'

'Possibly one of the few cases on record of

a university lecturer doing something useful.'

'Your lectures are useful. You challenge things.'

I said that because it was true, not meaning to flatter him. He took it without embarrassment so I risked another comment.

'I'm surprised you're coming with us. I'd have thought you had a lot of other things to do.'

'I've got a book to finish and Oxford smothers me sometimes, especially in July and August. I want fresh air and light-hearted company.'

'I hope we come up to scratch then.'

This time he didn't smile, just looked at me as if the remark had said more than I'd intended.

'You think there might be some failure of light-heartedness?'

'I think there might be tensions.'

'Ah.' He took a long drag on his cigarette. 'Beston, you mean?'

'He is fathoms deep in love. I think Kit may be as well, but he hides it better.'

I was amazed to find myself saying it to him, as if we'd been on close conversational terms for years. He grimaced, but it seemed to be at the thing itself rather than at me for saying it.

'Odd, don't you think, that we've managed to convince ourselves that that's an enviable state. The ancients didn't think so. Being in love was a madness the gods wished on you, like an illness.'

'Yes.' I stared out of the window, thinking about something I certainly wasn't going to tell him about. Then I saw, from our reflections, that he was looking at me as if I had.

'Luckily most people seem to recover,' he said. Then, after a little silence, 'So you think that's all that's worrying Beston?'

'Should there be anything else?'

'It struck me that the nearer we get to his uncle's place, the more nervous he's becoming.'

'Perhaps it's because we've all built the old man into a kind of mythic beast. He's probably not half as interesting in reality and Alan thinks he'll come as a disappointment.'

'It struck me that he's not quite sure we'll all be welcome.'

'But his uncle sent him a telegram and told him he could bring his whole tribe.'

'Is that the telegram he's carrying around with him?'

'Is he?'

'He dropped it on the floor when he was getting out his penknife and scooped it up as if he expected it to run away from him.'

I thought of Alan's face in the torchlight. Meredith obviously decided not to press the subject.

'We must be getting near Carlisle. Will you excuse me if I go and start getting my things together?'

We'd been told that it would be easiest to go all the way up to Carlisle then change on to the line that went south-westwards down to Maryport on the coast. The nearest town to where Alan's uncle lived was about halfway along the line. There was nearly an hour to wait for our connection so we piled our bags and cases and hampers on the platform and strolled up and down in the afternoon sun. A line of coal wagons clanked past, a reminder that this little corner of the country had mines as well as farms. It was a part of England I'd never set foot in before but the pleasure of being on the edge of a new place was clouded by wondering about Alan. I saw him standing on his own at the far end of the platform staring down the line and went over to him. He turned round, looking alarmed.

'Everything all right, Nell?'

I decided to come straight out with it. 'What did your uncle say in that telegram?'

His eyes went to Imogen, sitting with Midge on a bench at the other end of the platform.

'Has she asked?'

'No. But there's some problem, isn't there?'

'It depends what you mean by a problem.'

'He doesn't want the whole pack of us, is that it?'

I thought I'd understood. If his uncle had

withdrawn the offer of hospitality when faced with an invasion by four men and three women, Alan was in a dilemma. It would have been sensible to break the news to us before we left Oxford but that would have meant losing his chance to spend most of the summer with Imogen, and when was a man in love ever sensible?

'Oh no, he's quite happy for us all to stay. Only...'

'Only what?'

He licked his lips and looked back along the platform again, though Imogen was nowhere near within hearing.

'You won't tell her?'

'If there's a problem she'll find out soon enough.'

'There might be nothing to find out. It probably isn't anything... His idea of a joke.'

'Suppose you just show me his telegram?'

He took it out of his pocket and slipped it into my hand like a man passing a bribe. I opened it and read BRING YOUR WHOLE TRIBE AND WELCOME. My brain was just registering that I'd misjudged him when my eyes took in the next phrase – PROVIDED THEY DON'T MIND STAYING WITH A MURDERER. I stared at Alan as he held out his hand for the telegram.

'What on earth does he mean?'

'I haven't the faintest idea.'

Chapter Three

We arrived at the local station in the early evening, tired from a long day's travelling, skin prickly from railway upholstery and clothes smelling of engine smoke. The train went on its way down to the coalmines and the coast and left us standing on the platform while Nathan and an old porter organised our pile of luggage. There seemed a lot of it for seven people intent on living simply. As well as the knapsacks and cases of books I counted at least three food hampers and a small crate of bottled ale. The porter heaved three cases and a hamper on to his trolley and looked towards the empty station yard.

'Where to, sir?'

Nathan looked at Alan. Alan looked worried.

'There isn't a cart or anything to meet us?'

'Where from, sir?'

'Studholme Hall. Mr Beston's place.'

The porter's face was weather-beaten and as wrinkled as a hippo's hide. It wasn't the kind of face that changed expression easily but I had a feeling he didn't like what he'd heard.

'No sir.'

'Is there anywhere we can get a cab?'

'Cab's away to Carlisle. Thank you sir.'

He accepted a tip and strolled away. Alan called to him to wait, but he didn't seem to hear.

'We can't stay here all night,' Imogen said.

Meredith looked amused. 'We could if we really had to, but there may be alternatives.'

I guessed that he was deliberately holding back. As the oldest one of us he might have taken the lead, but it was his pupil's party. At the moment Alan looked far from happy about that, but he took the hint.

'Kit and I'll walk up to the town. There'll probably be a pub with a fly or something to hire.'

He and Kit went off at a good pace. The remaining five of us finished off the strawberries and lemonade and then Nathan got his pipe going, always a considerable performance. He smoked a particular kind of tobacco mix that a shop in Oxford compounded to his recipe. It smelt of old rope and overripe apples and he'd brought a dozen tins with him. Once the pipe was fuming away to his liking he produced a length of string from his bulging pocket and did tricks to entertain us – knotting his own wrists together until it looked as if they'd take hours to undo, then releasing the whole cat's cradle with one tug of his teeth, pipe still in mouth. Only Midge managed to work up much interest and while he was showing her how the trick was done Alan and Kit came back. Alan looked angry and, I thought, a little scared.

'We can't get one.'

Kit said, 'There's a fly in the pub yard but they won't hire it to us. They say there's something wrong with the axle. Alan offered them a sovereign if somebody would just drive us a few miles to his uncle's place, but they weren't interested.'

From Alan's expression, he wished Kit hadn't told us that.

Imogen asked, 'So what do we do now?'

It was about seven o'clock by then, three hours or so of daylight left. I think we were all waiting for Meredith to make a suggestion but he just stood there, politely interested.

'We could walk,' I said.

I'd brought a map with me and had been looking at it while we were waiting. Studholme Hall was marked, no more than five or six miles away by country lanes. Five or six miles uphill as it happened, but it was no good depressing them even more. Midge asked what we should do about all the luggage.

'We'll have to leave most of it here and have it collected tomorrow. We can put the things we shall need for overnight in the rucksacks.'

It took some time for us all to root out our hiking boots and get essential things packed into the three rucksacks we had among the seven of us. All the time the sun was sliding down the sky and our chances of getting under a roof before it was dark were going with it. That didn't worry me or Midge – who'd led a tomboy life with her brothers – but I could see Imogen was unhappy. There was a point in the repacking when one of the men's shaving kits and her nightdress and washbag were lying jumbled together on the platform and she gave me a look of pure panic. Then Nathan found a flat wagon at the end of the platform and we loaded all the rest of our luggage on to it and pushed and pulled it under a lean-to shelter by the ticket office, with a note in block capitals saying it was to await collection. By that time a group of boys around nine or ten years old had gathered by the railings separating the platform from the station yard and were watching us, not offering to help. I said to Meredith, who happened to be next to me on the cart handle, 'Those boys worry me.'

'Why?'

'When a boy passes up a chance to earn a shilling, there's something odd going on.'

At last we were organised with Kit, Nathan and myself carrying the rucksacks. Alan had tried to take mine from me, but I wouldn't let him. The road from the station passed between terraces of workers' cottages on the outskirts of the small town. There were strings of faded red, white and blue flags looped across the street and a poster in the corner shop window announced 'Mafeking Relieved' with a portrait of Colonel Robert Baden-Powell. It had happened six or seven weeks before, and if we'd had more energy the signs of celebration might have sparked off a discussion. In our group, all of us had our doubts about the Boer War but with most of the country in a patriotic frenzy you had to be careful about how and where you voiced your opinions. I had a cousin serving with the cavalry in South Africa and hated to think of him risking his life in what seemed to me a piece of imperial bullying. By the look of it, this part of the country was solidly behind Queen, Government and Empire. Some of the families along the street probably had sons in the army. It seemed a sociable place if you lived there. People were out on their front steps, chatting to each other and enjoying the evening. The boys who'd been watching us back at the station had fallen in behind us, still at a distance. It was natural that we'd attract attention but odd that none of the people on the doorsteps answered when we said good evening to them. One man even turned away and went inside.

'Don't seem to care for strangers round

here,' Nathan said. Just after we passed the last house in the terrace the stones started flying. They came from the boys following us and the first flew over our heads and landed at Alan's feet. Then two or three more, one of them thudding against Kit's rucksack. He whirled round and ran back along the street towards the boys, Alan and Nathan following. The boys yelled out something in shrill voices, both scared and defiant, and disappeared behind the houses. Suddenly all the front doors had shut and there was nobody watching, just rows of closed windows glowing orange in the low sun.

Imogen called to the men, 'Come back. Come back, it's no good.'

They came unwillingly, furious.

'The little...'

'Their parents didn't even try to stop them.'

We walked on. I was glad when we'd left the town behind us and were on the uphill road. It was a deep lane with ferns and red campion growing up the banks, thick hazel hedges at the top so it was already deep dusk.

Alan and I led the way at first but after a while I let him have the map and dropped back with the other two women because I was worried that Midge might still be having trouble with her ankle. She was stoic as usual and insisted it wasn't bothering her. Imogen had gone silent and was walking in the plodding automatic way of somebody who can't imagine the journey ever ending. The first of the bats were flying across the lane before she said anything.

'Those boys, Nell, did you hear what they were shouting when they ran off?'

'I'm not sure.'

'It sounded like "murderers". Could it have been? What did they mean?'

'They were just boys. Don't worry about it.'

I tried to take my own advice and stop worrying because walking in the country on a fine night like this was what I'd pined for when shut up indoors. The clouds had cleared and a warm breeze was blowing, with wafts of hay and wild flowers coming off the fields and the sound of little streams. Above all there was the sense of the high hills not far away with a different smell about them that was difficult to define but somehow harder and older than the fields, perhaps the smell of the bare rock itself that you don't get in the soft south. Although I couldn't see them I knew that the Uldale Fells were to the east of us and the foothills of Skiddaw a little way to the south. We had the landscape almost to ourselves except sometimes we'd pass a track with the dark shape of a house at the end of it, the glow of candlelight or lamplight in a window and a dog barking. Once we saw a man checking a cattle trough at the side of a field with his back to us. Usually I'd have called out good evening but this time I said nothing. The others walked past in silence too. I think the experience with the boys had made us all unsure of our welcome. If he was aware of us, he must have found us a strange intrusion. It was too late in the day and too far north of the popular Lake District tourist areas for a rambling party. Besides, we didn't look like one. Our clothes weren't right and there was no spring in our steps, no sense of being pleased with ourselves.

We tried to keep together but got strung out. Alan and Kit walked in front. I could see Alan was torn between his responsibility as leader of the party and concern for Imogen because he kept looking back at her. For most of the time, Michael Meredith walked on his own a little way behind them, moving with a good easy stride and looking as if he, at any rate, might be enjoying it. Then there were the three of us, plus Nathan who was carrying the heaviest rucksack and kept up a continuous flow of jokes and silly remarks that were obviously intended to keep our spirits up and worked after a fashion, more because of his good-heartedness than the quality of the jokes.

By the time we'd gone five miles or so it was too dark for the leaders to read the map, so they had to keep stopping at crossroads and striking matches. Although we knew we must be getting near Studholme Hall it was difficult to navigate with rutted farm tracks all looking alike, and of course nobody had brought a compass. Alan got argumentative and led us half a mile in the wrong direction before admitting he'd made a mistake. By then we were all tired, hungry and ready to snap at each other. As we trailed back the way we'd come, tripping over ruts and being snagged by briars, a voice said close to my ear, 'I congratulate you all. Nobody's said it yet.' Meredith's voice, low and amused. I was about to ask, 'Said what?' then realised it was like a serve in tennis and I was supposed to return it, not let it fall.

'The most pointless of remarks, but sometimes the hardest to resist.'

'Yes. Once voiced, it would end our philosophic party before it got properly started.'

Matches flared again up ahead and Alan shouted that this time it was definitely right, his voice full of relief. We hurried to him and he struck more matches to show a sign on a five-barred gate. The sign was done in amateur poker-work on a piece of plank. It read 'Studholme Hall' and underneath, in larger letters, 'Keep Out'. The gate was closed across the top of a drive between unkempt hedges. The smell of crushed pineapple weed was rising around us and even by match light you could see that grass and weeds were growing thickly in the gateway. Alan stooped and fumbled with the catch of the gate. When he pushed it open there was a sudden carillon of bells, tuned to different notes like Alpine cowbells. At any other time the effect might have been welcoming but, with our nerves already stretched, it made everybody jump back. We filed through the gate and Nathan pushed it shut, setting the bells jangling again. Below us, quite a long way down the steeply sloping track you could make out the dark rectangle of a house against the slope of a wooded hill with lamplight in one of the upstairs windows. We started walking down the track, Meredith still alongside me.

'It's something to see a light,' I said. 'I was beginning to think Alan's uncle had forgotten about us and gone away.'

There was a new-looking post-and-rail fence on our right, a tall hedge on the left. Alan and Kit were striding ahead.

'I agree his hospitality's been unobtrusive so far.'

'But then, different people have different ideas of hospitality.'

At that point the night exploded. There was a flash, a blast of noise then a second blast. After that silence for the space of a heartbeat apart from a sound like rain pattering on the hedge. Then a voice shouting, 'Go away. I warned you. Go away.'

Alan and Kit had disappeared. Ahead of us on the track where their shapes had been there was only night sky. A sound came from Imogen behind me, part gasp, part sob. Then Alan's voice, unsteadily from ground level, 'Uncle? Uncle James, what's happening?'

'Alan?' The voice down the track was doubtful at first, then horrified. 'Alan, I haven't gone and killed *you* now, have I?'

'Not quite, Uncle, but you had a bloody good try.'

Kit laughed, high and shakily, also from near ground level. Meredith said to me entirely calmly, as if there'd been no break in our conversation, 'It isn't granted to many of us to be proved right so quickly, Miss Bray. Beston's uncle clearly has a refreshingly original view of hospitality.'

Below us, Alan was getting to his feet. A figure came out of the dark, wrapped itself round him then released him.

'Alan, my dear boy. I'm very sorry. I took you for some other people.'

It was an elderly voice, but powerful and unexpectedly attractive, with the deep, rounded quality of an old-fashioned actor. There was something actorly too in the man's power of recovery. The horror when

55

he thought he'd killed his great nephew had been obvious but now he sounded as if the thing had been some boisterous joke. Kit was on his feet by now, but there was something odd and awkward about his silhouette. Then the Old Man's voice, uncertain again.

'Who are you? Have I hit you?'

'I bleed sir, but not killed.' Kit was an actor too and had got his composure back, but he was holding his left arm stiffly away from his body.

Alan yelped, 'Kit, he hasn't gone and shot you has he?'

'Only winged, I'm sure. Could we go inside and have a look at the damage?'

'Yes, come in. All of you, come in.'

The Old Man hurried Kit and Alan down the path towards the house and the rest of us followed.

Chapter Four

Our procession went in single file round the side of the house to where light was spilling out from an open door. We walked in silence, still too shaken to say anything. The open door led into a lobby cluttered with boots, walking sticks and oddments of harness, then to a big farm kitchen, brightly lit by two oil lamps hanging from a beam. It was the size of two or three normal living rooms and looked comfortable in a haphazard way with a coal fire burning in the grate, a fat white and sandy coloured dog asleep on a rug in front of it, a big scrubbed table and five or six armchairs, all well-worn and none matching. A saddle was hitched over the arm of one of the chairs and the table was strewn with bits of horse tack, sponges and a tin of saddle soap, surrounding an old stone cider jar filled with wild flowers.

'Now let's see what I've done to you,' the Old Man said to Kit. He was still carrying the shotgun, now folded harmlessly over the crook of his arm but we found it hard to keep our eyes off it. Perhaps he noticed this because he hooked it over the arm of his chair, next to the saddle. His grey eyes glinted with the manic brightness you get sometimes with short-sighted people. He had the build of an old jockey and probably didn't weigh much more than Midge, with legs that looked thin even in the leather gaiters he was wearing. Old age had drawn skin and muscle tight over his prominent bones. His face was as brown as the leather of the saddle he'd been cleaning, with a beaky nose and high forehead under a thick thatch of silver hair that came almost down to his shirt collar. He wore a beard that was the same bright silver as his hair, but clipped to a neat point. When he spoke he showed lines of teeth as regular as a young man's but the colour of milky coffee. Kit turned to show him his left arm. The white shirt sleeve was spattered with blood, ripped in several places. Alan gasped and stepped towards Kit but his uncle waved him towards the table.

'Scissors there somewhere, she uses them for bacon rinds. Now, my friend, if you'll sit there under the lamp where we can see...' Kit let himself be guided into a chair. He was pale but calm, unlike Alan who was shaking. Imogen had to help him find scissors among the detritus on the table. The Old Man grabbed them from him and cut round the shirt sleeve at the shoulder. When it fell away Imogen gasped and hid her head in my shoulder. The damage wasn't so serious. Maybe half a dozen or so shotgun pellets had pierced the skin but trails of blood made it look worse than it was. The Old Man nodded, produced a pair of tweezers from a pocket and started digging away in Kit's arm.

'Not hurting you am I, my boy?'

Kit shook his head, tight lipped. Alan tried to protest but Kit signalled with his eyes not to interfere so Alan had to watch, his face registering pain with every prod of the tweezers while Kit's was almost impassive. The only sound was the gentle roar of the lamps and the occasional ping of a shotgun pellet falling on to the stone floor.

'Seems to have got 'em all. Somebody get the carbolic. She keeps it under the sink.'

Midge and I searched under the stone sink in the far corner and found a cloth-stoppered bottle that, from the smell, was household disinfectant.

'Oh no,' Midge said. 'It will kill him.'

'It'll need something strong after those tweezers. Goodness knows what he used them for last.'

Some equine activity, I guessed. We carried the bottle over to the Old Man. He tore off a relatively clean piece of Kit's shirtsleeve, soaked it in disinfectant and clapped it on his arm. Kit reacted with no more than a shiver and a sharp intake of breath. In his place I'd have howled like a timber wolf.

'Pudding cloths, in the table drawer.'

At least the Old Man seemed to have a good grasp of what went on in his kitchen. There were several pudding cloths, newly laundered. He converted one of them into a pad over the wounds and used two more as a bandage. I had to admit it was quite a neat effort in the circumstances.

'Right, you'll do.'

Meredith had found Kit's jacket, dumped in a pile of our luggage by the door. He held it for Kit to get his uninjured right arm into the sleeve, then draped it carefully over his bare and bandaged left arm. Kit nodded a thank you. The Old Man took a deep breath.

'So that's that dealt with. You are all welcome. My home is your home. Alan, my dear boy, please introduce me to your friends.'

It looked doubtful for a moment whether Alan was going to obey his great uncle or hit him. But custom and politeness won.

'Miss Bray, may I introduce you to my Uncle James.'

As it happened, these formal introductions were the last time any of us heard him called Uncle James. Everybody called him the Old Man, almost as a title of honour. He even used it of himself. He shook my hand, Imogen's and Midge's, peering at us closely as if he wanted to be

60

sure of recognising us again. I noticed that when Alan introduced him to the men he repeated their names, obviously memorising them, which he hadn't done in our case.

'Sit down, all of you. Alan, there's brandy on the sideboard over there. Do the honours. I expect the ladies will take tea.'

Most of us settled in various chairs. The Old Man poured our tea himself into cups that looked like survivors of several different tea sets from a smoke-blackened clay pot that had been nudged up close to the fire. The tea was as dark as a peat bog, served without milk or sugar, and tasted as if it had been brewing all day. After all that had happened I'd have preferred brandy. The sideboard was Jacobean oak, carved with biblical scenes including a little pot-bellied Adam and Eve holding branches in front of their loins. As Alan walked over to it to get the brandy a few shotgun pellets pattered off his clothes on to the stone-flagged floor.

'Not bad shooting anyway,' the Old Man said.

Alan didn't answer. His uncle got glasses from the sideboard and watched closely as Alan filled them.

'Properly, my boy. More than that. This is a celebration.'

Alan did as he was told, pouring until the bottle was empty. I could see that the dazed feeling was wearing off and being replaced by the anger most people feel after being terrified.

'You've got a good steady hand,' the Old Man said. 'I'm glad about that.'

'You are, are you?'

Alan carried brandy over to Kit, Meredith and Nathan then took a gulp from his own glass and faced the Old Man. If you allowed for at least fifty years difference in age there was a family resemblance, particularly the prominent facial bones and – it struck me – a ruthlessness about getting what they wanted. Alan had wanted Imogen there, and got her (though, from her thoughtful expression, probably not for much longer.) The Old Man had wanted Alan and got him, although why he wanted him was anybody's guess.

'You don't think you might have warned me?'

'But I did, my boy. I sent you a telegram.'

'I thought it was some kind of joke.'

'The whole thing's a bloody joke.'

Nathan was sitting next to me and I could see him wincing at swearing in front of ladies. I signed to him not to worry.

'So it's a joke, is it? It's a joke that you nearly killed my oldest friend? It's a joke that you've let me bring my friends here without letting me know you've managed to start another civil war with your neighbours?'

'Civil war, you say?' In spite of Alan's anger,

the Old Man seemed quite complimented about that.

'It's even spread to the town. Do you know they wouldn't hire us a cab or even a cart to come out here? As soon as they knew where we were heading, the whole town was against us.'

'I'm sorry for that. I'd meant to have Robin waiting for you with the wagonette but we thought it was tomorrow you were coming.'

'They threw stones at us. Actually threw stones as we were hiking out of town. And when we get here at last, what do you do? You start blazing away at us as if we were a gang of poachers.'

The Old Man looked hurt. 'Oh no, my boy. I'd never open fire on poachers. Some of my best friends are poachers.'

'Well, thank you for that. You wouldn't shoot poachers, but you've no scruples about shooting my friends.'

'My dear boy, please don't be so angry. It was a misunderstanding. I told you I wasn't expecting you until tomorrow.'

'So who did you think it was? You were out pretty quickly with that shotgun, weren't you, and you've got warning bells rigged up on the gate. What's happening?'

The Old Man sighed, 'Isn't this discourteous to our guests? Shouldn't you and I discuss it after we've all eaten?'

Meredith said, quietly and politely, 'I think we'd all be interested to know, sir.'

It was the first time any of the rest of us had spoken since the introductions. The Old Man swivelled his head round towards Meredith, gave him a long look and nodded as if acknowledging that he had a right to an opinion.

'In that case, I'll tell you. Alan, sit down for goodness' sake. You're not addressing a meeting.'

Unwillingly, Alan sat down on a straight-backed chair by the sideboard and the Old Man settled himself into the armchair with the saddle and shotgun beside him, crossing his gaitered legs. The plump dog by the fire stirred and developed two heads, one at each end. As it got up I saw that what I'd taken for one fat dog was two thin ones, fine Afghans. They padded across the room to take up positions on either side of the Old Man, white head on his left knee, sand-coloured on his right. He sat very upright, like a tribal chieftain between bodyguards.

'It started with the Relief of Mafeking.' The short-sighted eyes ranged round us as if that should tell us what we needed to know. To nudge him along I asked, 'The celebrations?'

His glare focused on me. 'Celebrations! You think it's something to celebrate – that we're killing honest hard-working farmers because we think we know how to run their country better than they do? Shooting men off the backs of their own horses on their own land – is that something to put out the flags for and light bonfires for and get drunk and march round the town singing songs for?'

I started saying that as a matter of fact I agreed with him, but he didn't take any notice.

'I lived with the Boers for two years. I rode with them, worked with them, ate with them. They're some of the straightest men on earth and this wretched government's sending our young men out there to kill them. And when I dare to stand up and say it's an abomination, I get ruffians invading my land, trying to burn down my stables with my horses inside, and where are the police? Nowhere.'

He paused for breath and Alan slipped in, 'But why are people accusing you of murder?'

'Let me tell it my way. After the Mafeking nonsense, I'd had enough. I decided it was time to tell the people round here what was really going on. They're mostly farmers, you see, just like the Boers. I thought they'd understand if I explained it to them.'

From behind me Meredith sighed under his breath, 'Another optimist.'

'So I hired a hall and put up posters. We drew a big crowd, nobody can deny that.'

Alan asked, 'Who's we?'

'Robin and I. Dulcie wanted to come but we made her stay at home. Just as well. No place for women, as it turned out. They howled me down. Howled me down and dragged me off the platform. Probably would have torn me limb from limb if Robin hadn't pulled me out and driven back here like a bat out of hell. So we got home, put arnica on our bruises and I thought that was that. At least I'd tried to keep faith with my Boer friends.'

I asked, 'So did somebody get killed?'

'No, that wasn't until the next night. We were back home here, just Robin and Dulcie and me. It was about ten o'clock and I'd gone out for a last look at the horses, as I always do. Most of them were out in the fields but we had Sid in his box that night and a couple of mares and foals in the main stables. Anyway, as soon as I got outside the door I smelt burning and there was the new hay barn alight and people capering round it cheering and shouting like savages. I went back inside to fetch Robin and my shotgun. When we got outside again some of them were coming this way shouting they were going to set light to the stables. Well, what would you have done? I ask you all, what would you have done?'

He waited as if he really wanted an answer. There were tears running down his cheeks. He'd started crying unashamedly when he talked about the mares and foals.

'Can you imagine the sheer wickedness? Wanting to set light to stables with horses inside, and him the son of a horseman.'

'Who?'

'The one I'm supposed to have killed. Mawbray's son. Mawbray the magistrate's son. I heard his voice giving orders to them. I shouted to them to stop but they kept coming so I fired both barrels. Robin fired too. They shouted a bit. I reloaded and fired again, then they were all running and squealing like a rabbit with a weasel's teeth in its gizzard.'

'Except Mawbray's son?' Alan asked.

'As far as I knew at the time, he scuttled off with the rest of them.'

'But if you're supposed to have killed him...'

'Perhaps he died in a ditch somewhere. Perhaps Old Nick took him straight down to hell to save the trouble and expense of a funeral. All I know is, I shot at where his voice was in the dark and nobody's seen hide nor hair of him since. And if that's murder then you're all under a murderer's roof and you'd better make the best of it or go elsewhere.'

Silence, except for a lot of deep breaths round the room. Then Alan said, surprisingly mildly in the circumstances, 'I wish I'd known.'

'Would've cost a fortune to put all that in a telegram. So if you'd known you wouldn't have come?'

'No, I'm not saying I shouldn't have come, but I shouldn't have brought my friends.'

The Old Man seemed to relax a little. 'Understandable, my boy. We'll feed and water them and get them bedded down for the night, then Robin'll get out the wagonette in the morning and take them back to the station.'

'Yes, I think that's best.'

'But you'll stay, my boy?' It was almost a plea.

Alan only hesitated for a moment. 'Yes. Yes, I will.'

Kit said, 'In that case I'll stay too.'

'Please yourselves. All of you are welcome to stay or go as you like. Anyway, you'll eat now. We eat late these evenings, because of keeping watch.'

He got up suddenly, dislodging the dogs' heads from his knees, went to the outside door and yelled into the darkness, 'Robin.'

Imogen, looking shaken, mouthed, 'Who's Robin?'

Alan shook his head. Soon afterwards there was a stamping of boots in the lobby and one of the best-looking men I'd seen in a long time came into the room. He was probably in his mid-twenties, quite tall with dark curly hair and eyes that looked black in

68

the lamplight. He wore moleskin trousers, a coarse white shirt open at the neck, a red neck-cloth with white spots and an old black waistcoat. He'd walked into the room as confidently as a horse into its meadow but when he saw us all sitting there he looked on the point of bolting. The Old Man took him by the arm.

'Alan, Robin. Robin, this is my great nephew and these are his friends.'

That seemed to be all the introduction anybody was going to get because the Old Man then walked across the room, drew back a curtain that had been hiding a flight of stairs and yelled up, 'Dulcie, suppertime.' There was the sound of feet hitting bare boards overhead. He dropped the curtain back and explained, 'Dulcie's been catching up on her sleep.' Then he went to pick up his shotgun, stopped, shook his head, un-hitched a heavy driving whip from the back of the door instead and went out.

If any of us had made a sudden move or said anything I think Robin would have run out after him. He stood with his weight forward on his feet ready for a quick move, like an animal that had strolled accidentally into a circle of predators. I couldn't blame him. Although the kitchen was a big room the seven of us filled it and we were oddities there. The men had got to their feet out of politeness on being introduced, but with the four of them standing together and him on his own it must have looked more like a threat. We all stood there frozen until the silence was broken by the pad of feet downstairs and a rattle of rings as the stair curtain was drawn back.

'Well I'm gloppened. What o'clock is it? Why didnae somebody wake me?'

The men spun round and four jaws dropped in unison. If Robin looked like an animal among predators, this woman – Dulcie presumably – was as thoroughly at home and self-possessed as a lioness lolling on a tree branch. She wore a lilac-coloured velour wrap patterned with bunches of purple grapes, with a shawl collar that fell open to show a pink chemise pushed out by a swell of uncorseted bosom like a wave just before it breaks. Her hair was chestnut brown with a few strands of grey in it and reached down to her waist. She'd made a token move towards controlling it by taking the two front hanks and knotting the ends loosely at the back of her head. Her face was too plump and round for beauty but when she smiled – and she was smiling at all of us – she looked so pleased with herself and everything else that it was like being given a present. She was quite a lot older than we were, but her little white teeth and plump brown feet seemed almost childlike.

'I'm Dulcie,' she told us, 'Dulcie Berry-man.'

The voice was pure Cumberland, with the 'I' coming out as 'Ahm'. The accent had an extra warmth and laziness about it in her case, as if it came from the depths of a goosefeather bed. We introduced ourselves in a confused way that couldn't have left her with much impression of who was who but it didn't seem to bother her. She picked Alan out.

'Your uncle will be reet glad you're here. You've seen him?'

Alan managed to stammer out the understatement that yes, he'd seen him. Dulcie's appearance seemed to have shaken him at least as much as being shot at. I was struck by her self-possession, as if she came down every evening to find her kitchen full of strangers. She might have felt gloppened – whatever that might be – but she'd recovered quickly. She made no comment on the double shotgun blast not far from the house that must surely have woken her, or the fact that one of her unexpected guests had an arm bandaged with her pudding cloths and the room reeked of carbolic. An unworthy thought came to me. The floors upstairs must be bare boards because I'd heard her feet on them, so sound would travel. She must have been aware that there were a lot of people downstairs, probably even heard what was being said. She'd have known too that at least some of the company was male so could have dressed more formally if she'd chosen. I'd been dragooned into enough amateur theatricals in my time to recognise somebody making an entrance when I saw it.

'You'll be clemmed with hunger, poor things. Get the dishes, Robin lad.'

At least with her there to protect him Robin didn't look as if he intended to bolt after all. He walked round the men, keeping as much space between himself and them as the furniture allowed, opened the sideboard cupboard and took out a stack of plates.

'Kneyves and fawks, somebody. Left-hand drawer.' She'd picked up the Old Man's habit of casual command. Midge and I started getting up but Nathan was there first. Cutlery rattled down on the table, chairs were dragged from all corners of the room while Dulcie knelt at an oven beside the fire. A blast of heat came out and the smell of rabbit stew got stronger, fighting the carbolic. Without being told, Robin took a half-gallon brown jug out to the lobby and when he brought it back a strong whiff of ale added to the atmosphere. No nonsense this time about tea for ladies. We all got ale in a variety of containers from pint mugs to green-stemmed glasses meant for hock. I'm pretty sure it was the first time Midge and

Imogen had tasted ale and I could see Imogen wincing as she sipped. She still looked shaken, which was hardly surprising.

Kit ate neatly with a fork, one-handed, but didn't say much. Nathan did most of the talking, mainly for Dulcie's benefit, making a joke of our hike and the arguments over the map, no reference to shotguns. It was clear that he and Dulcie had taken to each other. Between them they managed to make an indoor picnic of what might have been an embarrassing occasion. There were only two rabbits in the black stewpot and that meant everybody got just a few inches of shoulder or saddle or a little pale leg, plus a spoonful of gravy and a floury potato with some of the eyes and black bits left in. But there was plenty of flat oat bread, or clapbread as Dulcie called it when urging us to take another piece, and endless quantities of ale. Robin went out several times to refill the jug, walking in wide circles round us. He still seemed to be trying to decide if we were a threat and if so what sort. When Dulcie had whittled most of the meat off her little share of rabbit she picked up the bone and gnawed the rest with her pretty little teeth. Nathan laughed and gnawed too and soon our plates were all strewn with a litter of delicate bones sucked as clean as driftwood. All except Imogen's. She'd hardly touched her meal. Midge looked at the empty stewpot.

'Oh no, we've eaten all of it. What about the Old Man?' Then clapped her hand over her mouth from embarrassment at calling him that.

Dulcie didn't seem to mind. 'The maister says guests come first, like when he was in the desert with the Arabs.' Then, a little sadly, 'Besides, he eats nobbut a bite or two these days.'

It was enough to break the temporary spell of the meal. The uncurtained windows were dark now and I suppose all of us thought of the Old Man patrolling outside, alone and unfed.

Alan asked Dulcie, 'Were you here on the night it happened?' His tone was uncertain because he obviously had no more idea than the rest of us who Dulcie Berryman was – housekeeper, landlady or perhaps some unusual species of nurse.

'What night was that?'

'When he... When the barn got burned and so on.'

Dulcie stood up and started stacking plates, not ignoring him but not especially attentive either. 'Yes, Ah was here.'

'Did you see what happened?'

'He told me to stay inside. Anyway, it was dark when they came.'

She held out her hand for my plate. As I handed it over I looked into her eyes. Brown didn't begin to describe the colour of them properly, more a very dark amber with the light shining through it. They gave nothing away, even at Alan's next words.

'My uncle thinks he killed somebody.'

She added my plate to the pile, reached for Imogen's. 'He has some reet queer notions sometimes.'

She had the plates in the crook of her left arm. With her free hand she picked up the piece of rabbit leg Imogen had left, stripped the meat off the bone with her teeth and carried the plates over to a stone sink in the far corner, still munching.

'You mean, you don't think he did?'

She didn't turn. We never knew whether she'd have answered or not because there were footsteps outside then the door opened and the Old Man came in.

'Robin, would you go and have a look at Sheba? She's not settling.'

Robin got up and went out without a glance at any of us. He didn't say a word. In fact he hadn't said a word throughout the meal. The Old Man hooked his whip on the back of the door and grinned at us.

'You've eaten well?' Then, after our ragged chorus of thank yous, 'Dulcie makes the best rabbit stew in the county, don't you Dulcie?' She was clattering things over at the sink. He reached up and unhooked one of the lamps from the beam, standing on tiptoe to do it. Alan was on his feet, towering over his uncle but almost conciliatory now it was clear that Kit wasn't seriously hurt.

'Let me do that, sir.'

'Not yet, my boy. Your turn will come.'

He carried the lamp over to a hook near the sink, to give Dulcie more light. It swung gently, sending our shadows dancing over the walls, more lively than we felt. We were all of us dropping from tiredness and perhaps the effect of the ale.

'Now, where shall we put you all? There's a parlour next door. You can bed down there once we've found you some cushions and blankets.'

Midge glanced at me. At least she seemed to be finding it funny. Neither of us dared look at Imogen.

Alan said, 'What about the ladies, sir?'

'The womenfolk can have Dulcie's bed. That alright, Dulcie?'

She nodded without turning round from the washing-up. We started protesting that we couldn't possibly.

'Nothing wrong with Dulcie's bed. Best one in the house by a long way. Plenty of room for three.'

'But we can't–'

'Dulcie will show you upstairs when she's finished. Now if the rest of you come through here we'll get you bedded down.'

Nathan, Kit and Meredith followed him

obediently. Meredith had been almost as silent during the meal as Robin and I supposed he must be wishing himself back in his comfortable set of college rooms, smothering or not. Alan stayed behind and dropped down on one knee beside Imogen who was still sitting at the table, head resting on her hand, looking weary and confused beyond thinking.

'Imogen, I'm so dreadfully sorry about this. We'll get you back safely tomorrow.'

She didn't move or make any reply. He got to his feet, looking wretched. 'Look after her, Nell.' Then he followed the others. From next door we heard sounds of furniture being moved around and Nathan's laugh. Midge and I started sorting out the contents of the packs, putting the men's things and our things in separate heaps. By the time we'd done that Dulcie had finished the washing-up.

'If you want to go somewhere before you go upstairs it's across the yard next to the cart shed.'

We wanted to go somewhere. Outside the night was full of stars, with no sound but the brook flowing and a horse whickering not far away. We found the black shed by its smell and waited for each other outside. As we walked back across the yard, Midge took hold of Imogen's hand and squeezed it.

'Don't worry, things won't look so bad in

the morning.' No answer from Imogen. She was moving like a woman in a trance. Dulcie was waiting for us in the kitchen holding a candle in an enamel holder.

'Mind the third stair. It's loose.'

If she was annoyed about giving up her bed to us she didn't show it. She pulled back the curtain and we scooped up armfuls of nightdresses and shawls and followed.

It was one of the biggest beds I'd ever seen, an enormous four-poster with all the hangings gone except for a tattered pelmet of faded velvet around the top. The bottom of it was filled by an enormous feather mattress that looked as thick and white as an Alpine snowfall in the candlelight, with a ruckle of sheets and blankets pulled back and a bolster wide enough for four or five heads to lie side by side. The room was large but the bed took up half of it. The rest of the furniture was as oddly assorted as down in the kitchen – a sagging chintz armchair, a big china jug and washbasin on a marble-topped stand, a huge wardrobe with an oval mirror in the door, cracked from top to bottom. It all had the feel of a house rented ready furnished by people in a hurry and I remembered what Nathan had said about the Centaur travelling light and always moving on.

'Has ta got all ta need then?'

I said yes thank you and Dulcie went padding back downstairs, still barefoot. Midge threw herself backwards on to the feather mattress and almost disappeared into it.

'Wheee. It's like clouds.'

Imogen sat down on the edge of the armchair. 'I've never shared a bed with anybody before.'

'Never?' Then I remembered that she was an only child.

'When I was a child, I suppose, with cousins at Christmas time, but not grown-up.'

'Well, I don't suppose Nell and I have got fleas or any awful diseases. Do you snore, Nell?'

'Not as far as I know.'

I sat on the side of the bed, trying not to tip backwards, and unlaced my boots. My stockings were sticking to my feet from heat and the walking. 'Is there any water in that bowl?'

Midge hauled herself off the bed and took the candle over to see. 'Yes, but it looks as if Dulcie has been washing in it. There's some fresh in the jug though.' She opened the window and threw the dirty water out, then giggled. 'I hope Alan's uncle wasn't underneath. I don't want him chasing me across country with a shotgun.'

Imogen said, 'Don't,' and shuddered. At least she was talking to us. I guessed the

79

next thing she'd say was what Meredith had congratulated us earlier on not saying – 'I wish I hadn't come'. If anybody was accepting bets on who'd be going back to the station in the wagonette in the morning, Imogen would be first favourite and Meredith second. As for me, I'd already made my decision but there was no point in talking about it and starting an argument. Midge and I worked out that there was enough water for us to have about half a pint each to wash in. None of us fancied going back down to the kitchen to get more. Midge went first, stripping to bodice and petticoat and rooting out a sponge and towel from our baggage. Imogen slowly unlaced her boots, walked over to the window in stockinged feet and looked out for a while then came to sit on the side of the bed.

'These must be the sheets she slept in. She didn't have time to change them.'

'I'm tired enough to sleep in anybody's sheets, aren't you?'

'It smells of her.'

It was true the bed did smell, although not unpleasantly. There was the faint candlewax smell of dried sweat, of new hay and something less easily definable, rather salt and sea-like. When I put my hand on the mattress I felt her warmth still hoarded in the feathers.

Imogen said, 'How old do you think she is?'

'Thirties? Forty even.'

'Quite old. Who is she?'

'Cook-housekeeper, I suppose.'

'Do cook-housekeepers usually walk around like that?'

Midge said, tactless but muffled as she was putting on her nightdress, 'Do people usually open fire on their guests? Anyway, she seems to think he was imagining killing anybody.'

Imogen said, 'Were those boys back in town imagining it too? You heard what they were shouting.'

Midge didn't answer. Under her nightdress she was unbuttoning her bodice and petticoat. It was odd how bashful we were about getting undressed in front of each other.

Imogen insisted, 'You heard them, didn't you Nell?'

'Yes. Why don't you get washed and get into bed? You're too tired to think about anything. Tomorrow you'll be on your way to your aunt's and...'

'I'm not going. I'm staying here. I don't care what you two are doing, but I'm staying.'

Midge and I stared at each other. A few days ago she'd been fussing about chaperones, now this. Imogen was sitting bolt upright on the edge of the bed, hands clenched together and pressed against her thighs. She'd started shivering though it wasn't a cold night. Delayed shock.

I said, 'Just get into bed and get warm for goodness' sake. We'll discuss it in the morning.'

'There's nothing to discuss. I'm not going and leaving him here – after what's happened.'

'Him being Kit?'

I thought, 'oh dear, wounded warrior'. The sight of Kit, brave and suffering, must have tipped the balance towards him after all. If so, what had been a bad day for Alan had just become a lot worse.

'No. Of course I'm sorry for poor Kit, but I mean Alan. I thought he was dead. I heard that mad old man firing his gun and saw Alan go down and I thought he was dead.'

She'd started crying, tears running down her cheeks and glinting in the candlelight. Midge kicked away the underwear from round her feet, sat beside Imogen and put an arm round her.

'He's all right, you saw that. It didn't touch him.'

'It isn't that. When I thought he was dead I ... you can't imagine. It was like someone reaching inside my chest and putting a hand round my heart and crushing it.'

Midge went on making comforting noises. 'Yes, but it's all right now. It was a terrible shock but it's all right...'

Imogen pulled away from her. 'No, it's not all right. When I thought Alan was dead I realised I love him. I really love him.'

Then she leaned against Midge and sobbed as if she'd been overtaken by some great catastrophe, which she probably had. Ironic, I thought, that Kit was the one who'd had the unlucky day and Alan, if he only knew it, would be thanking his trigger-happy uncle. We got Imogen to lie down at last in the warm dip in the middle of the mattress with Midge and I on either side, both trying not to slide down on top of her. It was a long time before we got to sleep and by then we'd acknowledged that we'd all be staying. Imogen for the reason stated, Midge because she wouldn't desert Imogen and I – well, they didn't need to know my reasons. I was just staying, that's all.

Chapter Five

The window curtains were as thin as tissue paper so I woke up early, at about four o'clock, just as the light was coming in. The other two were probably awake as well but they said nothing as I got up and fumbled about for my clothes. I needed to go to the place across the yard, but since that meant getting dressed I might as well walk round and take a look at the place. After moving as a pack the day before I wanted to be on my own for a while. There was nobody in the kitchen and the fire was out. I went through the porch, unlatched the door and walked round the side of the house to the walled yard. It had a gap broad enough for a farm wagon to get through on one side. The facing side consisted mostly of a high open-fronted cart shed with an old haywain and a neat wagonette parked inside. There was nobody visible, human or animal, but a cow was mooing not far away and the soft churring sound that hens make when they're waking up was coming from a chicken shed in the angle between house and wall. Underfoot was mostly hard beaten earth, with shallow craters where the chickens had been scratching, but some-body had dug a vegetable patch along the wall at right angles to the cart shed and planted onions, carrots and a few cabbages. The place didn't look poor exactly, but not very prosperous either. The Old Man and his little household obviously lived a spartan life. When we'd decided to inflict ourselves on them I suppose we'd envisaged more of a country house existence, or at least some-where surrounded by rosy-cheeked country folk with trugs of fruit and jugs of cream. This was more like a place under siege and the supplies we'd brought with us were only enough for a picnic or two. We'd have to discuss that later, along with a lot of other things, but meanwhile being up so early was like stealing the best part of the day and I intended to enjoy it.

I strolled out of the yard and on to a farm track that ran uphill between hedges smothered in honeysuckle and dog roses, frothed with white cow parsley. The sky was clear blue with a few clouds towards the west, the air cool enough to blow away the itchiness of the long day's journey and restless night. A little way up the track the view opened out and suddenly there were sea and hills, the sapphire glint of the Solway Firth and beyond it on the Scottish side the southern uplands misty and paler blue with the sun not yet on them. I stood leaning on a gateway enjoying them until I realised that something was happening nearer at hand. The gate led into a paddock of fine grass scattered with buttercups and cuckoo-smock, sloping up to the edge of the wood. A horse was cantering towards me, such a horse that might have been made by the old gods to go with the place and the morning. Technically he was a grey, but the effect was shining silver. He wasn't large, probably no more than fifteen hands, but well proportioned and fine boned, with his long mane flying up and his tail streaming out like a pennant. He moved as if the grass had springs under it. A few yards from the gateway he came to a halt, looking at me wary-eyed, blowing gently through wide nostrils. He'd been expecting somebody else. When I reached out he let me stroke his muzzle, but guardedly. I was talking to him, telling him he was beautiful and so on, when I heard footsteps swishing in the grass and looked up to see the Old Man. When I arrived he must have been at the top of the field near the wood or I'd have seen him earlier. He was carrying his carriage horsewhip and I wondered if he might have been there all night, on guard at the high point of his land. The horse turned and went to him, nuzzling against him.

'A fine horse,' I said.

He smiled, arm over the horse's neck. 'Seawave Supreme.' Like a herald announcing a title. 'You like horses?'

'Yes.' It was practically a guilty secret because most of the people I knew thought that liking horses went with everything we despised, such as country squires and Conservatives. 'Especially Arab horses.'

Which was true. For me, they'd always had a kind of gallantry about them that made the heart lift just to see them.

'Want to see the others?'

'Yes please.'

He vaulted over the gate, head down and heels up, almost as easily as a young man and straightened up beside me, pleased with himself. We fell into step together back down the track. It was my first taste of what was to be one of the oddest things about that summer – the feeling of at least two worlds going on at the same time, side by side. The evening before he'd confessed to murder, I'd spent most of the night lying awake wondering if he'd meant it but there we were, strolling along with the sun coming up as if we had nothing to think about but horses. I suppose I might have started quizzing him about Mawbray's son and all the rest of it – an older version of myself might have done just that – but it would have been an intrusion, brutal bad manners. Besides, it was such a fine morning and I liked him. We walked down past the house then up again along the track we'd been on when he'd shot at us the night before. He pointed with his whip.

'That's the barn they burnt. It was empty because we hadn't got the hay in at the time, but they didn't know that, the devils.'

It was up near the road. We must have passed it in the dark without seeing it. A few blackened timbers stuck up at odd angles and the grass all round it was burnt brown. We looked for a while then he opened a wide farm gate to the left of the track and we went into a broad meadow that sloped up to the road on one side, down to a curving line of willows and alders on the other. From where we were standing you could hear a river but not see it and I guessed it was hidden in the trees. I found out later from the map that it was a tributary of the Waver that ran down to the Solway Firth. There were some pockets of mist down by the river. When the Old Man stood by the gate and whistled, heads and necks of horses came out of the mist and the little herd came galloping uphill to us. They were mostly mares, three bays and two greys, with a couple of youngsters.

'Two year olds,' he said. 'Sid's first sons.'

'Sid?'

'Seawave Supreme. Sid's his stable name. He's one in a lifetime, that horse. Best stallion I've ever bred.'

'Why Seawave?'

I hoped he might confirm at first hand the story Nathan had passed on, about bringing the original mares and stallion from Arabia.

'You want to know? Come with me and I'll show you.'

He stroked the necks of the nearest mares then pushed them gently aside so that we could get back through the gate. We went back down to the house and when we went through the gateway to the yard we found Robin letting out the hens. He said 'Good morning, sair' to the Old Man and gave me a diffident little bob of the head. The two Afghan hounds were sniffing around and came up to the Old Man to have their long heads caressed.

'Morning, Robin. We'll be needing the wagonette. When you've finished in the stables, will you go and get Bobbin. He'll be down by the river as usual.'

Robin just nodded and walked away through a gap in the wall next to the cart shed.

'Robin's not very talkative with human beings,' the Old Man said, 'but he understands horses better than anyone you'll ever meet. Came over on the boat from Ireland a couple of years ago and stayed.'

He followed Robin through the opening by the cart shed. It opened into another enclosed yard larger and more prosperous looking than the one by the house. It was paved in sandstone with a water trough and pump in the middle, loose boxes around three sides and a two-storey brick building backing on to the other yard. He opened the door of the building and let me into one of the finest tack rooms I'd ever seen. The walls were newly distempered, with saddles and bridles ranged on supports and hooks along them, all supple and newly cleaned. Gleaming window panes let in the light and gave an uninterrupted view of the stable yard. There was none of the casual muddle of the house. Everything was bright and orderly as a cavalry stables.

'That's it,' the Old Man said.

He was looking at the wall at the end of the room. It had no saddles and bridles on it, just one huge painting. It was an oil more than ten feet high, almost filling the wall, and showed a group of Arab horses galloping along a beach with white crashing surf in the background.

'Who painted it?'

'Can't remember. Got some young chap to do it for me, but I told him what to put in. Like the poem.'

There was a gilt-edged panel under the picture, with lines of poetry inscribed on it. The Old Man started reading.

'With flowing tail, and flying mane,
Wide nostrils never stretch'd by pain,

90

Mouths bloodless to the bit or rein,
And feet that iron never shod,
And flanks unscarr'd by spur or rod,
A thousand horse, the wild, the free,
Like waves that follow o'er the sea.'

Long before he got to the end I realised that he was reciting from memory, not reading. He repeated the last two lines, his eyes on my face. 'Seawave, you see. Free as a wave on the sea. Know who wrote that?'

'Byron. It's from *Mazeppa*.' A fierce tale about a young man who made love to another man's wife and in revenge was tied to the back of a wild horse to be galloped to death.

'That's right, *Mazeppa*. Greatest poem in the English language.'

I could tell it wasn't an occasion to indulge in literary discussion and he'd said it the way he recited the lines, like a matter of religious faith. He stood in silence, staring at the picture then suddenly turned to me.

'I'm taking Sid on a ride to the sea, any day now. Want to come with me?'

'Yes.'

'As long as there won't be any trouble about it. Had enough trouble. Which one of them do you belong to?'

'I beg your pardon?' I stared at him wondering what he meant. College, political party?

'Which one of the men? If you get all that straight at the start, saves trouble later.'

I suppose I just stood there, gaping at him. He grinned.

'I should hope my nephew's taken the pretty one and the man with the laugh's got his eye on the little one. Can't make out you and the other two, though.'

There was no need to draw myself up to my full height because I was already taller than he was.

'I can assure you for the three of us that we're not in the ownership of any man and we never will be.'

'Of course you will. You all seem healthy nice-looking girls. You've got a bit of a temper by the look of it, but some men like that. You'll marry all right.'

'*If* we decide to marry we shall enter into a free relationship of equals. The idea of a wife being subservient, let alone *owned*, as you put it, is downright disgusting.'

I could tell he was enjoying himself, that he'd wanted to provoke an argument, and that made me more angry.

'It's a law of nature, girl. You saw Sid. He's the only stallion here and the mares are his mares. If another stallion came and tried to take them, they'd fight and tear out one another's throats with their teeth till one of them gave in and probably dragged himself away to die.'

'So you're implying that men and women are no better than horses?'

'Wouldn't dream of it. Most of us aren't nearly as good. Have you ever seen a human being as much of a real nobleman as my Sid?'

'I wonder if his mares think so. But I don't suppose they have much choice in the matter.'

'They don't need choice. They're happy.'

'Don't women need choices, then?'

'No. Doesn't make them any happier and only causes a lot of trouble and confusion.'

'So that's why we don't need votes, I suppose.'

'Nobody needs votes. Whatever side you vote for you end up with meddling idiots.'

'If parliament gives women the vote, perhaps we won't keep getting idiots elected.'

'Give? They'll never just give it to you. If you want anything, you just have to go and take it. If you all wanted it enough, you'd have had it by now.'

It's always seemed odd to me that this remark, from an old man I thought was certainly misguided and quite probably mad, turned out to have more influence on the next twenty years of my life than all the sober good sense I'd heard from my friends and teachers. I'd grown up with the idea that because the logical case for giving us the vote had been made over and over again, it was only a matter of time before it would happen. Only it hadn't happened and it was beginning to dawn on me that something more than asking politely might have to be done about it. So what he'd said stung me more than he deserved. I don't know what I'd have answered because at that moment a little door through from the cart shed opened. We turned round and there was Dulcie Berryman, more or less conventionally dressed this time in blue serge skirt and jacket and blue cotton blouse. The only odd note was that her feet were in leather Turkish slippers much too big for her. She shuffled towards us.

'Robin's asking when you want the wagonette round.'

'When they've had their breakfast. Are they up yet?'

'Some of them.'

The Old Man had turned back to look at his picture of the horses, rather wistfully, and she went to stand beside him.

'There's nobbut tea and clapbread and butter,' she said.

'No eggs?'

'Nobbut three. The hens are out of kelter.'

'Clapbread and butter then.'

There was something curiously intimate about the little conversation, more like two friends than employer to housekeeper. Then I noticed the Old Man's right hand. Slowly but quite deliberately it was caressing

Dulcie's serge-covered haunch much as he'd stroked the neck of the horse in the meadow. She showed no sign of resenting it any more than the horse had. It was a casual almost automatic gesture, as if he'd done it many times, and yet I was sure it was connected with our discussion. It meant ownership and he meant me to see it. When he turned and looked at me over his shoulder I was quite sure of it. I said something, I don't know what, and blundered out through the little door, embarrassed and angry, through the cart shed and back to the yard by the house. Then, as luck would have it, the first person I saw was Meredith just when I was feeling at my least intelligent and philosophic.

'Good morning, Miss Bray. Is anything wrong?'

He'd been standing in the middle of the yard staring up at the house and looked as fresh and tidy as if he'd just come from his college bathroom, close shaven with a jaunty black felt hat on his head, which he raised to me. There was something ironic in the gesture – conventional manners in a mad situation.

'No, nothing thank you.' I was still hot with confusion and embarrassment and didn't want to talk about it to anybody, least of all him.

'Did you all sleep well?'

This was altogether too ironic. 'No, we

didn't, and I don't suppose any of you did either.'

'No. At least it gave us a chance to come to some tentative conclusions.'

'You mean on whether the Old Man really has killed somebody?'

'Oh no, nothing like as precipitate as that. The main question at issue was go or stay.'

'I thought Alan and Kit had decided.'

'Under some pressure, in an emotional situation. It seemed my duty to put the other argument.'

'As a tutor?'

'Not quite, but I have some duty to protect them, don't you think?'

'So you advised Alan to leave the Old Man to sort things out for himself?' Although I was angry with the Old Man I felt a twinge of conscience about that. I remembered how he'd cried in front of us all.

'I didn't advise him of anything. I just wanted to be sure he was thinking clearly.'

'And the result?'

'He's staying. You're looking pleased about that.'

'Am I? I suppose I'd have thought less of him if he hadn't.'

'So would I – logical or not.'

'So he's staying and Kit's staying.'

'We're all staying.'

'You too? You won't get your book finished with all this going on.'

'There are some things more important than books. This kind of opportunity isn't likely to come more than once or twice in a lifetime.'

'Opportunity?'

'We've all been talking about philosophy, particularly moral philosophy, which means choices. It's not often that you get a chance to put it into practice.'

'So we're all in a kind of philosophical laboratory, are we?'

'You disapprove?'

'No. I know you like experimenting with people.' Again, I was amazed at what I found myself saying to this man on such a short acquaintance.

'That makes it sound a very clinical process, as if I were outside it.'

'What happened to that scout's son – the one you coached?'

For a split second he looked surprised, then laughed. 'We keep in touch. He has a good job with a solicitor, if that reassures you.'

Did I look as if I needed reassuring? While we were talking, Robin had come through the arch from the stable yard, leading a big dark bay cob. He tied it to a ring outside the cart shed and started manoeuvring out the wagonette.

'You'll need to get ready for the journey back,' Meredith said. 'We shall come to the station to see you off.'

'We're not going.' He looked startled, I thought. 'We had our own discussion last night and came to the same conclusion.'

'So you're determined to be moral experimenters as well?'

'I suppose so.' I certainly wasn't going to tell him about Imogen's thunderbolt.

If he had been startled, he recovered quickly. 'Then you must join our college. In the hay barn after breakfast.'

'There's nothing left of the barn.'

'There's another one at the top of a field by the wood. I've just been to look at it.'

'Nell.' Imogen's voice. She came out of the house and saw us. 'Where have you been? We thought something else must have happened.'

Meredith raised his hat again and walked away.

'Nothing's happened,' I told her. Except a silver horse and a stroking hand and a maverick philosopher bent on experiment. 'Nothing.'

In the end the wagonette did go to the station with Robin driving it, but only to collect our luggage. By then we'd all had our breakfast in the kitchen and were in the yard to see it drive off. As it went away up the drive, Meredith looked at Alan and waited. It struck me that all the men except Meredith seemed worse for wear, with bags under their eyes and crumpled collars. Kit's left arm was in a sling. When I asked how it was he told me Meredith had dressed and rebandaged it. The skin was still inflamed from the Old Man's application of carbolic, but the wounds were clean and all the shot pellets out. Midge and I probably didn't look any better than the men and although Imogen would still be elegant after a night in a dog kennel she was paler than usual. I'd been curious to see how she'd behave with Alan at breakfast. After the passionate declaration the night before, I was worried that she might do something unthinkable like running up to him and putting her arms round him. I'd underrated her there, thank goodness. She poured tea and buttered oatbread quite calmly and, if anything, was more distant and formal with him than usual. Anyway that problem would have to keep while we sorted out more immediate ones.

Alan said, 'Meredith's found a barn that might do.' (Although the rest of us were on first-name terms, he remained Meredith. It was a careful judgement by his former pupils. A 'Mr' in front of it would have been too formal, but he was still a don and too senior in years to us to be 'Michael'.)

After a little hesitation Alan led the way across the yard and through the gate to the uphill track where I'd walked earlier in the morning. Just past Sid's field there was a gate on the other side, leading to a field of pale grass that had been shaved close for its hay. In the top corner below the wood was a grey stone barn that looked older than the house, pierced by narrow window slits.

'Behold our college,' Nathan said.

We walked up the field in silence. The view from outside the old barn was even better than from the track, across the flat green fields of the Solway Plain to the sea and the Scottish hills. As we went inside a flock of startled house martins came skittering out over our heads and swung up into a cloud-less blue sky. Inside was shadowy and sweet smelling, with shafts of sunlight coming through the window slits and illuminating random areas among the shadows. The new hay crop that had been taken off the field was stacked along one wall but the barn was so big there was still a lot of empty space. Alan and Nathan took the lead in piling up some of the hay trusses to make seats near the open doors of the barn where the light was best, seven hay piles in a semicircle, looking out at the view. We settled ourselves self-consciously, as if on a stage set and waited for somebody to speak. It was Nathan who broke the silence.

'It's not far from here to the sea, is it?'

Kit said, 'I don't think we're here to discuss the geography.'

'I mean, it would be quite easy to get the Old Man away. Down to the coast, off in a fishing boat and in France or somewhere before they know he's gone.'

We all stared. Meredith asked gently what the purpose of that would be.

'Well, as far as I can see it's either that or wait until they come and arrest him, and we can't do that.'

'Why not?' Meredith again.

'Well, he's Alan's great uncle and he seems a nice enough old chap in his way when he's not blazing away at people with shotguns. I take it if we've all decided to stay it means we're on his side and the main thing is to stop them hanging him.'

Midge gasped, 'They wouldn't hang an old man like him, would they?'

'Is it worse to hang an old man than a young one?' Meredith asked.

Midge started saying something, but Kit cut in, 'I suppose you might argue that it's not so bad, because an old man hasn't got so much life left anyway.'

'But death's an absolute. You can't look at it as if you're slicing cheese–'

'If you go down that road, you'd say it wasn't so bad to murder an old man as a young man–'

'Anyway, if he'd wanted to go he'd have gone by now wouldn't he, so–'

Everybody talking at once, then we all

stopped at once, waiting for each other to go on. Meredith broke the silence.

'So we have one practical proposition from Nathan, that we should help a murderer escape justice. Any comments on that?'

Midge said quietly, 'After all, a man's dead. I don't see how we can get away from that.'

I started saying something, then stopped because Kit was speaking.

'So you're arguing that we should let justice take its course?'

'It depends what you mean by justice.' A groan from Kit. 'It wouldn't be justice to hang an old man for accidentally killing somebody, but–'

'What do you mean accidentally? By his own account he fired a double-barrelled shotgun twice at a crowd of people.'

'People who were threatening him,' Midge said. 'It could count as self-defence.'

'Are we talking about justice or law?' Meredith asked.

'Both, I hope.'

'Essentially you're arguing that we should let the law take its course, but do what we can to influence that course?'

'By helping him prove self-defence, yes.'

'So you're against Nathan's proposition of helping him to escape?'

Sounding impatient, Alan said, 'He wouldn't go anyway. He wouldn't leave his horses.'

It was his first contribution to the discussion. Up to that point he and Imogen had been the sitting at the far ends of the semicircle, not saying anything. Nathan looked disappointed. He'd clearly been enjoying the prospect of night escapes and fishing boats.

'So we wait until the police come for him, then get him a good lawyer, is that it?'

I said, 'Doesn't it seem odd that the police haven't arrested him by now? After all, it must have happened more than a month ago. If it did happen.'

'Something happened,' Alan said. 'He thinks he killed somebody, even knows who.'

'Mawbray, son of the magistrate, whoever he may be. But all we know is that on a particular night your uncle fired on a group of people in the dark and since then nobody's seen Mawbray's son. Even that assumes that your uncle's account is more or less what happened – and that's making a big assumption.'

'You think he's lying, Nell?'

'Not lying exactly. But he's a man with a strong sense of drama, to put it mildly.'

'There's the other barn,' Alan said. 'It really was burnt.'

Midge said, 'Then there were those boys.'

'Yes, shouting "murderer". But even at best, all that would prove is that some people think he's a murderer – or choose to pretend

103

they think he's a murderer.'

Nathan clutched his head and groaned. 'Any minute now she's going to start talking about that tree.'

We stared at him. 'What tree?'

'You know, the one in the quad and whether it still exists if there's nobody around to see it existing. No?'

'Not unless you want me to.'

'No. So you're saying it's all moonshine – the Old Man never killed anybody and nobody thinks he did, they're all just pretending to think he did.'

'Has Nathan given a fair summary, Miss Bray?' Meredith sounded amused. I knew I'd pushed my argument further than it deserved, but didn't want to back down.

'Fair enough.'

'Can you explain why they should all be acting in this way?'

'Let's go back to that Mafeking meeting of his. Accepting for the sake of argument that it happened more or less as he told it–'

Alan interrupted, 'I accept that at any rate. It's exactly the kind of lunatic thing he would do.'

'Or brave,' Midge said quietly.

'Lunatic or brave,' I said, 'we accept that he did it, and it obviously made him enemies. Let's take another jump and assume some people really did come on to his land and burn down his barn, and he and Robin really did go out and fire at them.'

'So you're accepting his story after all?' Kit said.

'No. Here's where I start questioning it. From his account, the only reason for thinking he killed Mawbray's son is that nobody's seen the man, or the boy or whoever he is, since that night. Doesn't that allow two possible interpretations?'

'More than that,' Meredith said quietly.

Nathan cut in, more loudly, 'I think I see what Nell's getting at. The Old Man shoots at Mawbray's son in the dark and misses. Mawbray's son goes into hiding and his friends pretend he's dead to get the Old Man hanged.'

I think we all wished that he wouldn't talk so breezily about being hanged. It gave the thing too much hard reality.

'They might not intend to go that far. Perhaps when they decide he's suffered enough, Mawbray's son will come out of wherever he's been hiding – or back from wherever he's gone – and they'll pretend it's all a great joke.'

'Pretty cruel joke,' Kit said. 'So what Nell's saying is nobody's dead at all?'

'I'm suggesting it's a possibility.' I'd been carried along by the argument and wasn't as sure as I'd pretended. I'd never have admitted it at the time, but I can see now I wanted to impress Meredith. If I had, he was showing no obvious signs of it.

Imogen said slowly, 'One thing about Nell's version – it explains what the housekeeper woman was hinting at last night – that we shouldn't believe the story. If she'd heard local rumours...' Her voice trailed away and we waited for her to go on, but she didn't. She was carefully not looking at Alan.

'If she knows it's all a nasty joke, why doesn't she tell the poor old chap?' Nathan asked.

And Kit answered, 'Maybe she doesn't like him.'

I opened my mouth and shut it again. She'd shown no sign of dislike when he was stroking her haunch, but I couldn't bring myself to tell them about it.

There was silence for a while, then Meredith asked if we thought we'd made any progress. Kit, who seemed to have taken on the job of group spokesman as usual, thought not.

'We haven't even gone round in circles, we've gone backwards. We started with what our ethical responsibilities would be if the Old Man's a murderer, then we were talking like lawyers about reducing it to manslaughter, now we're wondering if anybody's dead at all.'

'Fair summary,' Meredith said. 'Any conclusions?'

Midge said diffidently, 'At least we're

talking about facts. Either Mawbray's son is alive or he isn't.'

'Indisputable,' Kit drawled. For some reason, Midge seemed to annoy him.

'All right, stating the obvious. But surely there's something we could do to find out.'

Nathan said, 'We might start by finding out who he is, or was.'

So we gave up any pretence of philosophic discussion and got down to ways and means. The problem was that we had only three possible sources of information at Studholme Hall. Of those, one was the suspect himself, another Dulcie Berryman who had offered one questionable piece of evidence, and then there was Robin who'd hardly uttered a word since we arrived. Widening the net was essential but that meant going back to the town or around the Old Man's neighbours and we felt we were in hostile territory. It was odd how quickly that feeling had grown on us. I supposed we simply weren't used to people disliking us and were too young to have developed thick skins.

It was Nathan who came up with both the simplest and most alarming suggestion – that we ask the police. He pointed out that it could hardly make things worse. If they were on the point of arresting the Old Man, at least we should know about it. If the whole thing might be the yokels' idea of a joke, we should know that too. At the very least, the police would know about Mawbray's son. Since we could hardly descend in a body on the local police station, Alan and one other should go. Alan looked unhappy, but agreed.

'You've got standing after all,' Kit said. 'I suppose you're the nearest relative.'

'My father's probably that, but he and the Old Man quarrelled decades ago, so I'm the nearest one on speaking terms.'

Meredith agreed to go with him. As Alan's tutor (or more strictly, former tutor) he'd add weight to the deputation. The next question was when. Obviously not that day, because we'd been talking all morning and it would be too late for them to walk to town and back. Tomorrow then? But the next day was Saturday, so by the time they got to the police station it might be closed for the weekend and Sunday was out of the question. Monday morning then, a good comfortable few days away. On Monday morning we'd definitely start doing something. It seems strange now to think how fast and how slowly time seemed to move that summer – as if we were living simultaneously in both centuries, the more leisurely nineteenth and the hurrying twentieth into which time had just tipped us. While we sat up there in our barn below the wood at the top of the hill we could enjoy the view and choose to be part of it or not. And if we chose to be part of it then we could take our time, make our own terms with it. Even on that morning the barn was already becoming for us a kind of sanctuary, a philosophers' porch. Which was why nobody seemed very surprised when Alan made his proposal.

'We'll live here. I don't see how I can stay under the Old Man's roof and go calmly down to the police station and ask if he's killed somebody. There's enough hay to sleep an army, we've brought some food with us and we'll get more from town. We'll move our books in and do some reading the way we'd intended.'

Instant agreement from Kit. Nathan added, 'Anything but that confounded parlour again.'

Alan said, 'I'm sure the Old Man will find you a room in the house, Meredith. After all, you're in a rather different position.'

'On the contrary, I'm in exactly the same position as the rest of you. It's a perfectly good barn.'

I thought wistfully how good it would be to go to sleep in the sweet-smelling hay and wake up to the house martins' twittering but knew it would be no use.

'What about us?' Midge said.

'You'll stay in the house. At least you have a bed there.'

Imogen said instantly, 'I'm not staying in Dulcie Berryman's bed.'

Alan turned from anxious to downright miserable, as he always was when he thought he'd offended her.

'I'll speak to him. We'll find somewhere.'

I asked if we weren't bound, like the men, by the ethical impossibility of staying under the Old Man's roof but didn't get an answer because somebody spotted the wagonette going down the drive to the house, loaded with all our luggage. There was a surge downhill, Nathan running to get to it and start setting up their camp, Kit following at good pace in spite of his injury, then Midge and Imogen. Alan hung back to talk to me.

'What's wrong with Imogen?'

'What do you mean?'

'She's been avoiding me all day, hardly said a word to me.'

'She's tired.'

'It's more than that, isn't it? She blames me, doesn't she? Blames me for bringing her here.'

'No, I'm sure not.'

'Is it the business with the Old Man, then? She thinks I'm doing the wrong thing?'

'Not as far as I know.'

'Then for pity's sake, what *is* it?'

I told him he'd just have to ask her, then stepped out fast to catch up with Midge and Imogen. Five words would have answered all his questions, but I wasn't the one to say them.

Chapter Six

We settled in over a weekend of sun and showers and everything was such a change from our protected college life that the holiday feeling couldn't help creeping in, murder or not. Most of the time was spent sorting out sleeping space. Alan had a talk on his own with the Old Man and came back looking strained but with a satisfactory outcome. The stone barn or anything else around the place was ours for as long as we wanted it. Kit asked if he'd minded that we were making our own arrangements.

'He didn't get a chance,' Alan said. 'I told him I felt I'd placed you all in an ambiguous situation and this was the best all round. And I told him Meredith and I are going in to see the police on Monday.'

'How did he take it?'

'Calmly enough.'

The question of where Imogen, Midge and I were to sleep had been settled too. It turned out that most of the upstairs rooms in the house were unsuitable owing to falling ceilings or being packed with odds and ends but there was a long empty loft above the tack room, looking out over the stable yard.

At one time it must have been used for storage because there were rough wooden shelves all round it but there was plenty of space on the bare boards for three pallet beds and good light from three windows once we'd brushed the cobwebs off them. There weren't any spare mattresses in the house, but dozens of clean feed sacks in the fodder room and endless quantities of hay. We found waxed thread in the tack room along with some big curved needles and sat cross-legged on the bare floor, stitching away like tailors. The men sent Nathan as an ambassador from their barn, begging us to sew them mattresses too. We gave him a lesson instead – he was a quick learner – and sent him back uphill loaded with sacks, needles and thread. There was one odd encounter as a result of that. Because we'd given Nathan our needles I volunteered to go downstairs to the tack room to get more. There was a little narrow stairway leading straight down to it from our loft and halfway down I realised that the Old Man was there. He had a bridle on a hook and was fixing a different bit to it, absorbed and looking quite content. When I said good morning from the stairs he turned round unsurprised, as if he'd known I was there all along.

'Oh, it's the argumentative one, is it? Good morning.'

As opposed to the pretty one and the little

one, I supposed. He seemed determined not to learn our names, but otherwise quite friendly. I explained about the needles and asked if we could borrow more.

'Course you can.' He rummaged in a drawer, found none, started trying to open another drawer. 'Dulcie's bed not good enough for you then?'

This with a grin over his shoulder at me that seemed to say a lot more than the words. I said politely that it had been kind of Miss Berryman to give up her bed to us for one night, but we couldn't deprive her of it any longer.

'Mrs Berryman. Not that she cares.'

'Widowed?'

'Long time ago. Husband was a Solway fisherman, lost at sea.'

'I'm sorry.'

'She wasn't. Drank and knocked her about.'

He seemed to be having trouble with the drawer. It was sticking and wouldn't pull out. I went across to help him but he waved me away and kept tugging and swearing at it. When it gave at last it came out with a rush that sent him staggering backwards. The drawer crashed to the tiled floor and a confusion of straps and curb chains and spools of thread scattered all over the place. The Old Man kept his feet but staggered and ended up leaning against the opposite wall. I got on hands and knees to pick things up and it was some time before I realised that there was something wrong. His head was bent over and his breath was coming fast and shallow. I went to him but he waved me away.

'It's all right. Don't make a fuss, woman. For God's sake don't fuss over me.'

I went back to picking things off the floor, but kept an eye on him. After a while his breathing became more regular. He straightened up and smiled but still looked shaky. 'Heart misses a beat or two sometimes. Comes back again – anyway, always has so far.'

I only just caught the last few words because they were said under his breath as he turned away from me. He was looking up at his picture of galloping horses and sea waves.

'Have you seen a doctor?'

'Bloody waste of money. And don't go gossiping to Alan. I'm not going to let them make an invalid out of me. Understood?'

I didn't promise. When he'd finished looking at the picture he helped me collect up the oddments and we got the drawer back. I thanked him and started back upstairs. When I was halfway up he called after me, 'That ride – are you still game?'

'Of course.'

'Next week, when the moon's full.'

The men showed us their hay mattresses,

ranged along one side of the barn with old apple boxes in between for their books and spare clothes. One of the mattresses was at some distance from the others with a pile of hay in between – a defence against Nathan's snoring, they said. They were proud of themselves and had organised a lunchtime picnic on the grass outside – cheese, cold sliced beef, pork pie, bottles of ale for them and tea made in a big kettle they'd borrowed from the kitchen, hanging from a tripod of hazel rods lashed together over a fire made from dead branches they'd collected in the wood. Like most of the practical things, the fire was mostly Nathan's work. He'd even cut out a big square in the grass and rolled up the turves he'd taken from it as neatly as Swiss rolls so that they could be put back later. The flames from the fire were transparent in the sunlight and the smoke smelled sweet. As we ate we discussed the food supply question. The things we had brought with us were running out and we couldn't go on eating up the household's meagre stores. That meant shopping would have to be done in the town and our reception there so far hadn't been encouraging.

'Alan and Meredith have got to go there on Monday in any case,' Nathan said. 'If we borrowed the wagonette, we could get a crate of ale and a leg of ham and so on.'

'And come back at a gallop, chased by a

115

rabble yelling murder and throwing stones?'
Kit said. He was managing to eat neatly,
one-handed, but from the cautious way he
moved, it was clear that the arm was still
giving him pain.

Judging by Nathan's expression he seemed
to think that was quite a good idea.

I said hastily, 'It might be a good idea if
the three of us went. People are less likely to
throw things at women on the whole.'

Surprised looks from Midge and Imogen
at that. We'd agreed that we weren't going to
let the men cast us as providers of food and
washers of dishes. But I had my own reasons
for wanting to try the temperature of the
town. It seemed to me that we wouldn't get
any answers by sitting up there on our hill.
Alan's mission to the police was a step in the
right direction, but there were certain to be
people in the area who knew things the
police didn't. It was too much to expect that
I'd find out anything to the point on my first
visit, but it would be a start at least. As I'd
expected, the men took up the idea
enthusiastically. They made up a shopping
list that was heavy on things like ale, Stilton
and Bath Olivers and we all agreed to
contribute ten shillings to a pool.

'Some progress in our little republic,'
Meredith said. 'We now have food and
money in common.'

So from that, rather self-consciously, we

did what we'd intended to do – we sat on piles of sweet-smelling hay outside the barn and studied Plato's *Republic*. The classicists, Alan, Kit and Imogen, took it in turns to read a passage in the original Greek and translate. After that, we'd discuss it. *As to this justice, can we quite without qualification define it as truthfulness and repayment of anything that we have received?* Even though I couldn't understand more than one word in twenty of the Greek, it was good to lie back on the grass looking up at the sky, hearing words from more than two thousand years ago drifting past like clouds on the breeze. Imogen had a pleasant, low voice, Greek or English, and while she was reading Alan stared at her so intently that she must have been conscious of it, though she gave no sign. Later we carried plates and cups to wash up in a brook that ran out of the wood into a little pool with pebbles at the bottom. I'd been wondering on and off whether I should tell anybody about the Old Man's near collapse. I'd made him no promises but hadn't rushed to tell Alan either. So I compromised by getting Meredith out of earshot of the others, walking along the bank.

'It looked like heart trouble to me. The strain of all this might be affecting him worse than he pretends. The question is, should Alan know?'

'In spite of the Old Man not wanting it?'

'Alan might be able to persuade him to see a doctor,' I said.

'So we disregard his wishes for his own good?'

'Plato said you wouldn't give a knife back to a madman, even if it belonged to him and he asked for it.'

'A reasonable point. I take it you're not arguing literally that the Old Man's mad?'

'No.'

'So the question is whether he's such a poor judge of his own best interests that we have to intervene for him.'

'Yes. We're doing that already with the other thing.'

'And you're arguing that one intervention justifies another?'

'No. If anything, the reverse.'

The Old Man had annoyed me but I still liked him enough to want him to keep his dignity. Talking to Meredith, the decision seemed to have made itself.

'I don't think I'll tell Alan. Not for the time being at least.'

We'd come to the fence where the field met the wood. I turned to stroll back to the others but Meredith hesitated.

'Miss Bray, there's another thing – rather similar in its way.' He sounded unsure of himself, which wasn't like him.

'Yes?'

'Alan. Last night he confided in me. I don't

know whether I'm right to be telling you about it or not.' I waited. 'You remember that conversation we had on the train?'

'About his being in love? Of course.'

'He seems to think that he's done something to offend her quite badly but he has no notion what it might be. If that is the case, if there's been some kind of misunderstanding, then it might be useful for him to know.'

I stared down at the stream, visible only in snatches under a tunnel of fern and foxgloves.

'I don't think he's offended her.'

'What is it then? Until now he was under the impression that she didn't dislike him at least. I know I've got no right to ask, only...'

I looked up and saw the anxiety in his face. It was gone the instant he realised I was looking at him, but it had been far too sharp to be caused by any anxiety over a pupil. The whole landscape seemed to give a little skip, the way it does when you're adjusting to something new, and I thought 'Good heavens, he's in love with her too.' It was a jolt, but then why should it be? After all, men did fall in love with Imogen. She'd been sitting there through a whole course of his lectures and she wasn't a woman you could ignore. So it all made perfect sense in its way and there was no reason for this sharp little pain in my chest that felt horribly like envy but couldn't be. I was sorry for them, that was all. Sorry for all of them and perhaps a little angry over this business of love that confused things and made idiots of people and made it so hard to be honest and reasonable however much you'd agreed that men and women should be. Once I got that sorted out I knew I had to give him some kind of answer, if only to stop him hoping.

'It's for her to say, not me. But you can take it that she certainly doesn't dislike him and he hasn't offended her.'

I could see from his face that he'd taken my meaning, but he recovered quickly.

'May I tell him that?'

'I suppose so.' Then, thinking of the stunned way Imogen had been behaving. 'But could you give me some time to talk to her first over the weekend? You might tell him on Monday perhaps, when you're in town together.'

I hated having to plot like this, but sensed that Imogen was on the edge of a cliff. Whether the way off it was flying, plunging or simply walking back the way she'd come and waiting for another day, she should at least have time to think. He nodded and we went back to the others.

On Sunday the hot weather started and the sky was an almost metallic blue like the body of a dragonfly. We read Plato for a while after a picnic breakfast, then the men found a bathing place lower down the brook, in the big field where the mares were. They came back, wet-haired and pleased with themselves, for more tea and philosophy. Kit said the cold water had been good for his arm and Meredith rebandaged it for him. I lay on the grass, tried to memorise various tenses of the Greek verb *luo*, I loosen, and did my best not to watch Meredith standing in the sunshine, combing his dark hair. He seemed somehow more elegant, more finished than the other three men, even the handsome Alan. It was something to do with the way he moved, under control with no gesture wasted. Or perhaps... Concentrate woman. *Leluka*, I have loosened, *lelukas*, *leluke*. Should I warn Imogen that he was attracted to her? Probably not. It would only worry her and she had enough to think about, God knows. On the other hand... Damn. Why did people persist in landing me with their dilemmas as if I were some sort of oracle? Being two years older than Imogen shouldn't mean I had nothing to do but sit on the grass and dole out wise counsel – as if I knew anything, particularly about this business of loving or not loving. Why should the curve of a cheek, the colour of a lock of hair, a few inches in height more or less govern who you spent your life with or even what you did with your life? In the middle of the afternoon, with the Scottish hills hazy in the heat, Imogen, Midge and I decided that we'd go bathing too. We walked slowly down our field and into the lane. I noticed Sid grazing quietly in the shade of the trees and told them about the Old Man's picture and lines from Byron.

'It would be Byron, wouldn't it,' Imogen said. 'He belongs in another age, the Old Man.'

'I see what you mean. As if Queen Victoria never happened.'

Assuming him to be in his mid-seventies now, he'd have been a lad when she came to the throne more than sixty years ago, in an age when gentlemen at least didn't have to care too much about being respectable. Perhaps that explained a lot of things, including Dulcie.

'Poor Alan.' Imogen breathed it on a sigh. Midge and I looked at each other.

By the house we debated whether to collect our towels and decided against it. We'd get dry in the sun, Midge said. We saw nobody in the yard or on the track down to the big field where the mares were grazing. The grass in there was still uncut, so soft and cool looking that a few steps through the gate I took off my boots and stockings and went barefoot. After a while the other two did the same. We went in single file down to the river with the mares staring at us from the shade of the alders and willows, whisking their tails against the flies. The bathing place was a long way down the field. By then the brook had collected a few tributaries and become a little river. A bridge crossed it, made of flat stone slabs on supports of rocks piled up without mortar. Below the bridge the river broadened and deepened into a pool perhaps four or five feet deep and so clear that the pebbles at the bottom gleamed like jewels in a shop window. Nearly mad from the heat, I tore my clothes off and slid into the water. It felt bitingly cold. I struck out to the middle of the pool, turned downstream and went slowly with the current, moving just enough to keep afloat. A splash and a cry behind me and Midge was following, striking out at the water like a happy spaniel. We turned and took a few strokes upstream to where Imogen was still sitting on the bank with her skirt drawn up to her knees, dabbling her long white feet in the water.

Midge said, 'Isn't it nice without men.'

We stood with water up to our shoulders and teased Imogen to join us. After a while she said all right, stood up and started unbuttoning her skirt but so slowly that we could tell she didn't want us to watch her undress. We went off downstream again and when we came back she was standing there with the water up to her knees but the same dreamy look on her face she'd had since we got there, as if the coldness of the water made no impression. Midge and I grabbed a hand each and pulled her in, screaming, which at least took care of the dreaminess for a while. We had a mock water fight as if we were about nine years old, slapping the surface to send sprays of drops over each other, diving to grab at ankles, laughing and screeching so much that the mares turned their heads to see what was happening.

When we'd had enough we climbed out on the bank and slapped at ourselves with our skirts to dry off the worst of the water. We got back into our petticoats, chemises and blouses, loosely buttoned, but left our hair down and our skirts spread on the bank to dry while we lay in the sun, half asleep and half awake. For a while, with my skin still cool from the water and the scents of river and crushed grass all round us I felt totally, mindlessly happy as I hadn't felt for years. Then Imogen spoke.

'What am I going to do?'

I said, 'He thinks he's offended you. He asked me what was wrong.'

'What did you say?'

'That you were tired.'

She smiled up at the sky. 'It's funny, I've never felt less tired. I don't think I slept a moment last night or the night before, just lay there thinking – no, not even thinking, just being.'

'Interesting point,' Midge said. 'Are you suggesting that when we go to sleep we stop being?'

'No. I've had enough of philosophical discussion. I'm asking you both, what I'm going to *do*.'

'One way or the other,' I said, 'you're going to have to say something to him before he goes melancholy mad.'

'I know. That's why I've been avoiding him. I can't talk to him about the weather, or his uncle or anything else. If I speak to him at all I'll have to come straight out with it. "Alan, when you said you loved me, but I didn't understand, I understand now and I love you too."' She said it staring up at the sky. We didn't speak. She got impatient. 'Come on, say something. Isn't that what we all agreed a woman should do when she loves somebody? No coyness, no pretending not to understand, no little tricks to make it look as if it's all his responsibility, not hers. Simple, honourable statements from two people who happen to love each other – wasn't that it?'

Undeniable. We had discussed it – not all the time, of course, because there were plenty of other things to worry about – as part of the question of how a modern woman should manage her life.

'Haven't you ever felt like this, either of you?'

Midge shook her head from side to side against the grass.

I said, also looking up at the sky, 'Once, four years ago. There was this young German I met when my mother and I were in the Alps for the summer. It was crazy, I can see that now, but nothing and nobody else existed.'

'What happened?' Midge asked.

'His father found out and made him go back home. Just as well, probably.' Only it hadn't felt like that at the time.

'Well, Alan's not going away,' Imogen said, 'so I've got to make up my mind. Can either of you give any good reason why I shouldn't tell him?'

We gave her several: that things were complicated enough already, that her nerves were still too jangled to make proper decisions, that if she really loved him she'd still feel the same when they were back in Oxford in October and she could tell him then. She made the same point in reply to all of them: that she could hardly go through the next few weeks without speaking to Alan, and if she did speak to him, it would be impossible to tell him anything but the truth. All right, we said, go away. Next train south out of Carlisle and we'll come with you if you like. Total resistance there too. How could any woman who loved a man go away and leave him with an undoubtedly mad, probably murderous great uncle? All right, we said, the two of us will stay if you like and help protect him and write to you. She didn't even bother to reply to that.

'So when it comes to it, neither of you has got any argument against telling him.'

'We've given you half a dozen,' Midge said, 'only you won't listen.'

'So it's decided then, at the first opportunity, I tell him. Then what?'

Midge said, 'I suppose you get engaged but don't tell your colleges, ask your parents for permission and get married when you've done your finals.'

'But that's a year away. Anyway, my parents will hate it. Mummy's got half a dozen fledgling ambassadors lined up for my inspection next time I'm in India. Penniless scholars need not apply.'

'Penniless, is he?'

'Pretty nearly. Anyway, I'm twenty-one in October and he's twenty-one already. We could get married whether my parents liked it or not.'

'Leaving you penniless too,' Midge said.

'We're all going to work for our living, aren't we? Or have you gone back on that too?'

'We haven't gone back on anything,' I said. 'But there is the question of the colleges.' Students were not allowed to marry. Very occasionally exceptions were made for the young gentlemen, but this wouldn't be one. Somerville woman marries Balliol man was more likely to set alarm bells than joy bells ringing.

'I could leave and get a teaching job. Anyway, it's not as if they even let women take degrees.'

'You won't get much of a teaching job if you leave before you take your final exams.'

Imogen said, 'Oh, this is nothing to do with it. Nothing to do with it at all. Why worry about finals or jobs or money. I love him and he loves me now, now, now.' With every 'now' she beat the grass beside her with clenched fists.

'So,' I said, 'you go to him and you tell him you love him and nothing else matters?'

'Yes.'

Midge said, 'And you both wait until you can get married?'

Imogen turned her head to look not at Midge but at me and gave me a lazy smile, much more relaxed than she'd been so far.

'Did you wait, Nell?'

'I told you, he was sent–'

'Before you had time to–'

'Yes.'

'And if you'd known he was going to be sent away?'

'That's a hypothetical question.'

'That means yes, doesn't it? You're

blushing, Nell. Yes?'

'It's hot.' I turned my head away.

She laughed. 'Yes.'

After a while we wandered back up to the barn, stopping before we got there to help each other put up our still-damp hair. The men pretended they'd been discussing Plato all the time we'd been away but we didn't believe them. Nathan was making a kind of chair from hazel rods and a section of tree trunk he'd found in the woods, Kit and Meredith were reading and Alan was pacing aimlessly up and down. Imogen's eyes followed him.

'Do you think he's worrying about what the police will say tomorrow, Nell?'

'Probably.'

'Do you mind if I don't come down to the town with you and Midge. I don't want...' Her voice trailed away. I wasn't sure if she couldn't trust herself in a wagonette with Alan or if she wanted him to keep his mind clear for a difficult interview.

'Not in the least. You can have a nice quiet time here reading Greek with Meredith.'

I usually try not to be waspish, but it was hot and I'd had enough. Luckily she wasn't paying me much attention. I walked up the field to look at the view and get myself back in a good temper. The sound of Midge's and Nathan's laughter followed me. I think he was trying to persuade her to try sitting in his chair. Further down, a solitary figure was walking away from the house, along the track towards the mares' field, the sun glinting on his silver hair – the Old Man going about his business, apparently unconcerned with all of us up there debating what should be done about him. A surge of sadness came over me that he might be taken away from his land and his horses and I knew I wanted to do something to prevent that happening. It was a question that had very little to do with liking and nothing at all with any definition we'd found so far of justice. A question of rightness, I supposed, though I was glad nobody was asking me to define it.

Late that night, well after midnight when Midge and Imogen were asleep on their hay pallets on either side of me, I heard soft footsteps in the tack room below then the door to the stable yard opening. I looked out to see the glow of lamplight on the cobbles of the yard and the familiar figure, horsewhip in one hand, lamp in the other. It was the Old Man again, keeping watch against enemies who might or might not exist. I remembered a sentence that Imogen had translated from the Greek: *For, Socrates, old age lays only a moderate burden on men who have order and peace within themselves.* I thought he had made a kind of order for himself, but it didn't look like peace.

Chapter Seven

I was in the stable yard around seven the next morning when Alan came to ask the Old Man for the loan of the wagonette.

'Take it, my boy. My house is your house. Only you'll have to hitch up Bobbin yourself. Robin's up in Sid's paddock seeing to the fence.'

We went down in a bunch to collect the placid cob from where he was grazing by the river. Alan and I buckled the head collar on and led the horse up to the yard. He and Nathan pulled the wagonette out from the cart shed while Midge and Imogen collected the harness from the tack room.

'Which way round does it go?' Midge stared at the mass of straps and buckles.

'Let me see it.' I had hold of Bobbin at the time and, forgetting about the arm, handed the head-collar rope to the nearest person who happened to be Kit. He almost dropped it.

'I'm not good with horses, in any case. Unpredictable animals, cherished by irrational people.'

He was keeping as much distance as he could between himself and the cob. Without fuss, Meredith took the head-collar rope from him. We managed to get Bobbin harnessed to the wagonette, although I noticed Imogen too was keeping her distance.

'I'm not good with horses either. I prefer bicycles.'

Meredith took the reins, Alan climbed up beside him and Midge and I sat facing each other on the seats at the back. Nobody said much on the way into town. We arrived there at about half past nine and decided to stable Bobbin and the wagonette at a public house with livery stables at the back. Meredith went inside to negotiate while we waited in the yard and, I guessed, to test whether there was any open hostility. He came out looking relieved, followed by a grinning groom.

'They'll look after him. I've said we'll be back in a couple of hours or so. Will that be enough for your shopping?'

We said yes and agreed to meet in front of the public house at midday. Meredith had already got directions to the police station and we watched as they walked away through the arch into the street. Alan looked pale and nervous but then calling on the police to ask if a family member might have murdered somebody would put a strain on anyone. Midge took the shopping list out of her pocket.

'Where shall we start?'

'I thought we might go and have a look at the police court.'

'Oh?'

'I'm sure the magistrates will be sitting on a Monday. There are bound to be a few cases of fighting or drunkenness over the weekend, even in a little town like this.'

'And that interests us?'

'The magistrates do. About the only thing we know about the person the Old Man's supposed to have murdered is that he's a magistrate's son. If Mawbray senior is on the bench, I'd like to see him.'

'How will that help?'

'I don't suppose it will, but can you suggest anywhere else to start?'

'Apart from the grocers, you mean?'

'That can wait.'

She put the list back in her pocket and we asked directions to the police court. It turned out to be alongside the police station, but luckily there was no sign of Alan and Meredith by the time we got there. There was a constable at the entrance to the court. I asked him when the magistrates would be sitting and he said from ten o'clock onwards.

'Will Mr Mawbray be on the bench?'

'Major Mawbray's chairman of the magistrates, miss.'

Later in life I spent a lot of time in police courts, but this was my first experience of one. The public bench turned out to be quite crowded because the main attraction of the morning concerned a fight in a public house between two local poaching families, with most of the evidence delivered in such strong Cumberland accents that it was hard for us to follow what was happening. At least it wasn't difficult to pick out Major Mawbray. He was the middle one of the three magistrates on the bench, a thin and upright man with sparse dark hair and yellowish skin stretched tight over a broad forehead and narrow jutting chin that gave his head the shape of an angular pear. He was clean shaven, apart from a thin moustache, and when he spoke to ask a witness a question his voice was sharp and soldierly, with no trace of local accent. He kept taking little sips from a glass of water. From that and his complexion I guessed that his health wasn't good. Digestive problems possibly, which might account for the sharpness of his tone.

Midge and I were squeezed as a buffer between friends of both parties of poachers and kept getting jostled and nudged in the ribs when some particular allegation or piece of evidence made our line hiss and quiver like a breaking wave. At one point the usher threatened indiscriminately to have us all thrown out and Major Mawbray backed up the threat with a glare at the public bench. He noticed the two of us and the glare turned into a puzzled look. He probably knew all the wrongdoers and their relatives in the whole town and country around, and we were strangers. As far as I knew, he had no reason to connect us with the Old Man but we seemed to bother him all the same. We stayed until the end of the case (three months all round, groans and sounds of protest from friends quelled by another warning from the usher, a promise from Major Mawbray, sounding infinitely weary, of more serious sentences if they came up before the bench again) then we walked out into the sunshine.

It was past eleven by then and we'd have to hurry if we were going to get the shopping done. The day had turned bakingly hot and it was a relief to get into the cool cavern of the grocer's shop with a yellow tiled floor, bins of flour and oatmeal around the walls, shelves with red lacquered tins full of different teas and coffee beans. A smell of ham and coffee hung over everything and soft-voiced male assistants sliced bacon and slid sugar and rice and dried peas from the shiny bronze bowl of the weighing machine into brown paper bags. We ruthlessly edited the men's shopping list, leaving out luxuries like Carlsbad plums and Gentlemen's Relish and adding two more legs of ham, several large cheeses and patent soup in slabs. They'd all insisted on Cumberland sausage so we bought pounds of it from the butcher's shop next door, though we were worried about how long it would keep in the heat. Naturally there were no fruit or vegetables on the list, but we found a greengrocers and added a sack of potatoes, a dozen large cabbages and half a dozen punnets of big golden-skinned gooseberries. As we were doing all this, we got some curious looks from shop assistants and other customers, but at least no sign of hostility.

We were walking back to the public house with ten minutes to spare, feeling pleased with our work, when Midge said, 'We've forgotten the butter.' We were just crossing a side street and further up it there was a dairy with shining milk churns outside and a blue sunblind. The woman inside had grey hair and quick little hands. She carved a lump of butter out of a big tub in the cool at the back of the shop, weighed it, slapped it into shape on a marble slab with a pair of ridged wooden butter pats then picked up a wooden stamp and pressed the outline of a cow on the top. I said I was afraid the cow would have melted by the time we got it home.

'Oh,' she said, 'Ah like to mek it conny.' Her accent was as strongly Cumberland as Dulcie's, but not so languorous. She asked if we had far to carry the butter. Experimentally, and because she seemed friendly, I said 'Studholme Hall' watching to see if her expression changed. She beamed.

'You'll be staying with Mr Beston. How is the gentleman? Tell him Dolly Wilson sends her regards.'

Far from being hostile she couldn't do enough for us and hustled us through to a little garden behind her shop, carrying the butter wrapped in paper.

'Rhubarb leaves'll take care of it.'

The rhubarb was growing against an outhouse wall. She pulled three stems and twisted off the floppy leaves, her small hands unexpectedly powerful. As she wrapped the butter in rhubarb leaves to keep it cool I asked if she knew Mr Beston well.

'He's always been a very civil man to me and that gannanlad of his cured our little cuddy when it was ganging cockly.'

Midge gave me a look as much to say, 'You're supposed to be the linguist.'

'Gannan-lad?'

'The Gypsy lad. The little donkey that pulls our milk cart went lame. Mr Beston saw me in town fair greeting for worry over him so he said he'd send his lad to see to it and now he trots as well as any creature in the county. Say what you will about gannan-folk, they've got their ways with a hoss or a cuddy other folk don't know.' She secured the rhubarb leaves with a twist of raffia from her apron pocket and handed the little package to me. I offered her some coins, but she shook her head.

'With my good wishes.'

A clock was striking midday. Midge signed to me to hurry up, but now we'd found somebody on the Old Man's side I wasn't going to give her up so easily. I thanked her and said not everybody in the district seemed to think so well of Mr Beston.

'Oh, that's nobbut politics. They'll get over it in a while.'

'Some people seem to think he shot Major Mawbray's son.'

'Some blatherskites will say anything. If Arthur Mawbray and his gang of gowks go making a shindy and firing an auld man's byre, they should expect to cop a bit of a shooting.'

'As I heard it, nothing's been seen of young Mawbray since the night they set fire to the barn.' She gave me a sideways look that said a lot. 'You have your doubts, then?'

She took her time answering, then, 'It wouldnae be the first time that young man had taken himself off. When he was no more than fifteen, just after his mother died, he quarrelled with his father and went off on a fishing boat. They brought him back from somewhere way up in Scotland and sent him away to college for a fair while, but folk

138

say it didna make any great difference.'

'How long ago was that?'

'Four or five years, maybe. I'm not saying there's any great harm in the lad, only he's got no more sensible as he's got older and he's given his father a deal of trouble.'

Midge was practically dragging at my sleeve by now so we thanked her again for the butter, promised to give her regards to Mr Beston and hurried to meet Alan and Meredith outside the public house.

They were waiting for us and Alan was looking impatient and careworn. Before Midge or I could ask any questions he said, 'Do you mind if we leave it until we're all together? I don't want to have to go over it twice.'

That didn't sound as if the interview with the police had brought any good news and it clearly wasn't the time to start talking about the woman in the dairy. They'd already been into the stable yard and asked the groom to harness up Bobbin so we decided to drive the wagonette to collect the stores we'd bought from the various shops then head for home. Whatever had happened in the police station, I think we were all relieved that our appearance in public hadn't resulted in stone-throwing or insults. While Meredith was paying the groom Midge and I got on board and stowed the butter in a shady place under the seat. As I was straightening up, I noticed an envelope. It was coarse in quality, tied to the side rail of the wagonette with a piece of string knotted through a hole punched jaggedly in the top right hand corner. I unknotted it, already apprehensive and saw the name J. BESTON ESQUIRE in pencilled capitals. Alan climbed into the front passenger seat and saw me looking at it.

'What is it now?'

'It's addressed to your uncle. I have an idea it might not be friendly.'

Meredith finished paying the groom and swung himself into the driver's seat. Alan showed him the envelope.

'It might be a threat of some kind. I think I ought to open it.'

Meredith nodded and Alan tore open the envelope and took out a single sheet of notepaper. He read, started to say something, then handed it to Meredith. When I thought he'd had time to finish – and there were no more than two lines of writing – I leaned over and held out my hand for it. If the message to the Old Man were being treated as public property I thought we had a right to see as well. Alan made a movement probably intended to spare my eyes from it, but Meredith passed it over. I held it so that Midge could see too. It was different paper from the envelope, thin and yellowed as if from a pad in a household where not many letters were written. The message was all in capitals with no signature.

DID YOU ARSK DULSIE WHO HER BAS-
TARDS FATHER REALY IS.

Alan had his head in his hands. 'Oh God, isn't it ever going to stop?'

I gave the letter back to him and we drove home.

Chapter Eight

The others must have heard us on the road because by the time we got down to the yard outside the house Imogen, Kit and Nathan were waiting. There was no sign of the Old Man or Mrs Berryman though Robin appeared, silent as usual but smiling, to take Bobbin and the wagonette when we'd finished getting things out of it. We portered armfuls of bags, boxes and bottles up to the barn and stowed them away in a corner. When we were ready to talk it was still so hot that we stayed inside the barn for shade sitting on our heaps of hay, except for Nathan who'd brought his chair inside and went on working at it. Alan looked round the semicircle, hesitated then plunged in.

'The police aren't sure one way or the other, but they think he might have done it.'

In the silence, you could almost hear hearts dropping.

Midge asked gently, 'Were the police very... Were they rude to you?'

'No, awfully polite in the circumstances, wouldn't you say?' Alan glanced at Meredith, who nodded. 'In fact, Meredith and I got the impression they were almost relieved to have somebody from the family to talk to. The desk sergeant was a bit slow at first and we had to wait and see the inspector – Armstrong his name is, decent sort of man – and he explained things to us pretty straightforwardly. But he didn't try to hide that it looks bad for the Old Man and they're treating it as a possible murder case.'

'Not manslaughter?' Kit asked.

'No, for two reasons. The first one is that they never found a body. They accept that it could have happened more or less as the Old Man says – he fires in the dark and young Mawbray dies – but if it had been an accident wouldn't he have tried to get medical help, or at least if he was beyond help see that the family got his body back?'

'He might have panicked,' Nathan suggested. He'd found a piece of gritty stone from somewhere and was using it to rasp at a rough place on his chair. Alan went on with his story, not bothering to reply.

'Inspector Armstrong thinks the Old Man hid the body or got rid of it. What my uncle didn't tell us was that the police had a dozen people up here for two days after it happened, turning over every room in the house and all the outhouses, looking round the fields for any freshly dug patches. They even raked over the ashes of the other barn that got burnt, in case he'd stuffed the body in there while it was still alight. Nothing.'

'That should be in the Old Man's favour,' Kit said. 'With his age and build, he couldn't go dragging bodies all over the country. I suppose this Mawbray fellow was an average sort of size.'

'Yes. The police have their theory on that as well. They think Robin helped him, possibly Mrs Berryman too.' Alan looked, if anything, even more unhappy. 'Robin's a Gypsy and Mrs Berryman has, well ... has a bit of a past. We got the impression that Inspector Armstrong didn't think much of either of them.' Again he glanced at Meredith for support and got a nod.

Midge said, 'Just because he's a Gypsy–'

And Imogen, speaking at the same time, 'What sort of past?'

Alan blushed. 'She used to be housekeeper to somebody else and apparently rumours got around that she was ... well, more than just a housekeeper.'

Imogen said, 'You mean she had a sexual relationship with her former employer?'

'Well yes, we gathered that's what the rumours were though he didn't come straight out and say so. I suppose he...' Alan was floundering. Imogen had sounded very sharp with him and he didn't seem to guess it was from her own embarrassment.

Midge said, 'Even if she did, I can't see what that's got to do with helping her next employer hide bodies, any more than being a Gypsy does.'

'Police tend to proceed by association rather than logic,' Meredith said. He'd been silent until then and was probably taking up the story to give Alan a chance to recover from his confusion. 'There are a lot of Gypsies in this part of the world. They come over from Ireland for horse trading and the local people tend to hold them responsible for everything from stealing chickens to starting fights in public houses.'

'It's still a long way from that to hiding bodies,' Midge said stubbornly.

'I agree with you. The police answer to that is that Robin is particularly loyal to the Old Man because of his horses and would do anything he wanted.'

Nathan said, 'There's quite a lot of land here, Alan. The paddocks, the wood and so on. You'd need an army to search it properly.'

'Your point being?'

'Well, if the police are right and the three of them did make away with the body, then it's probably still round here somewhere.'

Involuntarily our eyes went to the inside of the barn with its dark corners and piled-up hay.

'It's all right,' Nathan said cheerfully. 'It's not in here anyway. I've had a good look.' Our eyes came back to him. 'Well, don't all stare at me like that. It stands to reason that if the man's dead there's a body somewhere, and if he's not there isn't. You don't have to be Aristotle to puzzle that out. If the main reason the police think it's murder is that they haven't got a body our best course is to find the body alive or dead, wouldn't you say?'

Meredith said gently, 'Could you have missed a few logical steps there, Nathan?'

'How would that help? He'd still have hidden him,' Alan said, recovering. 'Anyway, hypothetically disposing of the body is only part of it. There's the Mawbray question. His father's chairman of the local magistrates and the police practically jump up and salute when the name's mentioned.'

Midge and I glanced at each other. We still hadn't told the others about our visit to the police court.

Kit asked, 'So why is a magistrate's son out in the dark burning people's barns down?'

'If he was,' Meredith said. 'Remember we've only got the Old Man's word for that so far.'

Alan said, 'But Inspector Armstrong didn't question he was there. He didn't really seem surprised. He wouldn't say much, but we did get the impression that the young Arthur Mawbray might have been a bit of a wild lad.'

'Isn't arson and attacking old men a bit beyond the bounds of wildness?' Nathan

146

said, still rasping away.

'The police attitude seems to be that it was mostly high spirits that got out of hand and my uncle pretty well brought it on himself by being pro-Boer. He seems to have upset people round here more than you can imagine with that meeting.'

'What I can't understand,' Kit said, 'is all the uncertainty about what happened. Nobody seems to be disputing that a gang of people attacked this place, so even in the dark the others would have heard or seen something. Surely the police have witnesses to what really happened.'

'Meredith asked them that,' Alan said, glancing at him.

'Yes I did, and got nowhere, as I deserved. If reality depends on witnesses, then none of this is real. There are none. Or at least, none that the police have been able to question.'

'They ran off,' Alan said. 'After the shooting the whole gang of them ran off. I suppose they knew they'd be in trouble about burning the barn down. According to the inspector, the police have made inquiries about who was in the gang and got nowhere.'

'In a country area where everybody knows everybody? I don't believe it,' Midge said.

I pointed out that country areas where everybody knew everybody were good at closing ranks against the police. It was a fair guess that every farmyard for miles around had a young man or lad working in it who'd been out that night.

'Of course,' Alan said, 'that's a bit of good luck for the Old Man in its way. If the police haven't got witnesses and haven't got a body, they'd have a job proving anything happened. But it can't go on like this. They can't just throw up their hands and say if there's no material proof, then it never happened.'

'Logically speaking, they could,' Kit said.

'Except you don't find the police playing logic games when it's the son of the chairman of magistrates missing believed dead. Anyway, there's another thing about the Mawbrays and the Old Man.'

'Worse?'

'Yes. There was a history of trouble between him and the Mawbray family practically from the time he got here two or three years ago. The Mawbray land's just over the hedge near that place in the river where we bathed. A stallion belonging to Major Mawbray got into my uncle's field and … um … paid his compliments to one of my uncle's mares.' Nathan made a strangled sound, trying not to laugh. 'All right, I know it sounds very funny, but in my uncle's case that was quite enough to start a war with a neighbour over.'

I said nothing but knew he was right. I'd already seen the Old Man's reverence for his horses and his possessiveness in questions of sex.

'So there was bad blood between them even before this latest business. In fact, the inspector seemed to think the Old Man might have organised that meeting as much as to annoy Major Mawbray as support the Boers. The Major used to be in the cavalry.'

There was silence for a long time. I wondered whether Alan intended to tell the others about the anonymous note on the wagonette. It seemed not. He'd been embarrassed enough talking about Dulcie Berryman's past even without that and thought he'd offended Imogen again. Imogen was looking at Alan but now he was staring at the ground, not her. How long before that bomb exploded?

I said, 'Not everybody in the town's against the Old Man, and Arthur Mawbray's run away from home once already.'

Heads jerked up all round us. I told them about the conversation I had had with the woman in the dairy. Meredith was looking at me particularly intently, but I couldn't tell if he approved or not.

'I don't think that proves anything,' Kit said. 'The fact that he ran away years ago – assuming it is a fact and not just gossip – doesn't prove he's done it again.'

'I'm not saying it proves anything in itself, but it is some weight on the other side of the scale. Young Mawbray does something he knows is wrong, he gets on badly with his father in any case so he decides to disappear for a while. Isn't that as tenable as the theory that he's dead?' The bad news from the police station had made me realise how much I wanted the Old Man not to be guilty but I could see I wasn't convincing them. I threw another little weight on to the scale. 'Mrs Berryman agrees with me at any rate. You heard what she said on our first night here about the Old Man having some queer notions.'

Imogen said, 'I'm not sure Mrs Berryman would be a very good witness for anything.'

That annoyed me. Imogen didn't know about the anonymous note, but the malice and grubbiness of it had put me on Dulcie's side. 'Why not? Because there's gossip about her? I dare say there's been gossip about many a housekeeper, particularly if she looked like Mrs Berryman.'

Alan blushed deep red. Frank talking on matters of sex was something we all believed in theoretically, but we hadn't had much opportunity to practise it yet.

'The police seemed to think it's relevant,' he said.

'Why? It sounds as if they've been gossiping like a lot of old market women. What has Dulcie Berryman's last position got to do with whether she helped the Old

Man hide a body?'

'It's a matter of who she worked for.'

'Who?' Then, as soon as I'd thrown the question at Alan, the answer dawned on me. 'Not...?'

'Yes.'

Kit said, 'Since the rest of us don't go in for mind-reading, would you mind telling us?'

Alan looked towards Meredith for help and got an almost imperceptible nod. Even so he said it reluctantly. 'Until about a year ago, Mrs Berryman worked for Major Mawbray.'

Silence, broken suddenly by a great bark of laughter from Nathan. 'The Trojan war all over again.' He went on laughing, while we stared at him. 'Come on, you classicists. Major Mawbray as whatsisname – Menelaus – and Mrs Berryman as the lovely Helen who gets stolen away. Do you suppose the Old Man carried her off across his saddle bow?'

I couldn't help laughing and Midge laughed too, but Alan was furious.

'I'm glad you find it so funny. He's my relative, remember, and for all we know the police could be up here arresting him tomorrow. I suppose you'll make a joke of that as well.' He got up and stalked off out of the barn. Imogen put out a hand to stop him but he didn't see and her hand fell back down.

151

I mouthed at Meredith, 'Have you told him?' and got a shake of the head.

'You'd better go to him,' I told Imogen. She gave me a wild and wide-eyed look then stood up and went after him. Midge meanwhile was trying to reassure a shocked and penitent Nathan.

I think we were all shaken, as much by this first quarrel in our little republic as by any news about the Old Man. Through the hot afternoon we went our various ways, collecting things to eat and drink from our new supply of stores as we wanted them. Meredith stayed in the shade of the barn to work on his book. Kit disappeared for a walk on his own. He seemed preoccupied, probably because his friend was in trouble and he could do nothing to help. Nathan tried to make practical amends by promising chairs for everybody and persuaded Midge to go into the woods with him to look for more materials. As the two of them scrambled through the fence that separated wood from field, Nathan looked back at me with a worried expression.

'What happens if we find him, Nell? Do we leave him or don't we?' For once he wasn't joking.

'You're expecting to find Arthur Mawbray's body?'

'Not expecting exactly, but you have to

admit if you were trying to get rid of something it would be better in a wood than a field. You could put dead leaves and branches over the place where you'd buried it and–'

Midge said, 'Come on and stop being morbid,' and practically dragged him through the fence. At least that meant I didn't have to try and answer his question.

I decided a walk might clear my mind so went down the field and crossed the lane into the paddock where Sid was grazing. I said a few friendly words to him in passing, then contoured round the side of the wood to the open hillside. Up there it was rough pasture, with sheep newly sheared and looking as leggy as goats wandering in and out of clumps of bracken and gorse. You could see the whole of the Old Man's land from there, identifiable by the new post-and-rail fences round his paddocks, and beyond it to the railway shining in the sun and the little town. Westwards towards Aspatria a cluster of chimneys and winding gear marked the collieries, then a strip of green along the coast and the sea. Nearer at hand to the left, in another clump of woodland, the red roof and chimney-pots of a large house were just visible: Major Mawbray's house possibly, and if so more hostile territory.

Just by being there we'd taken on the Old Man's battle whether we liked it or not, in local eyes at least. The trouble was, we hadn't quite. When I looked down at Studholme Hall I saw the Old Man walking slowly across the stable yard and Robin leading Bobbin down the track. The thin line of smoke coming up from one of the chimneys meant that Dulcie had the fire going for her oven, even on this hot day. Rabbit stew for them again? They were going about their normal lives apart from us. We were polite and even friendly when we saw each other, and yet we'd just been discussing whether somewhere under all this green of pasture and woodland they might have buried a man's body. And we still hadn't decided what to do about it.

After a while I turned away from the house and walked straight uphill, criss-crossing from one sheep track to another. A little breeze came off the sea and as I got higher first the hills around Skiddaw Forest came into view, then Skiddaw itself. That made me feel better, not because I'd forgotten the problems back at Studholme Hall but at least it reminded me I could walk away from them if I wanted. I was crazily tempted to do just that, even though I had no pack or money with me. As it was I stayed up there longer than I should have and by the time I turned downhill the light had taken on the golden glow of late evening, with the sun on its way down to the sea. Walking fast, I was back within sight of the house while there was still some light left, probably nine o'clock or so. I followed the wood round the top of Sid's pasture and saw the horse standing there under an oak tree. When I heard a voice I thought for a mad moment that Sid himself was speaking. It was a kind of low crooning, the sound a pigeon makes on a roof on a sunny morning. I caught a word, 'acushla' and realised it was a man talking to the horse in a soft southern Ireland accent. The horse saw me before the man did. He'd been totally relaxed listening to the crooning, but suddenly his neck came up and his nostrils flared, 'Hrrrh?'

'Who's there? Who is it?'

The voice was still soft, but alarmed. Robin had an arm over Sid's neck, lifted high in the air now with the horse's sudden movement. His eyes looked very bright in the half-light under the trees.

'Just one of the visitors,' I said. Who had he expected? 'Nell. I'm sorry if I scared him.'

He looked at me for so long I wondered if he talked only to horses. Then, 'It's a grand evening for walking.'

'Yes.'

'I come up here sometimes for a bit of crack with him.'

The horse had relaxed again now we were talking. Robin slid his arm along the shining neck and down the shoulder. The horse turned his head towards him, blowing a long breath through his nostrils. Robin replied with a similar gentle breath and Sid rubbed his muzzle up and down his arm, giving little playful pushes.

'Thinks I'm another horse, so he does.'

He was perfectly friendly and seemed more relaxed out here than in the farm kitchen. I apologised again for disturbing them, said goodnight and went on my way, leaving man and horse breathing at each other under the trees.

From the lane, I heard louder voices up by our barn and smelled woodsmoke. All of a sudden I was hungry and thirsty, longing for a mug of tea or even a bottle of ale, bother whether it was ladylike. I wondered if Alan was back from his own walk and if Imogen had made her simple, honourable statement yet. Within a few seconds of opening the gate into our hayfield, I had my answer. They were walking slowly along by the hedge at the bottom of the field, about as far as they could get from the fire and the voices, side by side and hands not quite touching. They had their backs to me but everything about them from the matching curves of their necks and shoulders to the swing of her skirt and their feet sauntering on the close-cropped grass said that yes, the words had been said. They must have heard the latch of the gate click because they turned. Imogen called out, 'Hello Nell,' probably thinking that she sounded normal, but so bubblingly happy that she might as well have let rip with war-whoop at convention and caution and anything in the world that argued against being where she was and what she was doing. He said, 'Good evening, Nell. Everything all right?' There was a laugh in it – not a bad-natured one but as if he couldn't take the presence of anybody else in the world except the two of them entirely seriously. I said good evening back, raised my hand to them and turned away quickly up the field, so that they wouldn't think I was coming to interrupt. The air seemed crammed with the scent of honeysuckle. The moon was rising over the field, bronze-coloured and three-quarters full. It was one of those crazily beautiful evenings when anything seemed possible, like taking off from the field and flying. As it was, I joined the other four by the fire outside the barn and was informed by Midge that they'd kept me some scramlette.

'Scramlette?'

'Nathan made it. It was meant to be omelette, but it ended up more or less scrambled eggs.'

Meredith was sitting on the grass with his back to the barn, forking some spongy substance carefully into his mouth. I accepted my plateful, picked up a half bottle of ale and a cup and sat down beside him. The ale was flat and warm but I was so thirsty I downed it in a couple of gulps, then looked up to see he was watching me.

'Did you enjoy your walk?'

'Yes. Is the book going well?'

He shook his head. 'Couldn't concentrate, I'm afraid, so I took myself off for a walk as well. I followed the river down.'

'Wouldn't that have taken you into Major Mawbray's land?'

'Yes, I suppose it did. I didn't see anybody.'

'Were you looking for him?'

He put the fork and plate down, with most of Nathan's offering uneaten. 'Perceptive, aren't you Miss Bray?'

Only slightly mocking. I said that some people would call it inquisitive. I had the idea that he was making conversation with me to keep his mind off something and noticed that he was carefully not looking at the two people strolling by the hedge, no more than silhouettes now in the fading light. Was Imogen why he couldn't concentrate on his book?

'I think it's more than inquisitive. I have the impression of a mind that progresses by grasshopper leaps.'

I thought about it and decided that this was not a compliment, coming from a philosopher. 'That sounds a little too much like women's instinct as opposed to man's pure reason.'

'I didn't mean it. Besides, is there any such thing as pure reason? All we have are our own minds to reason with and we're impure creatures, even the best of us.'

We'd both given up any attempt at eating by then. Kit, Nathan and Midge had gone off somewhere so the two of us seemed very much on our own, perched above a sweep of woods and fields caught between light and dark, not quite real.

'And yes, I admit it,' he said. 'I half-intended to look for Major Mawbray, but how did you guess that?'

'Because he's probably the man who can answer the one question we need answered.'

'Only one?'

'The one to start with anyway. Is his son alive or dead? If there are rumours around that he's alive and hiding, he'd surely know them.'

'So we walk up and ask him? That was what I was wondering when I was walking on his land. What happens if I do meet him?'

'We'd ask, I think.'

'And would he tell us?'

'Probably not, but we might learn something from the way he didn't tell us.'

He laughed, 'Do we do it then?'

Even if he was only trying to keep his mind off something else, I was pleased he wanted my opinion. 'I think we probably should, only...'

'Only?'

'It's hard to put into words, but it's as if once we start asking questions properly we make it real in a way it hasn't quite been before.'

'It seemed real enough down in the police station.'

'Yes, but we're sitting up here and the Old Man and his horses are up here and – I know this isn't at all logical – but it feels as if while we don't do anything it can't touch us.'

'So we do nothing after all?'

'And then one day the police come down the drive and arrest the Old Man. Perhaps they'd only lock him up in a lunatic asylum, but I think he probably wouldn't live long, shut up and away from his horses.'

'You care about him?'

'Yes, I think I do. He's one of the most infuriating people I've ever met and his views on where women belong are worse than a sultan's in a harem. But I admire anybody who's lived life the way he has – making the world behave the way he wants it to.'

'Until now.'

'Exactly. There's a sadness about him as if he's only just come up against the limits of what he can do.'

'If he's managed to get into his seventies before that's happened to him, he's been a fortunate man.'

The hedge and the field edge closest to it were dark now although the sky was still white-gold. You couldn't see the two silhouettes any more.

'So you think finding out more will help him?'

'We need some more facts,' I said. 'There aren't enough of them.'

He laughed, 'You sound as if you could go out and buy facts, so much a dozen, like this.' There were a few eggs left over from the scramlette. Somebody, Midge probably, had bedded them down on a little heap of hay by the barn wall. He picked up one of them and held it in the palm of his hand. 'But they're an awkward commodity, facts. They tend to change their nature depending on who's looking at them.'

'But an egg stays an egg,' I said.

And all of a sudden the little pale oval was up in the air between us. He'd thrown it. Almost unthinkingly, I put my hand up and caught it. It nestled unbroken in my palm as if the hen had laid it there. Meredith and I stared at each other, surprised.

'Is it still the same egg, now it's in your hand instead of mine?'

'It wouldn't have been the same egg if I hadn't caught it. Was that what you meant?'

Instead of answering he laughed, an ordinary open sort of laugh as if some problem had been solved, though I couldn't see what. 'It's getting dark. We should see you all back to the house.'

He stood up. I put the egg carefully back with the others, started to get up, caught my skirt hem on the heel of my boot and stumbled. He put out a hand to me and pulled me up.

'You're tired. It must have been a long walk.'

I wanted to explain that it wasn't tiredness at all, just the confounded hem, but when our hands met a pleasurable little shock went through me. He was still talking.

'Midge says you know this part of the world well. Perhaps we might take a walk together one day.'

'Nell, Midge?' Imogen was calling from the field. 'Are you there?'

Her voice was still full of happiness, but just a little uncertain. When I answered from the darkness she sounded relieved. 'Alan's walking with me back to the yard. I think we should all go.'

So we made up a party down the track, Alan and Imogen in front, then Midge,

Meredith and me. Back in our loft over the tack room the moonlight came in through the windows, unsettlingly bright. It kept us awake for hours, that and Imogen telling us what good friends we were, and how right we were about being completely honest with men and how lucky we were to be alive now in this century and this summer.

Chapter Nine

Next day the old man announced that he was taking Sid on his ride to the sea and we were all welcome to come along or not as it suited us. He made the announcement to me, like issuing a challenge, as I was walking back across the yard from the earth closet just after sunrise.

'We're going first thing tomorrow. Still game to come with me, then?'

It took me a moment to remember about the ride and I must have hesitated, because he laughed. 'Yes,' I said quickly, 'I'd love to.'

'No side saddles here. You'll have to ride leg-over.'

Was that meant to put me off? I said that was all right as well and had the satisfaction of seeing him look a little disconcerted. The fact was, although I'd been taught to ride side-saddle like any other young Victorian lady my brother and I had spent a few harum-scarum summers with the cousin who later went into the cavalry, riding tough little moorland ponies astride with only a blanket to sit on. Later in our wanderings round Europe I'd ridden ponies and mules high up in the mountains where it didn't matter if you rode astride, sideways or backwards hanging on to the tail as long as you stayed on.

'Think any of your friends will want to come?'

'Why don't you ask them? We'll all be up at the barn this morning as usual.'

He came walking up the field at about ten, when we'd cleared up the breakfast things and were just settling down to the *Republic*. Progress on it had been slow so far. He was wearing jodhpurs and gaiters as usual, bareheaded although the sun was already hot. The men got to their feet when he arrived but he signed to them to sit down.

'Taking the horses for a bit of exercise tomorrow. Want to come?'

I'd warned them so they'd had time to think about it. Alan and Nathan said immediately, yes please. So, rather to my surprise, did Meredith. I'd imagined horses hadn't played much part in his scholarly life. Midge said honestly that she hadn't ridden a horse since she was ten and didn't mind if she never did again. Kit gestured at his bandaged arm by way of an excuse and although the Old Man probably knew men who'd broken both arms and ridden on with the reins in their teeth he accepted it with good grace.

'You can look after the womenfolk then. Sleep in the house, use my bed if you like.

Dulcie will feed you. The rest of us will be starting as soon as it gets light tomorrow. We'll be sleeping out by the beach, so you'd better all bring blankets with you if you think you'll need them.'

He walked away down the field, leaving some consternation among the horse contingent.

'Sleeping out?' Nathan said. 'Is it going to take that long?'

About fourteen miles as the crow flies, I told him.

'Please God my horse knows what it's doing.' (That, come to think of it, was the first time I'd heard him make even a passing reference to things theological.) We worked on Plato for a bit longer but our minds weren't really on it and around lunchtime we all walked down to the stable yard to find the Old Man and Robin making preparations for the ride. With bits of tack and saddlebags lined up along a wall in the sun it looked like a nomad camp preparing to move off and in the middle of it the Old Man seemed happier than at any time since we'd arrived. Some of the horses needed shoeing. Robin was about to go to the lower paddock for two of the mares while the Old Man went up the lane for Sid, then Robin would take them in a bunch to a forge somewhere between there and the town. Alan and I went with Robin. The mares were right down by the river so by the time we got back with them, Sid and the Old Man were already in the stable yard. The little stallion looked as fine as ever, coat gleaming, mane and tail like spun sugar. He had his head up, sniffing the air. Robin was worried that one of the mares had been kicked on the hock and the Old Man said he'd come and have a look at it.

'Hold on to him.'

He threw the end of Sid's head-collar rope to Alan who was standing next to him. Alan caught the rope, turned to say something to Imogen and–

'Hold him! Don't let him!' the Old Man yelled.

The whinnying squeal from Sid, heard from a few feet away, was as loud as if we'd been standing beside a steam whistle. The stallion's front legs came up and for a split second he stood almost vertically on his hind legs, pawing the air. His hind hooves were slipping on the flagstones and it looked terrifyingly as if he might go over backwards.

'Keep *hold* of him.'

But the rope had been twitched out of Alan's hands as soon as the horse raised his head. He made a brave grab for it but stumbled, then Sid's front feet came smashing down within a few inches of his hand and the horse galloped off across the yard, still whinnying, to where the Old Man and Robin were standing with the mares.

Midge said, shakily, 'Would you believe it? He doesn't like being parted from–'

But it was the kicked mare Sid was making for, not his owner. Robin tried to pull her out of the way, but Sid reared himself up on her hindquarters, clasping her firmly with his forelegs. His teeth were bared and the steam-whistle noise was fit to crack the sky. The mare snaked her neck round, looking terrified, and tried to bite Sid but his legs held her clamped firm and she couldn't reach. Robin was shouting something, in Irish I thought, and trying to pull the mare away. But the Old Man ran to her head.

'Too late now. Better let him get on with it.'

They held the terrified mare's head between them, stroking her sweating neck, murmuring things meant to calm her, while the stallion got on with his work. After all the noise it was over remarkably quickly. Sid slid off the mare, clumsily, snorting, the Old Man grabbed the rope and led him away into a box while Robin calmed and gentled the mare. At that point I noticed two things. The first of them was Imogen's face. I think she'd probably gone running to Alan when he slipped because she was standing beside him, but not looking at him now. Her eyes were on the mare and she was as pale and horrified as if she'd just witnessed a fatal accident. The other was Dulcie, who must have come into the yard at some time while it was going on. She was looking at the mare too, but smiling. None of us spoke until the Old Man came back and the mare was led, still sweating and quivering, to a box on the far side of the yard.

Alan said, sounding wretched, 'I'm very sorry sir. I couldn't hold him.'

The Old Man put an arm round his shoulder. 'Don't you worry, my boy. Anyway, I should have noticed she'd come into season. It wasn't the time of year I'd have chosen for her, but you can't argue with nature and with luck we'll get a good foal out of her next year.'

Then he went over to Dulcie and quite openly, in view of all of us, did what he'd done in the tack room and slid an arm round her haunches. He put his mouth to her ear and said something. I happened to be standing next to them and heard, or perhaps misheard. It sounded like, 'You'd think he'd know when he'd done it, wouldn't you?' When he'd put his hand on Dulcie her smile hadn't changed, but now it faded suddenly and her face was anxious. She looked on the point of saying something but decided against it. Robin came out of the mare's box with bucket and sponge, looking apologetic.

'Will I get Senta from the field instead, sir?'

'Yes. Check her shoes and take her down

169

with the others if she needs it. Tell Kerr I'll be down separately later with Sid.'

That night when Imogen, Midge and I were in our room, the moon through the window was so bright that we didn't need to light a candle. I was sorting out things for the ride. Luckily I'd brought with me the rational dress designed for bicycling. In fact, we'd all scraped together the money to have the outfits made back in Oxford, though hadn't so far dared to wear them there. They consisted of a pair of bloomers in fine tweed ending just below the knee, worn with boots and thick stockings, and a rather dashing jacket to match the bloomers, hip length with bone buttons and green facing on the lapels, reminiscent of a German huntsman's costume. I put mine on and swaggered up and down in it a bit, so the other two tried theirs on as well and the swagger turned into a kind of country dance without music, on the bare board floor in stockinged feet in the moonlight, whirling and spinning each other round, bowing and clapping palm to palm, but quietly so as not to disturb the Old Man if he happened to be down below in his tack room. I thought he probably was and wondered what he'd make of the slip and slide of our feet over his head. The dance got wilder, the spins giddier until the three of us collapsed on the hay pallets, breathless and weak from silent laughter. After a long silence, Imogen spoke.

'Nell, that mare...'

'Well?'

'She didn't look as if...' Such a long silence that Midge told her to get on with it. 'Well, would you say she was *enjoying* it?'

Midge giggled and said it didn't look like it, but there was something in Imogen's voice that told me she needed a careful answer.

'I suppose it depends what you mean by enjoy and whether animals experience things like human beings do.'

'Aren't we animals too?' She was staring up at the shadows on the ceiling, her face still flushed from the dance. 'Do you think women enjoy the sexual act or need it like men do?'

'I think they should,' I said, knowing it wasn't an answer.

'It must be awful to be a man,' explosively, from Imogen. It was a new and surprising doctrine. Up to then, we'd all agreed that ours was a world designed for and by men, and everything came to them unfairly easily. Midge asked what she meant and Imogen poured it out as if it had been on her mind for a long time.

'Wanting something so much, being ill for not having it ... knowing somebody you care for and who cares for you could give it to you if she wanted to ... if she had the courage...'

171

'I'm not sure that it really makes men ill,' I said. I was, after all, a doctor's daughter.

'But it must be torment, wanting something so much all the time you can hardly concentrate on anything else. Don't you remember how desperately, really desperately, we all wanted to go to college when we were about sixteen?'

'It's hardly the same thing is it?' Midge said.

'But wanting something – wanting anything so much. You must see what I'm talking about.'

I said, 'I assume Alan has asked you to take part in sexual activity with him.' I really didn't know how else to put it. After all, most of what we knew – and it was precious little – came from high-minded and carefully phrased books or discussions with other women who knew no more than we did.

'Not yet, no. Not exactly, but... You see, sometimes when he kisses me I feel I want ... really want it and not just because he does. Then I think of that horse and so on and whether it will hurt a lot and... Oh, I'm such a coward.'

I started assuring her that no, she wasn't, but Midge cut in. 'What would happen if you did and got *enceinte?*' (Even advanced women still put 'pregnancy' in French.)

'I asked that. Alan says there are ... ways.'

Which just showed how far the discussion

with Alan had gone. We talked about it for a bit longer and came to no conclusion, beyond that it was a very serious step for a woman and that Imogen should think carefully before doing anything and she said she was thinking, of course she was. Only I remembered certain evenings in Alpine meadows and what undoubtedly would have happened if his father hadn't taken him away, and knew that there were limits on what thinking could do to help you. So I went to sleep, because next morning the Old Man had ordered us all to be up early for the ride.

We assembled in the stable yard soon after it was light, around five o'clock. The aim was to do a fair part of the ride before the sun got too hot, then find somewhere in the shade to rest and water the horses and finish the journey to the sea in the evening. The horses we'd be using had been kept in overnight and were looking out of their loose boxes. There were saddles ready on the loose-box doors, bridles on hooks beside them. Robin was doing most of the work. When he saw me he grinned, happy as a schoolboy on holiday. I tried not to imagine him helping to carry Mawbray's dead son as easily as he was carrying hay bales and water buckets. For these two days, I was going to enjoy myself and try to forget about it. The horse I'd been allocated was a palomino mare named Sheba. When I went into her box to tack her up she turned to me confidingly and nudged her nose against the green lapels of my jacket. It was a while since I'd had anything to do with horses, but Sheba was cooperative and by the time the Old Man called from the stable yard to come out and mount up we were ready. It was the first chance I'd had to see my companions on horseback. Nathan was hauling himself on to the back of the good old cob, Bobbin, not very expertly with a lot of laughter from Midge who'd come out to see us off. Meredith was already mounted on an Arab mare about a hand taller than mine and looked more at home than I expected. Next to him, Alan was adjusting the girth of a useful-looking dark bay gelding I'd seen in the paddock with the mares, not pure-bred Arab. Imogen was standing beside him, their heads close together. Robin led another bay gelding out of a box. This one looked a handful, raw-boned, around sixteen hands high and probably young. It tried to bite him when he tightened the girth and whirled round and round when he put his foot in the stirrup, but he said something to it that calmed it enough to let him swing himself up with the easy grace of a man who spent more time with horses than human beings.

The Old Man had disappeared for a while, but as soon as Robin was settled in the saddle he came riding back into the yard on Sid, or Seawave Supreme to give him the title he deserved from the way he looked that morning. The Old Man was hatless, his hair and beard gleaming silver in the sun as bright as the stallion's mane and he had the air of a patriarch come to lead his people. He looked all round at us and if I hadn't guessed he was short sighted I'd have been sure he was checking every strap, buckle and curb chain. He nodded at Kit, who was standing by the wall of the yard with Dulcie and Midge on either side of him.

'Look after them well, now. Don't stand for any nonsense.'

Alan had got himself into the saddle by then, none too expertly, so it was just as well the Old Man wasn't looking. Imogen had a hand on the horse's neck and as Alan adjusted the reins he took her hand, leaned down and dropped a quick kiss on the back of it. She bent her head and the back of her neck blushed pink. I don't know what made me look towards Kit at that point. Perhaps the sheer intensity of the way he was staring at them both was a kind of magnet. His head was up, his whole body tense and his anger seemed to sear the air like a lightning flash. I don't know if anybody else saw it – certainly not Alan and Imogen because they were too absorbed in each other. Here was yet another complication to our philosophical summer. It seemed clear from that look that Alan and Kit's long-standing friendship might not survive the choice she'd made. I thought that if she'd chosen Kit, the brilliant one, Alan might have accepted it more easily. But Kit wasn't used to taking second place to his friend and hurt pride was part of his loss. Still, I didn't have long to worry about it because the Old Man raised his riding whip as a signal and we were away, in no particular order down the lane to the mares' paddock, where Robin opened and closed the gate for us without needing to dismount, though his big bay was still trying to spin round.

We went at a walk alongside the river, with the loose horses leaving their grazing to crowd beside us. This early, there was still a wide band of mist marking the line of the little river. The only sounds were the water, the horses' hooves swishing through the long damp grass and the clink of bits and curb chains. We passed the bathing place and came to a narrow gate at the bottom of the paddock. Here we had to wait, while the Old Man and Robin chivvied the loose horses away. Once that was done, Robin held the gate open while we filed through. I happened to be next to the Old Man and noticed that he was looking back uphill to the house, with a closed-in look on his normally expressive face, as if thinking hard about something. Then he saw me looking at him and grinned.

'You happy with Sheba, then?'

'Very. She's beautiful.'

'Let her have her way when it doesn't matter and insist on having your way when it does, then you'll get on fine – like any woman.'

I didn't try to answer that. The river turned a bend, round the bottom of a wooded slope. I was pretty sure that we were off the Old Man's land now and on to Major Mawbray's. Just as we rounded the bend, Sheba gave a little shy at something up in the wood. I glanced there, expecting to see a squirrel or pigeon and did my own equivalent of a shy. There was a man standing there, watching us. He was no more than a few yards away from us on the other side of the stream, but so nearly hidden in the leaves and so still that even the other horses had gone by without noticing. He was wearing a tweed suit and brown felt hat but was unmistakably the same man I'd seen two days before on the magistrates' bench, Major Mawbray. Just for a moment his eyes met mine and the enmity in them was so stark that I almost cried out. Sheba, catching the alarm, surged forward and our eye contact was broken. When I looked back there was no sign of the man, just leaves. I decided to say nothing to the others. I wondered how he knew we'd be passing that way or whether he was out there early every morning. Was he looking for his son or looking for the man who'd killed his son? It was some time later, not until we'd had our first canter and the sun was high, before I got the chill feeling out of my spine.

After that, we had the ride of a lifetime. The Old Man was grandly unconscious of the laws of trespass and seemed to take it for granted that we could ride where we wanted as long as we didn't trample crops or scare cattle. Nobody seemed to resent it. Once we were a few miles clear of Studholme Hall people working in fields waved to us and children on the outskirts of villages ran to see the horses, not to yell insults. I hadn't realised until then how the feeling of being besieged and at odds with our neighbours had grown on us in such a short time, and being clear of it and back in the normal world made the air smell even sweeter. We followed the river down for a while then struck westwards and crossed the railway line. The Old Man halted Sid between the rails and stood guard until we were all across, as if his presence would be enough to stop a coal train in its tracks. Then we took a long loop to the north to avoid

Aspatria and its coalmines.

The land flattened out as we got nearer the coast and there were long stretches where we could gallop, the horses surging along in a herd with manes flying, racing each other. Robin's big bay was usually in the lead at the end, with competitive little Sid not far behind. Alan's gelding hated being passed by the two smaller mares that Meredith and I were riding, but had to put up with it. On one of these occasions Meredith looked at me as we passed Alan on either side, so closely that our stirrup irons almost clashed, and gave me a smile of sheer triumph and devilment – most unphilosophic. Invariably Nathan and Bobbin ran way at the back of the field, still plodding at their lumbering canter with Nathan bouncing around in the saddle long after the rest of us had stopped for breath. It didn't bother Nathan at all. Best fun in a long time, he said. Sheba was by far the best horse I'd ever ridden, so responsive that it seemed I only had to think something and she'd do it. Like most Arabs her stamina was amazing. Minutes after a long gallop she'd be raising her head and sniffing the air for the next challenge. My rational dress turned out to be just as suitable for riding as for bicycling and the balance and freedom of sitting astride convinced me that side-saddles were an invention of men for making sure that women couldn't outride them.

At midday, with the sun hot and the horses and ourselves bothered by clouds of flies, we stopped by a little stream in a grove of willows and alders. We watered the horses then untacked them and let them roll in the grass while we settled on the bank under the trees. I hadn't thought to bring food and didn't know whether anybody else had, but anyway it was too hot for eating. After the early start most of us dozed or, more probably, slipped into that happy state where you're too near sleep to speak or move but just conscious enough to enjoy it. At one point I roused myself enough to worry that the horses might be wandering off but when I opened my eyes there was the Old Man, sitting upright with his arms round his knees, watching over them and us. I thought, 'Well, if you did kill him I hope he deserved it', and let myself drift back to the state where nothing mattered but the murmur of the stream and the willow leaves shifting in a private little breeze that seemed to operate only for them, nowhere else. Or perhaps one other thing mattered – the consciousness of Meredith lying on the bank a few yards away from me, not doing anything, not saying anything, just there.

In mid afternoon, when the sun had shifted westwards and was shining into our grove of trees we drank from the stream, saddled up the horses and went on our way. This second part of the ride was slower. The drowsiness of the midday halt was still clinging to us and the horses, and the temperature must have been well up in the seventies. It was freshened though by the consciousness of the sea being near, though we couldn't see it yet. There was a salt whiff to the air, the occasional gull flying overhead. The land under our hooves changed from the long grass of cattle pastures to cushiony turf with sheep grazing and thickets of golden-flowered gorse instead of trees. In the early evening we came to a line of low sandhills and beyond them the sea, calm and blue as the Mediterranean. We sat in our saddles and watched the white sails of yachts and the cargo steamers going in and out from Maryport to the south and Silloth to the north. Between us and the sea there was nothing but a long sandy beach broken by patches of shingle and small rocks. A small stream, probably the same one we'd dozed by earlier, ran between the sandhills and spread over the beach in a miniature delta of runnels in the sand and tumbled pebbles.

'Tide's just turned,' the Old Man said. 'Be in and out again by morning.'

He seemed pleased with himself. We'd gathered on the way that the plan was to sleep in the sandhills then get up at first light for a gallop along the beach before turning for home. This evening we simply walked the horses down to the sea, to cool their feet and legs in the waves that were breaking as slowly as a big animal breathing, with hardly any foam. Afterwards we tethered them to graze just behind the sandhills near the stream, so that nobody would have to stay up all night to watch them. Robin and the Old Man produced bread and hard cheese from their saddle-bags and shared them out, a few mouthfuls for everybody, washed down with water from the stream. Later we rolled ourselves in our blankets and slept in a hollow between the sandhills. The moon was full in a clear sky, turning the sea and sandhills black and silver. I lay awake listening to the sea and looking up at the moon, feeling some of the tension slipping away.

It was light at four. The Old Man was up before any of us. I saw him with the horses, standing beside Sid. He wasn't stroking him or talking to him, just standing there. The rest of us came awake slowly, stiff-limbed and heavy eyed because you never sleep as deeply outside as under a roof, unless you're used to it. Robin helped us sort out the tack. I knelt to drink from the stream, splashed water over my face and went to find Sheba with her head up and nostrils flared, sensing excitement. Most of the horses had come down to gallop on the beach before and knew what to expect. Only Bobbin, solid as a wagon, seemed unaffected and went on cropping grass. I felt a flutter of nervousness as I adjusted the tack. As far as I could see there was nothing to stop us between there and the Solway Firth and the pace was likely to be wild. Also, from what I'd seen the evening before, the beach needed more caution than it was likely to get with all of us going full tilt. Avoiding the rocky patches wasn't going to be easy. Still, the Old Man and Robin knew what they were doing and if I stuck close to them, all should be well. The Old Man was mounted before the rest of us and waited at the top of a sandhill looking out to sea. When we joined him he turned and smiled.

'Are we ready, then?'

There was a little edge to the smile and his voice. Perhaps even he was nervous too. Without waiting for an answer he pressed his leg lightly against Sid's silver flank, cantered down the sandhill and on to the beach.

We followed in an untidy bunch, backing into each other, hooves sliding on the sand. Once we were on the beach Sheba went off like a stone from a catapult, so fast that I could hardly think or even see beyond a blur and all my efforts were concentrated on staying in the saddle. When things cleared a little I saw Robin and his big bay ahead of me to the right, on the landward side, and the silver streak that was Sid further ahead, closer to the sea. Given the bay's wildness I decided that following the Old Man was the safer option and nudged Sheba over a little with my right leg. From the sound of several sets of hooves thudding along behind me, I guessed others had made the same decision. We galloped along, getting faster if anything, and with Sheba's smooth pace it felt like being suspended between sea and sky. The only worry was that we must hit a rocky patch soon and I wondered how we'd slow down. Then I saw the Old Man signalling with his right arm. He seemed to be telling us to bear right, back towards the shore. Sheba turned as soon as I thought it and the others followed. I glanced left, expecting to see the Old Man turning too but he was going straight ahead. Then suddenly, as I looked, he wasn't there. Only sea and sky and the silver stallion checking for a moment then turning, still at the gallop, in a long curve to join the rest of us, riderless. Robin must have seen it as soon as I did because he'd pulled the big bay round and was cantering towards where the Old Man had disappeared but I was nearer. Somehow I managed to pull Sheba up and turned her in the same direction. There was another rider beside me. Meredith.

'Has he fallen?'

I didn't say anything. We came back from a canter to a walk because the beach was dangerous now, first scattered pebbles, then larger stones and small rocks covered in green weed – just the place anybody with sense would avoid. We found the Old Man sitting on a rock. There was a gash on his forehead and tears running down his face. He looked at me.

'I've made a mess of it, haven't I?' he said. Then, 'Is Sid all right?'

'Yes.'

'I knew he would be. Sure-footed you see. Bred for it.'

Meredith was off his horse by then. He went up to the Old Man and offered him a clean handkerchief to put to his forehead. The Old Man waved it away angrily and tried to get up.

'Just sit there for a moment, sir. You'll be—'

But the Old Man ignored him and got to his feet, rather shakily and unmistakably furious. Meredith took hold of his arm and I slid off Sheba and tried to support him on the other side, but he pulled away from us.

'For Christ's sake don't make such a fuss about it. And don't tread on your bloody reins.'

By this time Robin had arrived and dismounted too. He got the same reception and the three of us walked back to where Alan and Nathan were waiting with the Old Man

185

striding ahead of us. Alan had hold of Sid's reins. The Old Man ran his hand over Sid's legs, then snatched the reins and swung himself into the saddle. Then, without a word, he rode off the beach and through the sandhills, not watching to see if we were following.

The ride home through the stifling day seemed endless. At one point, on a wide path through some woodland, Meredith came to ride beside me.

'A nasty fall for an old man.'

'It wasn't a fall,' I said. 'He deliberately threw himself off.'

'You're sure of that?'

'As I'm sure of anything. He wanted to kill himself.'

'I wondered. But I thought he wouldn't risk the horse.'

'He said Sid's sure-footed. The idea was to ride him as close up to the rocks as he could get then throw himself off and break his neck. Only his neck turned out to be tougher than he thought.'

'Poor man.'

'Yes. He thinks they'll either hang him or put him in a lunatic asylum. He'd decided to go the way he wanted, off a horse galloping by the sea. Only it didn't work.'

Chapter Ten

We got back in the middle of the afternoon. Imogen ran to Alan before he'd dismounted. Kit caught his eye and raised a hand in what might have been a welcome back to his friend, but not a very warm one. Midge jokingly helped Nathan down from the saddle and perhaps he needed the help more than in joke, because the ride had been a hard one for him. Dulcie stood at a little distance with a smudge of flour on her nose, smiling at everybody, seeming glad to have us back. There were the usual inquiries about whether we'd had a good time and we said yes – except for the Old Man who said nothing. As soon as we got into the stable yard he'd dismounted without speaking or looking at anybody, unsaddled Sid and led him to drink from the stone trough. It was only when he was leading Sid past the rest of us to take him back to the paddock that anybody noticed the gash on his forehead.

Imogen gasped, 'Oh, what happened?'

He glared at her. 'Bit of a fall. Nothing to make a fuss about.' Then he and Sid marched on out of the yard.

I was bending down undoing the girth.

When I looked up Meredith was looking at me across Sheba's back, signalling a question as clearly as if he'd said it, 'Well, do we tell them?' We'd discussed it on the way back and come to the conclusion, probably no. It was a long ride so we came to it from all directions. Ethically, it turned out that we both took the Stoic view on suicide, that there were circumstances when it might be the act of a rational man or woman. This was probably one of them. The Old Man was eccentric to put it mildly, but obviously capable of taking decisions. Legally it was a serious offence to try to kill yourself, but we agreed the law was an ass in that respect. What would-be suicide was ever deterred by the thought that the magistrates might not like it? Humanely – well, that was the problem and what we talked about most of the time. What was best for the Old Man? It was a pity for him that the thing hadn't gone as he intended, but as far as we could tell we were the only two who knew what had happened. Robin had given no sign that he guessed and Alan and Nathan had been too far away to see it. So it was up to us to decide whether to tell Alan.

'Or perhaps Dulcie,' Meredith had suggested.

'Why Dulcie?' I could guess, but wanted to know what he'd say.

'They're hardly trying to hide that fact

that she's more than his housekeeper.'

I liked the fact that he could say it to me, adult to adult, with no hypocrisy or sign of disapproval. So we changed the question to whether to tell Alan or Dulcie or both and decided tentatively against it. There were all sorts of reasons, but in the end it came down to the Old Man's pride. Meredith agreed with me that he was a survivor from a more buccaneering age and we both respected that. If we told either of them he'd feel diminished in their eyes by his failure. But our decision was provisional. We agreed that if the Old Man gave any signs of wanting help, then we'd speak to one of them – or both. His decisive rejection of Imogen's sympathy answered that question at least. If either she or Alan had pressed the point it might have been another matter but they had other things to think about, as I found out when she followed me up to our loft when I went to change back into a skirt. I asked her if anything had happened while we'd been away.

'Not really.' But there was something in her voice that said otherwise.

'What did you do?'

'Midge and I just lazed around and read mostly. We didn't see much of Dulcie, and Kit hardly spoke to us. Midge wondered if his arm might be going septic and offered to re-bandage it and he nearly bit her head off.'

'I wonder why.'

'Why that tone of voice?'

'Because you must have at least a suspicion why Kit's in a bad mood.'

'Yes. Only it's more than a suspicion.'

'So he did say something?'

'Not say exactly, no. But I found a letter from him. I'd left my copy of Plato up in the barn with the men's books and when I went up to collect it this morning, there was a letter from him inside it.'

'An angry letter?'

'Yes, no ... I don't know. Just so terribly *hurt*, Nell. Would you like to read it?'

'No!'

But she already had the letter in her hand. 'I want you to. I feel so sad about it and I want you to tell me it's not my fault. It really isn't.' She practically forced it into my hands so I sat down on my hay pallet and read in Kit's flowing black handwriting.

Oh my dear, the other and better half of me. I've tried hard to say nothing, even to see nothing, but it's like letting somebody you love stand there on the edge of a precipice and not calling out. There are so many things I could say to try to persuade you to step back – all the sensible rational things – but they would insult both of us. Simply, you know the path that you're taking is wrong. I sense that because there's not a

190

thought you can have that's not my thought as well, not a breath or a heartbeat of yours that isn't mine. Perhaps I should have spoken out, but I simply didn't think I needed to because I was so convinced you guessed – no, not guessed, that you knew – everything that's in my head. I'm still sure that is true but I can't stand the thought of seeing you take an irrevocable step that can only cause hurt and grief to you and your friends because of a few words not spoken, or written at least. I love you. K.

I looked at the envelope on the pallet beside me. It had no address, only a circle with two crosses through it.

'What's that? Kisses?'

She shook her head. 'It's more Plato. One of his characters makes this wonderful speech about how all human beings were once completely round in shape, with four arms and four legs. Then a jealous god cut them in half, so we're all looking for our true other halves.'

'And Kit is convinced you're his.'

'You can't choose who you fall in love with. For a while, yes, I thought it might be Kit. But I did nothing to encourage him, Nell. Nothing to cause this.'

She took the letter from me and folded it back in its envelope. While I washed and changed my clothes and brushed sand out of my hair she lay back on her hay mattress watching me.

'I'm trying to read your expression, Nell. Are you blaming me?'

'No.'

'I'm desperately sorry about Kit, but it makes no difference. I've made my decision.'

'What about?'

'You know, what we were talking about. While Alan was away it gave me the chance to think about it quite rationally and calmly and...'

'So you're going to,' I said.

'How did you know?'

'When anybody talks about being rational and calm it's usually a sign she's going to do something irrational and wild.'

'Nell!' She threw one of my rolled-up stockings at me. 'So you don't approve.'

'I don't approve or disapprove. You're a grown woman and I wish you luck with all my heart.'

She got up and hugged me and we went down to join the others. Obviously it hadn't been an occasion for talking about suicidal old men.

That evening we had supper together outside the barn as usual, slices of buttered bread and ham, sausages grilled on sticks over the fire, tea and bottled ale and the last of the golden gooseberries. The sun slid down towards the sea, the heat of the day faded to a perfect warmth and the martins on their last flights before roosting and the bats just waking up flew loops round each other. It should have been idyllic, but nobody seemed happy; even Nathan was too exhausted from the ride to make his usual jokes. Alan and Imogen sat apart from each other and talked more or less like rational beings but they were like two magnets parted, the air between them crackling with attraction. Kit couldn't have helped being aware of it but he sat staring out at the red setting sun, holding his mug of ale but not drinking much. Meredith talked about the year he'd spent at Heidelberg and led me into some stories of my wanderings in Germany, but that petered out after a while and once the sun was below the horizon we went to our various beds. Midge and I changed into our nightdresses and lay down on our hay mattresses. Later the moon came up over the roof of the stables and shone on Midge, curled up and making little contented noises too soft to be called snores and on Imogen standing by the window still fully dressed. I asked her softly, so as not to wake Midge, if she was going to bed. She shook her head.

'No. I'm going to meet Alan later, after the other men are asleep.' She sounded excited and nervous. I knew there wasn't much to be said and later whispered a good luck to her as she went softly down the stairs. She didn't answer. I dozed but woke later to hear her coming back up the stairs.

'I've done it, Nell.' Her voice was part-triumphant, but shaky as well. I suppose my reactions were those of any fairly well-brought up young woman whose best friend has just taken the irrevocable step – concern for her, curiosity, and annoyance that she'd got there first. Midge was still asleep, or pretending well.

'Aren't you going to ask me if I regret it?'

'Do you?'

'No.' There was a 'but' in her voice, though. Something hadn't been as she expected it. It struck me that she hadn't been gone very long and surely two lovers on a hay-scented moonlit night shouldn't part before dawn.

'What time is it?'

'Does it matter?'

I found my watch and looked at it in the moonlight. Quarter past one.

'Are you going to sleep now?'

'I don't know. I feel so ... I don't know ... so confused.'

She went to the window. It struck me that part of her attention was still on something happening outside. Perhaps Alan was down there, keeping watch on his beloved.

'Did Alan bring you back here?'

She shook her head. Something was wrong. Please the gods they hadn't gone and quarrelled already.

'Nell, when you said–'

I think she was on the point then of telling me what had gone wrong but Midge stirred and opened her eyes.

'What's happening?'

'Nothing,' Imogen said. 'I'm just going to bed.'

She undressed to her chemise and petticoat and lay down. I'm not sure if she slept. I did for a while but woke up at one point while it was still dark and realised what had disturbed me were soft footsteps down below in the tack room. I imagined the Old Man pacing, then I turned over, dozed again and woke up to find the room full of sunlight. Just after five o'clock by my watch and no hope of getting back to sleep. My head was muzzy, my skin prickling with bits of hay and insect bites and the idea of cool river water came into my mind. Midge was asleep, Imogen lying on her back with her eyes closed, still in her underwear.

I got dressed, grabbed a towel and went down the stairs to the tack room in bare feet, hoping not to meet the Old Man and have to explain what I was doing. No sign of him in the tack room or the stable yard and nothing in the yard by the house except sparrows taking dustbaths. I went along the lane and through the gate into the mares' field, wading through buttercups, my muzziness and itchiness fading with the clean morning air and the pleasure of being up and about before anybody else. There was a lot of mist, mostly down by the river as usual but reaching long fingers up into the rest of the field and collecting in the hollows, with the treetops standing out above it. It closed over me as I went down the slope to the river, like being under a milky canopy. There was a splash of something going off the bank and into the river that might have been an otter. When I tried the water with my toes it felt cold enough to question whether a swim would be such a good idea after all, so I got my clothes off quickly before I could change my mind and waded in. There's something about swimming on your own in the early morning that makes it better than other times, the little quiver of risk perhaps or the feeling that you might choose to float right away and not come back, turn into another person altogether. Not even a person necessarily – an otter or a fish. Being shut in under the mist made it seem even more of a private world and I stayed in the river for quite a long time, sometimes swimming, sometimes just kneeling with my head out of the water, watching two dippers bobbing up and down where the water broke over rocks. After a while the cold got to me so I swam back to where my clothes were, got dried and dressed but left my hair down to dry.

Going back up the slope I was in no hurry. I didn't have my watch with me but guessed it was still early, probably not seven o'clock yet. I'd climbed above the mist belt and was in sunshine but the mist wasn't dispersing yet. If anything it looked thicker than ever down the paddock towards the little gate where we'd ridden through to Mawbray's land. I was looking in that direction when I heard a horse whinny, high and sharp, then more whinnying. I wasn't too worried because horses turned out together sometimes have little quarrels but, remembering the mare that had got kicked, I thought I'd better wander down in that direction just in case. I'd taken only a few steps when it happened. A silver horse came galloping out of the mist, mane flying, with a rider on his back. I had no doubt it was the Old Man. Who else would be riding Sid? But from the first glance I knew that something was wrong. The Old Man was a superb rider and a very upright figure in the saddle. Now he was slumped forward, his head low down on the horse's neck. Sid knew it felt wrong there. He kept tossing his head, trying to get the rider back into position, but every time the head slumped down again. And the whinnying I'd heard had been the horse yelling out in fear and distress. He did it again as they came near me. I ran towards him and tried to grab for the rein but he swerved round me, his eyes wide and terrified, nostrils flaring so that you could see the bright red veins inside them. As he swept past, just missing me, I saw the Old Man's lolling head and open eyes and knew at once that he was dead. His heart. He'd gone out riding early and alone and his heart had gone, the way it nearly did when I'd seen him in the tack room. Sid was galloping up the field, making for the top gate. The mares had caught his terror and were thundering after him in a bunch. I had to jump aside as they went past and for a moment the tossing heads and manes looked very much like the Old Man's picture of the sea-wave horses in the tack room. Sid got to the gate and stood and yelled there for a while. Yelled, I'm sure, for the Old Man, not believing that the flopping thing on his back had anything to do with him. I wondered why he hadn't shaken it off in that mad gallop up the field. Perhaps, even in death, habit kept the Old Man in the saddle. Then when nobody came to the gate to help him Sid was off again, galloping across and down the field with the mares following. There was no hope that I could catch him so I ran up the field and into the lane. Before I'd gone far Robin came running from the direction of the house, looking anxious. I supposed the whinnying had carried up to the stable yard.

'What's happening?'

I gasped out something, then we both ran. Sid and the mares were at the far side of the field when we got to the gate, just standing. But they weren't standing because they'd calmed down. They'd reached the point in their collective panic where they didn't know what to do next. Perhaps our figures at the gate decided Sid, because he came galloping and bucking towards us, the mares trailing behind. When he bucked the figure on his back jerked upright as if it had come back to life for an instant then slumped down again.

'Why doesn't he fall off?' I heard my own voice saying it.

Robin didn't answer. He waited until Sid was within a few yards of the gate and let out a long, low whistle. Sid dug his hooves in and skidded to a stop, rolling an eye towards Robin, ready to gallop off again. Robin whistled again, the same low throbbing note, then vaulted over the gate and went towards the horse. When he came near Sid snorted and started backing away. I was sure he was going to turn and gallop off again but Robin was saying something to him – more of a chant than normal speech – and the terrified horse was listening. He let Robin go up to him and put a hand on his neck and only made a little flinch away when he picked up the rein. Robin stroked his neck until he was calm then led him over to the gate. After the first glance he hadn't looked at the Old Man. He knew as well as I did that he was dead.

I walked through the gate and went to meet them. Robin needed to keep hold of Sid's rein so I had to look at the Old Man. I'd seen dead bodies before but they'd been laid out neatly on beds and I wasn't sure that I could manage it. I made myself think of my father with his patients, pretend for a while that the Old Man might be alive and need help. Even so, I had to take it carefully, a bit at a time. Start with the feet. His feet must have got wedged in the stirrups, that was why he hadn't fallen off. I was looking at the leg and foot on the near side. He was wearing gaiters and short boots as usual and his foot was tight in the stirrup, but it wasn't wedged there, it was tied. It took me a long time to believe what I was seeing. The Old Man's ankle was tied with a leather thong to the stirrup iron. Then something worse. There was thick string tied to the stirrup iron as well. It went from there under Sid's belly, alongside the girth and when I went round to the off side I saw it was knotted to the stirrup iron there too. The offside foot was tied to the stirrup like the other one. That would have been enough to secure his body in the saddle, but there was more. His hands, brown and gloveless, were tied with more leather thongs to a broad leather strap round Sid's neck. Bound hand and foot to a terrified horse. Something stirred in my mind. I turned and found Robin looking at me, stroking Sid's nose.

'I think we'd better take him up to the house as he is,' I said.

Chapter Eleven

The clatter of Sid's hooves on the stable-yard flagstones sounded terribly normal, as if his owner had brought him in from any ride. The injured mare stuck her head out of the box and whinnied, but this time Sid wasn't interested. Even Robin couldn't persuade him to stand still and he went round in circles, rolling his eyes towards the thing on his back. Since Robin had to stay with Sid it was up to me to fetch help, and for a moment I hesitated. Imogen and Midge were nearest, but I didn't want them to see the Old Man like this. Dulcie Berryman was next nearest and probably down in the kitchen by now, but the same thing applied. I admit my first reaction was to run for Meredith. He was older, after all he was a don. He'd know what to do. It was only then that I thought of Alan and remembered he had the right to know first. Looking back, it's odd that the idea of sending for the police didn't come into my mind at that point. Perhaps we'd already got used to managing things for ourselves up there. I told Robin to hang on, I'd be back soon and started running but before I'd gone more than a stride, there was Dulcie. She was walking under the arch between the house and the stable yard, with a big apron over her dress and slippers on her feet. From the casual way she was strolling and the beginnings of her usual smile when she saw me, there was no idea in her mind that anything was wrong. Then her face changed. She looked past me at Robin and Sid.

'I should go back to the house,' I said. 'There's nothing you can do.'

She took no notice and ran past me, heels of her slippers flapping to show the hard, calloused feet of somebody who walks barefoot a lot. Odd the things you notice. Then she stopped and said, 'Oh.' It was the tone of a mother whose child has done something damaging – the moment of realisation and regret before scolding starts. I called again that I'd be back soon and went on running. I didn't tell them to leave the Old Man as he was until Alan got there because from the way Sid was behaving I didn't think they had much choice. I ran out of the yard and up the track, across the mown field to the men's barn. As luck would have it, Meredith was the first person I saw, standing outside the barn in his shirt sleeves, looking at the view northwards to the Scottish hills.

I said, 'The Old Man's dead.' Then,

because I didn't have much breath to spare put the rest into one word, '*Mazeppa.*'

Whether he understood it all from that I didn't know, because the other three came out of the barn in various stages of dress and undress. I told them as calmly as I could what had happened. Alan's face went sharp and pale.

'Why? Why was he tied to the horse?'

Now it was too late I saw that I'd done Alan a wrong twice over by not telling him about the Old Man's heart trouble or his attempt to kill himself on the beach. Trying to protect him had made for a worse shock now. He seemed unable to move and Meredith had to suggest gently that they should all go inside and finish getting dressed. He and I waited outside for them. He asked me if I wanted to sit down, offered to get me water from the stream but didn't fuss when I said no.

'I take it there's no doubt that he's dead, Miss Bray?'

'No. It was what he wanted yesterday on the beach, only...'

'I'm sorry, you don't have to talk about it yet if you don't want to.'

'Alan will have to know about him trying to kill himself.'

We told him while we were all walking down the track. He'd wanted to run to the stable yard but Meredith made him go slowly and listen. Alan walked head down, not responding, and I wasn't sure how much he understood. To get it over, I told him about the Old Man's near-collapse in the tack room.

Alan said, still head down, 'You're saying that he knew he was ill, he wanted to die?'

'Yes, I'm afraid so.'

I tried to signal to Meredith with my eyes, over Alan's bent head, that I wanted a word with him. He understood and we dropped back a few paces.

'We brought him up from the field just as he was,' I said. 'I thought we'd better leave him like that until somebody else could see, but it probably shouldn't be Alan.'

He shook his head. 'It's his right, don't you think?'

As it was, I needn't have worried. When we got to the stable yard there was no sign of Sid or his burden. Midge, Imogen and Dulcie were standing near the horse trough. When Alan saw Imogen he went running to her and laid his head on her shoulder. Unashamed, she put her arm round him and bent her head so that their foreheads were touching, not saying a word. I looked at Midge.

'We managed to untie him,' she said. 'Robin and Dulcie and me. He's in the tack room.'

'Where's the horse?'

'Robin's shut him in the stallion's box. He's still with him, trying to calm him down.'

Meredith, Alan and I went into the tack room. An old table that was usually scattered with bits of leather and mending tools had been cleared and the Old Man was laid out on it, covered in a yellow and red horse blanket. Dulcie and Midge must have done that because Robin had the horse to deal with. Meredith gently drew back the blanket from his face. The Old Man's eyes had been closed and his face was gaunt but calm, the red gash from the fall on the beach standing out on the thin, weather-beaten skin. The sun was coming in through the window, shining on the picture of the galloping horses and breaking waves above his head and the Byron quotation. There were bits of grass and leaves in the Old Man's silver hair, earth and grass stains on the sleeve of his shirt.

'It looks as if the horse might have rolled on him.'

My own voice, sounding terribly calm. I wished I hadn't said that with Alan there but shock seemed to have turned me into two people, one of them drowning in what was happening, the other one watching and analysing. Tears were running down Alan's face. Meredith moved away to the far end of the tack room to give him some time to himself and I followed.

'Did you make the *Mazeppa* connection at once?' Meredith asked me.

'Yes. I suppose ... something like that was in my mind after that business on the beach.'

'You mean you expected it?'

'Not expected, no. But when I saw his foot was tied to the stirrup I thought ... it was the kind of thing he might do.'

'In the Byron, doesn't Mazeppa survive?'

'Yes, the horse drops dead and some Cossacks cut him free.'

'The horse might have dropped dead this time. It must have been terrified.'

'He risked Sid's legs on the beach. There was a ruthlessness about him, wasn't there? Horse and warrior taking their risks together.'

He glanced at me. 'You understood him rather well, didn't you?'

'I don't know.'

Alan turned the blanket back over the Old Man again and left, his steps slow and heavy on the stone floor. I couldn't look at the picture of the horses any more or the shape under the blanket, so much smaller now the life had gone out of him. I stared at a saddle stripped down for cleaning, a bunch of leather thongs hanging from a peg. They'd been left untidy and uneven, unusual in this neat room. I knew if I was going to say anything it must be now and to Meredith.

'Those thongs – some like that were tying his feet to the stirrups. I ... I think I might have heard him last night coming in to fetch them, and the saddle and bridle too probably.'

'When was that?'

After Imogen had come back, but of course I couldn't talk about that even if all the men had guessed.

'Some time after one o'clock but before it got light. His hands were tied too. That's what scares me. At first I was sure he'd done it himself. You could tie your own feet to the stirrups, even tie the stirrups together under the horse's belly ... if you leaned down from the saddle, say, and hooked the string with a riding crop...' (As I talked, I was visualising the Old Man doing it) 'but I don't see how he could tie his own hands...' My voice was becoming unsteady. 'I'm sorry, forgive me, I'm talking nonsense.'

He looked at me and sighed. His hand, pleasantly cool, came round my wrist and I felt myself being guided over to an old armchair against the wall. Shock must have been setting in badly by then, because I didn't try to resist.

'I'm sorry,' he said. 'I'm afraid if you're starting this there are no half measures.'

'What do you mean?'

'If you begin following a logical course of

208

thought, you can't tell yourself that you'll only go so far then stop. Either don't start or go as far as it takes you.'

'I haven't had time to think.'

'You've had as much time as you're going to get. You know we have to report this to the police? In a few hours it won't be our private property any more.' It sounds brutal, but the way he said it wasn't. He was talking to me quite calmly, like an equal.

I said miserably, 'I think I've already started.'

'Yes, I think you have too. So you have to use your eyes and your brain and your instincts and go where they take you, whether you like it or not.'

'Like being tied to a wild horse?'

'Perhaps. You were saying that you didn't see how he could have tied his own hands. Did you say that to Robin?'

'I ... I don't think so. I told Robin we'd better get him back to the stable yard as he was. I thought ... I supposed he'd still be on the horse when we got back down there but Robin and Dulcie and Midge must have...'

'Did you call Dulcie?'

'No, she just walked into the stable yard, the way she does.'

'What about Midge?'

'No, but we sleep just over the stable yard remember. Midge must have heard something and come down.' I was amazed, when

I thought about it, at Midge's competence and calmness.

'You said it scared you when you saw his hands were tied. What did you mean?'

'I thought it meant somebody else must have known what he was planning to do – must have helped him.'

'Did you get as far as wondering who?'

'I don't see who it could have been except Robin. He could get Sid to stand still, tie the knots and ... oh.'

I pictured Robin in the grey light before dawn, tying the Old Man's hands to the leather strap and the Old Man watching calmly, probably giving him instructions on exactly how to do it.

'He'd do anything for the Old Man,' I said. 'You could see that.'

'You know assisting somebody to commit suicide is a serious crime. It would be no defence to say you were told to do it.'

'I know. So how can I be the one who puts Robin in prison? The police would probably be happy enough with that. You said yourself that Gypsies get blamed for everything round here.'

'What happened to the leather thongs and the string?'

'I don't know. I suppose they're still out there in the yard somewhere.'

'The police might want to see them.'

'Yes, if we put the idea in their heads. Do

we have to do that?'

Meredith didn't answer because Alan's voice came from outside the tack room, calling for him. When we went out to him he was dry-eyed but still shaken, standing close to Imogen.

'What happens now?'

'We shall have to inform the police. I suggest that you and I go down and get that over as soon as possible. As Miss Bray saw him on the horse it might be a good thing if she came with us.'

Meredith's tone was businesslike and that seemed to help Alan because he blinked and said yes, yes of course. Midge, Kit and Nathan were in the yard but there was no sign of Robin or Dulcie. I went over and took Midge aside.

'I'm sorry you had to see that.'

'It doesn't matter.'

'Do you know what became of the string and the bits of leather?'

'We got a knife out of the tack room and cut them. I suppose we just threw them down.'

I walked all round the yard as unobtrusively as possible, but there was no sign of them at all, not an inch of leather thong or string. Somebody must have tidied them away, but it would have been brutal to start asking questions about a detail like that. Besides, I wasn't sorry not to find them.

The next job was getting the wagonette ready to go to the police station. Nathan volunteered to go to the mares' field to fetch Bobbin and I went with him because I'd have to face it again at some time. Something was obviously worrying Nathan and as soon as we were away from the others he came out with it.

'You shouldn't have let her get involved.'

'Midge? But I had no choice.'

'You could have warned her, told her to stay upstairs.'

'I'm sorry, but there were other things to think about. I had to tell Alan.'

In different circumstances I'd have been amused by the assumption that Midge was a delicate flower who needed protecting, but I agreed with him. I wished I could have saved her from it as well. We walked in silence up the track to the mares' field. Now it was just any meadow on a fine summer's morning. The mist had burned away, the mares gone back to their grazing and Bobbin's placidity seemed entirely unaffected. The only strange thing was not seeing the Old Man. I hadn't realised until then how his presence had worked itself into every corner of the place. Back in the stable yard when we managed to get the harness into a tangle I expected him to turn up and sort it out for us with his brown bony hands.

As Alan got into the wagonette, Imogen

212

came up to him and took both his hands in hers for a moment. He bent and kissed the back of her hand that was clasped round his own, not in the tentative way he'd done when we went off on our ride but with a desperate need as if she were the only thing that made sense. I had a sudden, sharp memory of our evening in the college garden. *Dead, for my life! Even so; my tale is told.* It seemed another world already.

Meredith asked me to drive, which was typically sensible. For one thing it gave me something else to think about. For another, it meant he and Alan could sit in the back and talk. I couldn't hear what they were saying above the clattering of Bobbin's hooves and the jingling of the harness but I guessed it must be what we'd discussed back in the tack room. Put brutally, what exactly should we tell the police? It wasn't an easy thing to have to do, given Alan's obvious grief and shock, but decisions had to be made in the course of the drive.

We left Bobbin and the wagonette in the stables of the public house again and walked to the police station. We got some curious looks on the way but didn't take much notice because Meredith was talking to us quietly but firmly, back in tutorial mode.

'You should both keep in mind that the police aren't stupid. Don't on any account try to lie to them about any matters of fact. On the other hand, you're under no obligation to talk about what you surmise, guess or suspect. The same applies to questions about Mr Beston's health and state of mind. It's perfectly reasonable for you, Nell, to tell them about the time you saw him taken ill. When it comes to what happened on the beach, that's a more difficult question. It must be a matter for surmise unless you can say for certain that he threw himself off rather than falling.'

I didn't say anything to that. I was certain in my own mind that the Old Man had intended to kill himself, but it would be difficult to explain why to anybody who hadn't been on the ride. An old man falls off a horse, it happens all the time.

Alan said, 'What about the telegram to me, and shooting Kit and so on? Do I tell them that?'

'Probably yes. They're both facts, and witnessed by other people as it happens. His state of mind is relevant.'

'Because the police will think he killed himself because he murdered young Mawbray?'

'It would be a reasonable assumption.'

I said, 'And from their point of view quite useful. It closes an embarrassing case after all.' I was feeling rebellious and it must have come out in my voice because they both looked at me.

'Don't you want that to happen?' Meredith asked, not argumentative but as if he really wanted to know.

'But if he didn't kill young Mawbray—'

'Oh for Christ's sake, let's go in and get it over with.' It came from Alan as a cry of pain and I realised how thoughtless I was being. Even if he hadn't known the Old Man well, he was a relative and the one most closely affected. We crossed the street and went into the police station without another word.

The police officer we saw was the same Inspector Armstrong who'd spoken to Alan and Meredith on their first visit – a broad-shouldered man in his fifties, plump and balding. He spoke unusually softly for a policeman in a lowland Scots accent and had a relaxed, almost kindly air but shrewd eyes. When we were first shown into his office there was the business of introducing me and finding an extra chair, then Alan burst out as soon as we were sitting down.

'My uncle's dead.'

Once he'd got that out, he managed the rest well and calmly. His uncle had been found early that morning, tied into the saddle of one of his horses, dead. Armstrong listened calmly, not taking notes yet.

'Was it you who found him?'

'No,' I said. 'I did.' I told him all of it just

215

as it happened, going to the river to swim, seeing the horse coming out of the mist and knowing at once that something was wrong. 'But I couldn't get the horse to stop, so I ran for help and luckily I met Robin.' I realised I didn't even know Robin's second name.

'The Gypsy lad?' Armstrong said.

'Yes. He got the horse to stand still and we took him back to the yard.'

'Did he say anything?'

'Robin?'

'Mr Beston.'

'He was dead. I'm sure he was dead as soon as I saw him.'

'On the horse?'

'Yes.'

Inspector Armstrong sighed and sat back in his chair. 'Where is he?'

Alan glanced at us both. 'My uncle?' Armstrong nodded. 'Up at the house. In the tack room.'

Silence inside the room. Outside a cart rolled past and the window frame vibrated. Armstrong seemed to be thinking hard, eyes closed and chin propped on his fingers. After a long time he unpropped his chin and spoke.

'We'll have to bring him down for the doctor to look at him and we'll be wanting statements. I'm afraid you'll have to give one, Miss Bray, since you found him. It won't be too alarming, just tell the story as you told me and we'll write it down for you to sign.'

It annoyed me that he thought I needed reassuring, but I was glad to be spared any hard questions. He turned to Alan.

'Do you know who the last person was to see your uncle alive, Mr Beston?'

We looked at each other. Alan said, 'I suppose it would have been Mrs Berryman, in the house the night before.'

'Ah yes, Mrs Berryman.' A heaviness in the Inspector's voice. You could tell he didn't approve of her. 'We'll need a statement from her, and the Gypsy lad. Does that mean you weren't in the house with him last night?'

'We all slept up at the barn,' Alan said.

Armstrong made no comment on that. 'Are you Mr Beston's next of kin?'

'I think my father is, only he's in Baden Baden with my mother. I'll have to telegraph him, but...' Alan let the words trail away. I think the complexities of the situation were only just catching up with him.

Armstrong nodded. 'In any case, you'll understand that you can't make any arrangements to have your uncle buried until the doctor and the coroner have seen him. There'll have to be an inquest. They might open it and adjourn it and release your uncle's body for burial, but naturally we'll keep you informed.'

'Thank you.'

'Do I take it you've got quite a party up there?'

'Some college friends on a reading party.'

'Well, we'd take it as a favour if they'd stay until we sort out who we need statements from. We'll try not to inconvenience them any more than we have to. And if you don't mind waiting now, Miss Bray, we'll get your statement taken down.'

Meredith asked, 'May we go back after that or should we wait for the doctor?'

'He's been called to Ireby on another case. We'll send him up to you later.'

The sergeant who took me through my statement and the constable who wrote it painstakingly down were as careful of my feelings as Inspector Armstrong had been. As Meredith had suggested, I kept to the simple facts of what I'd seen that morning with no speculation. They didn't ask any questions about the Old Man's health or state of mind. I supposed that would come later and was more than ready to let it wait. When we'd finished Meredith was waiting for me on the far side of the reception desk, looking concerned.

'All right, Miss Bray?'

'All right, yes.'

Alan had gone to the post office to send a telegram to his father. We met back in the yard of the public house and although I felt quite well enough to take the reins going home, Meredith insisted on driving us. I sat in the back with Alan. He looked worn down with worry and kept biting at his knuckles, probably a habit from his childhood that came back at times of stress. I couldn't blame him. I had my straw hat in my lap and I knew my fingers were twisting the brim out of shape, the way I was told not to when I was about six years old.

'Did you tell them about the ride on the beach, Nell?'

'No. Did you want me to?'

'It will all have to come out, won't it? Isn't that the kind of thing they want to know at inquests?'

'I don't know. I've never been to one.'

We were all so terribly new to it and this wasn't at all the intellectual exploration we'd intended for our summer. We bowled along between banks of foxgloves and meadowsweet and I wondered how much practice it took to stop thinking things.

Chapter Twelve

The police doctor, a sergeant and a constable arrived in a gig around the middle of the afternoon. Nathan spotted them coming down the track and we waited for them in the yard outside the house, with chickens scratching round our feet. Alan introduced himself to the doctor, managing to sound pretty well in control of himself, and led him through to the stable-yard. The sergeant, a sweating red-faced man, said they wanted to speak to Robin O'Kane. It was the first time I'd heard Robin's surname. The sergeant didn't put a 'Mr' in front of it. I volunteered to look for Robin and found him sitting alone on an old trough on the shady side of the house with the Old Man's two Afghan hounds on either side of him, their eyes open and mournful, long ears flopping in the dust. He looked so terrified when I told him that the police wanted to speak to him that for a moment I thought he was going to run away.

'It's all right, it's only because you saw him on the horse. Just tell them exactly what happened and don't let them scare you.'

While he was with them I kept the

Afghans company and twice heard the sergeant's voice raised from inside the house. He sounded angry but I couldn't make out what was being said. It was half an hour before Robin came stumbling out into the sun. He was looking round in a dazed way and when I got nearer I saw that he was shaking.

'What's wrong?'

He shook his head, bewildered. I asked if he wanted a cup of tea and he nodded his head but I couldn't get him to come into the kitchen for it. The sergeant and constable were still in the parlour and that was too close for him. When I went into the kitchen the door to the parlour was closed and the sound of the sergeant's voice came from the other side, too low to make out the words. I guessed it was Dulcie's turn now. At least she wasn't being shouted at, even scandalous housekeepers being a cut above Gypsy boys. The kettle was on the fire as usual so I made tea for Robin, strong with three spoonfuls of sugar and took it out to him in the yard. He drank it in three or four gulps and uttered some words at last.

'What will I do?'

'What's happened? What did they ask you?'

'They were asking did I do that to him, did I tie him on the horse.'

'What did you tell them?'

'God's holy truth that I never did. Will you tell them, miss? Tell them it was you who found him and called me to him.'

'I've already told them that.'

He shook his head again, so bewildered it was painful to see. 'What will I do? What will I do without him.'

He was grieving for the Old Man. I should have realised before, but I think the rest of us were still too shocked for grief and, after all, we'd only known him for a few days. Robin had been with him for two years, up here in their own small world with the horses, his life governed by what the Old Man wanted.

'You liked him?'

A nod. 'I honoured him.' There was liking as well as respect in his voice.

'Do you think he killed himself?'

Another shake of the head, but no way of telling if it was a no or simple bewilderment. It would have been brutal to press further and I'd given him no answer to his question.

'Somebody's going to have to look after the horses,' I said. 'He'd have wanted you to do that, wouldn't he?'

'Should I put Sid back in his field or will the police be wanting him?'

I had to stop myself smiling at the idea of the stallion giving his statement.

'Put him back in his field, I should.' Then, because he was calmer now we were talking about horses I risked some more questions. 'Was Sid in his own paddock as usual last night?'

'Sure he was. You couldn't go putting him down in the big field on account of the mares.'

'When did you see Sid last – before it happened, I mean?'

'After supper. Mr Beston and myself went up to see was he all right, like we do every night. An' then I left Mr Beston up there with him an' came down to my bed.'

'Leaving him up there with Sid?'

'I always did. He liked to be on his own up there and watch the sun setting.'

'Were the dogs with him?'

'No. They stay shut up inside of nights.'

'Did he take Sid's tack up with him?'

'Why would he do that? He had no need of it, not meaning to ride him.'

And yet, some time between then and early morning the horse must have been brought down from his paddock and his saddle and bridle taken out of the tack room.

Robin stood up. 'Shall I be seeing after Sid, then?' Then, 'Are they after taking Mr Beston away to bury him?'

I said I didn't know, but when I was back in the yard and Robin had gone to see to the horse I had an answer. Midge came up to me, tense and white-faced.

'The doctor's taken the gig and gone. He's sending up a covered cart to take Mr Beston away for a post-mortem.'

'Where's Alan?'

'With Imogen somewhere. He had a talk with the doctor before he went. He won't say much before he does a proper post-mortem, but Alan gathered he thinks the horse might have rolled on him. He had some ribs broken and a bump on the back of the head.'

'That couldn't have been from the stones on the beach the day before. It was the front of his head he grazed then.'

It was a relief to be with Midge, matter-of-fact about everything as usual, but even she was looking worn out. It was so hot in the yard by now, with the afternoon sun full on it, that we thought we'd both be better for some air. We walked up the track towards the woods. A long way ahead of us, Robin was leading Sid back to his pasture.

'Nathan thinks I should have protected you from seeing him like that,' I said. 'I thought you were asleep.'

'I woke up. You weren't there and your towel had gone so I guessed you'd gone down to the bathing place. I was annoyed with you for not waking me to go with you. Then I heard the horse's hooves in the yard and your voice and guessed something was wrong.'

'When you went down to the yard, what exactly did you see?'

'He was still on the horse's back then. Robin was trying to get the horse to stand still and Dulcie was the other side. I think she must have been untying his foot from the stirrup. I asked what had happened and Dulcie said he was dead.'

'Nothing else?'

'No. So I went up to them and saw his wrists were tied as well. I started trying to undo one of them and Robin helped from the other side because he'd got the horse quieter by then, and Dulcie went and got a knife from the tack room. When we'd got him cut free Robin asked me to take hold of the bridle so that he could lift him off.'

'So you found the knots round his wrists were too tight to untie?'

'For goodness' sake Nell, why don't you come straight out and ask it? I haven't entirely lost my brains any more than you have.'

'Ask what?'

'Whether he could have tied the knots himself. Isn't that what's in your mind?'

'Yes.'

'In my opinion, no he couldn't. I know about knots. When we were children my brothers were always tying me to trees and playing cannibals or Indians. I got quite clever at escaping. Look Nell.' She stopped us beside the gate to the big hayfield. 'Imagine the gate's the horse. That gatepost is its neck and there's a strap round it. You might be able to tie your left wrist to the strap, using your teeth and your right hand ... he was right-handed?'

I tried to remember him doing something with his hands, but all I could picture was the arm sliding round Dulcie's hips.

'I think so.'

'Anyway, once you've got one hand tied, how do you manage the other?'

'I don't know. I couldn't find the bits of string and leather you cut.'

'I told you we just threw them down. It wasn't the first thing on our minds. Why? Have the police been asking?'

'They didn't ask me, but I think they've been giving poor Robin a bad time. You didn't notice him or Dulcie tidying them away?'

'I wasn't thinking about that.'

We walked on up the track. Just past the gate to Sid's paddock on the left there was a place in the hedge that looked as if it had been recently disturbed. A few hazel leaves had been torn away and were lying on the path, curled up in the sun. I wondered if a badger might have pushed through and looked at the bank under the hedge for more signs of it, anything to distract myself from what we'd been talking about. About halfway up the hedge, pushed in among the branches, there was something black and cylindrical. It wouldn't move at first and came reluctantly when I tugged at it, tangling and pulling out more leaves.

'What's that doing there?' Midge said.

She sounded alarmed and when I saw what I was holding I felt the same. It was the Old Man's carriage whip, the one he carried with him when he patrolled his fields at night, the long lash still caught up in the hedge.

'I don't know.' One thing I was sure about was that it hadn't been used on Sid. His fine silver hide had been quite unmarked.

'Did the Old Man put it there?'

It was possible, I supposed. If it had been simply lost or thrown away it wouldn't have been so deep in the hedge. It might have been his equivalent of breaking his staff of office if he'd decided to kill himself. I untangled the lash from the hedge and coiled it in my hand. It felt odd holding it, knowing that the last touch on it might have been the Old Man's, but we couldn't leave it lying on the track. We turned to walk back down and as we got near the gate to the hay field a voice called hello from the other side of the hedge. It was Nathan coming down from the barn with a pack on his back and a rolled-up hay mattress under each arm. He looked too hot and bothered to notice the whip.

'What were you two conspiring about?'

'We were trying to work out if Mr Beston could have tied himself to the horse,' Midge said, opening the gate for him. He made a noise that sounded like a strangled swear-word and dumped the mattresses on the grass. I'd known Nathan for more than a year and this was the first time I'd seen him angry.

'I've had more than enough of this. I was going to wait until I'd got the three of you together but you can tell Imogen when you see her. I'm driving us to the station tomorrow, and we're leaving.'

We stared. 'Who?'

'You two, Imogen and I. Alan should never have brought you into this, but since he's stuck here it's my responsibility to get you out of it.'

I felt like laughing. Back in Oxford, nobody had been clearer than Nathan about women's right to equality. Now there was trouble he'd reverted instantly to protective Victorian male.

'I can't go,' I said. 'I'll be needed for the inquest.'

That made matters worse. His face had been flushed anyway but now it turned as red as a peony.

'It's all wrong. You shouldn't have to stand up there in public and be questioned in front of a jury. I'll tell the police that we're going away and that's that.'

'Not on my behalf,' I said. It had struck me suddenly that Nathan was nervous of the police. Goodness knows why since his past – though not blameless by Oxford standards – was unlikely to have been criminal.

'It's not a game any more, Nell. It was different while it was just this Mawbray business but now–'

'It never was a game. That's why we can't walk away from it.'

He stared at me then at Midge, picked up the mattresses and marched away down the track.

'Poor Nathan,' Midge said, sounding more sorry for him than he deserved. After all, she'd been more closely involved in it than he had.

'Where's he taking those mattresses?'

'Down to the house. The men have decided to move back into the parlour.'

'To protect us?'

'I suppose so.'

It was a defeat, we knew. The end of our airy college above the world in the old barn. The Old Man's death had dragged us back from theory into a very real world. Midge and I started walking after him back towards the house. We could see Dulcie down in the yard, scattering feed for the chickens. At least the police hadn't kept her long.

'Going on just as normal,' Midge said.

'Chickens still have to be fed after all.'

'It was the same this morning. There we were, trying to get him off the horse, knowing he was dead, and she was behaving ... oh, I don't know ... behaving as if it were just any other problem that had to be solved, as if it were a basket of washing or something. Only ... only there were tears just flooding down her face.'

'I can't imagine her crying.'

'I can't now, but I didn't imagine it. And yet she's not somebody you can talk to, is she?'

'I wonder why not?'

But Midge was right. We weren't snobs – we were quite sure of that – but class came in to it. That and the fact that she was older and had a reputation. We approved very much of women exerting their freedom, it was just that we weren't used to them looking and sounding like Dulcie.

Midge said suddenly, 'I've been thinking about that anonymous note. Do you think Alan showed it to Mr Beston?'

'I shouldn't think so. He was too embarrassed.'

I thought of the grubby message: DID YOU ARSK DULSIE WHO HER BASTARD'S FATHER REALY IS. Hard to imagine Alan putting that in front of his uncle, even though it had been addressed to him.

'But Mr Beston must have known there

was gossip about her.'

'I don't suppose that would have worried the Old Man.' (I was already slipping back into that way of thinking of him, rather than the funereal Mr Beston.) 'He wasn't exactly a model of respectability himself.'

'But if it wouldn't have worried him, why was somebody telling him to ask her?'

'Because whoever it was didn't know him very well. He or she wanted to make trouble for Dulcie and was getting impatient because it hadn't happened. That note reads to me like one of a series. There was probably at least one earlier note telling him to ask her and whoever wrote it wants to know what happened.'

In the yard below Dulcie scattered the last of the feed, upended the bowl and went back inside with lazy, swaying steps. She never looked as if she was working hard, but somehow everything got done.

Midge said, 'If there was a child, where is it now? She could have had it farmed out, I suppose.' Then, tentatively, a few steps further on, 'You don't suppose ... Robin?'

'I was wondering that too. But would the ages fit? I'd guess he's seventeen or eighteen, maybe older. If she's in her thirties she could have had him when she was very young.'

'But he's Irish and she's from round here.'

'If she'd farmed him out to Ireland when

231

he was a baby...'

'And brought him back when she got the position with the Old Man?'

'It's possible,' I said, 'and you can imagine the Old Man being quite amused by the idea.'

When we got down to the house I propped the whip in the porch with an assortment of other whips and crops. The police had finished their questions and were drinking tea in the kitchen. We left them in possession, although they were a nuisance because the men were carrying their things down from the barn and had to pile them by the porch until they could get to the parlour.

The doctor had promised to send a covered cart up from town to collect the police and the Old Man's body but it was early evening by the time it came lumbering down the lane. We directed it through the arch into the stable yard and stood in a line watching as the two policemen took out a stretcher from the back and carried the Old Man's body from his tack room, still wrapped in the horse blanket. Robin was crying quite openly. With the suspicions about him and Dulcie in my mind I watched to see if she made any move to comfort him, but she was staring down at the flagstones, thinking her own thoughts. As the cart creaked away across the yard and through the arch I was surprised to find tears in my eyes. I wished I'd talked to the Old Man more when I had the chance – found out about seventy years or so of a life that sounded as if it had been bravely, if not wisely, lived. I knew that in spite of the differences in our views I'd already learned something from him and might have learned more, given time. There was silence after the noise of the wheels died away, then people started talking apologetically at first, then with more confidence, about the commonplace things of life going on. The parlour had to be reorganised and we'd all eat together in the kitchen, pooling our rations. I knew it was right and necessary but couldn't face it yet. Besides, there was something that had been worrying me since Midge talked about the bump on his head.

I walked out of the yard and down the lane to the mares' field on my own. My towel was still there on the gate, dried by a day in the heat. There was no mist by the river now, just long tree shadows from the sun slipping down in the west and a smell of hot earth and drying grass. It was the trees that interested me, willows and alders mostly. The willows were either leaning out over the water or pollarded with whippy little stems growing from upright trunks. The alders threw their branches out over the river with only scrubby twigs inland. Even if you'd ridden a horse at a canter straight along the bank, there were no overhanging branches to give you anything worse than a scratch. Next door though was another matter.

I walked on downriver to the gate that led to Mawbray's land and looked over it, confirming what I remembered from our ride. A wooded spur came down to the river on the opposite bank, mixed wood with some big oak trees. The wood extended a little way on this side of the river, again with oak trees. We'd had to duck under the boughs as we rode past. I remembered bits of oak leaf in my mare's mane. The question was whether any of the overhanging branches was thick enough to give a man a bad blow on the head. I stood at the gate a long time, trying to make out the shapes of them through the leaves then pushed it open and walked through. Trespassing now, with no excuse. I looked up into the wood on the far bank, half expecting to see the tall man glaring down at me again, but there was nothing. The oak branches on my side of the river were low growing and quite thick enough to do serious damage. The blow had been on the back of the head. If he'd simply galloped into a bough, it would have been at the front. The most likely explanation was that the horse had been rearing up on its hind legs at the time. There were hoofprints in bare patches of earth under the trees, but a whole pack of us had ridden that way and back in the last few days. There was no way of telling in dry weather if one set were more recent. Then it struck me that a horse rearing would have to take all its weight on its back legs. If I could find a place where there was a low branch and a pair of unusually deep hoof impressions underneath I'd be making progress.

The work absorbed me more than anything I'd done for a long time, so much that I almost forgot why I was doing it and the grief and confusion up at the house. It was a relief, after all the philosophical theorising, to have a practical puzzle that might even have an answer. Either something had happened or it hadn't. If it had happened, then happenings leave evidence. They wouldn't be happenings otherwise. And if there's evidence, it's simply a question of finding it or not finding it. Thinking that out as I looked at dusty hoofprints under those trees was the second thing that summer that had an influence on my life, far more than Plato or ancient Greek (which, by the by, I still haven't learned). The light was just right for the work, horizontal with the sun low, throwing every little detail in high relief. Twice I found pairs of prints deeply incised that might have been a horse rearing, but they were nowhere near the likely tree branches. One big branch at about the right height had a scuff mark on the earth under it that might possibly have been made if a horse had stood up on its hind legs then slipped, but it was near the gate with a lot of other tramplings round it, so inconclusive. Still, I liked that one best and went back to it, kneeling on the ground with my eyes only a few inches away from it. Suppose a horse, scared already, reared with a man tied to his back. Why at this place in particular, near the gate? If the gate had been closed, shutting off the horse from his home then somebody had opened it, the horse might have reared up the way they do sometimes before galloping off. I looked towards the gate, imagining a man there, opening it and might have screamed except shock punched all the air out of my lungs. There was a man there. From where I was crouching under the trees, looking up at him against the light, he was no more than a silhouette but he was watching me and I had the feeling that he had been watching for some time. I scrambled to my feet, catching my boot in my skirt hem and ripping it again, wondering which way to run. Then he spoke.

'Have you found anything, Miss Bray?'

Meredith's voice, not mocking, just interested. My heart started up again, thumping with relief and a little embarrassment.

'I'm not sure. Come and see what you think.'

Amazingly, my voice sounded almost

normal. He came through the gate and stood a little way from me, sensibly so as not to scuff the marks. I told him what I was looking at and why so he came forward and crouched down. The light wasn't quite as good as it had been a few minutes before so my scuff mark didn't seem so convincing.

'The earth's almost polished from the pressure,' I said. 'There was a lot of weight on it for a while.'

He looked down at it for a long time, then up at the branch.

'You know the doctor found a bump on the back of his head?' I said.

'Yes. He thought the horse might have rolled on him.'

'I can understand that would break ribs, but would it cause a bump on the back of the head?'

'The ground's hard,' he said.

'Oak branches are even harder.'

But the picture was too vivid in my mind as I said it and my rooting in the dust seemed suddenly disrespectful, in bad taste. Perhaps Meredith sensed that because he opened the gate for me to go back into the mares' field as if this were no more than an evening stroll.

'We were worried because you were missing supper, so I said I'd come and find you.'

'How did you know where to look?'

'I didn't. I've been wandering all over the

place.' We were back on our own side of the gate, walking along the river bank. 'I brought you some ham,' he said, 'in case you were hungry.'

The warm feeling that came over me was quite ridiculous, given the banality of the thing. I laughed, a release of tension probably, but it felt like a little gust of happiness. Here was a man I admired and wanted very much to think well of me doing something as simply kind as a friend or brother. I hoped the laugh hadn't hurt his feelings and perhaps it had because he added, 'I put mustard on it, but perhaps you don't like mustard,' in an almost humble voice. I assured him that I loved mustard and I was very hungry. To my surprise I suddenly was. He produced a greasy brown paper bag from his pocket and handed it to me.

'Rather crushed, I'm afraid. Do you want to sit down?'

We sat on the bank beside an alder with a clump of yellow irises at our feet and gnats whining up and down. The ham was sandwiched between two bits of bread, no way of eating it elegantly, and yet somehow I didn't feel self-conscious. He let me finish it before trying to talk, just sitting beside me and staring at the stream.

'So you were looking for hoofprints on the other side of the gate. Did you think the horse might have jumped it?'

'I'm sure not. It's a terrible take-off and Arabs aren't great jumpers. Anyway, there were other gates that had to be opened.'

'Yes?'

'Robin says the horse was in the top paddock as usual the night before. Somebody would have had to bring him down to this field, open and close the gate. The Old Man couldn't have done that himself if his hands were tied.'

'So you're saying somebody must have helped him?'

'I don't think help's what I mean.'

I wiped my buttery fingers on the grass. He had a way of looking at people that said 'Go on.' I'd noticed it in our discussions. It was one of his skills to make you bring the half-formed theories out of your mind and give words to them.

'We've all been assuming that the Old Man killed himself, probably with somebody's help.'

'Yes.'

'But there's an alternative, isn't there? You reminded me yourself that Mazeppa didn't want to kill himself. He was tied on the horse against his will.'

'Are you saying that's what happened?'

'When I saw him and Sid, they were coming from the direction of Major Mawbray's land. Major Mawbray's a cavalry officer. He thinks the Old Man killed his son. Even before that the two of them had quarrelled.'

'That's just a series of separate facts. It's not a hypothesis.'

'All right, if you want a hypothesis, here it is. Major Mawbray watched us when we were riding through his field on Wednesday. That's not just part of the hypothesis. I saw him and he looked furious. The next bit is hypothesis. That was the last straw, so while we're away at the coast he's thinking of a way to punish the Old Man. Everybody round here will know how much Sid means to him, so, on the first night we're back he waits until the Old Man's somewhere else on his rounds, goes up into the top paddock and takes the horse.'

'Wouldn't that be difficult. He's quite a spirited animal.'

'Yes, but biddable and used to human beings. And remember Major Mawbray was a cavalry officer.'

'Very well, we have Major Mawbray creeping on to his neighbour's property and stealing Sid. What next?'

'He wouldn't think of it as stealing. He probably didn't intend to keep the horse, but the Old Man would have gone to the top paddock as soon as it got light and found Sid gone. He'd have been furious and guessed immediately who'd taken him. So naturally he'd go looking for Major Mawbray.'

'Who manages single-handed to overpower him and tie him on Sid's back?'

'It might not have been quite as cold-blooded as that. Suppose there was a fight and he managed somehow to knock the Old Man unconscious? It might have seemed a good idea to humiliate him by sending him back that way – only it went too far.'

'That still leaves us with a middle-aged man...'

'In poor health too, I admit that.'

'...knocking out an old man and tying him on a restless horse single-handed.'

'Does it have to be single-handed? What if he's got a strong young son hidden away somewhere?'

He sighed, 'So we're back with Mawbray's son again?'

'Yes, we are. I've thought all along he might still be alive. I'm almost sure of it now.'

'Because your hypothesis demands him. You're getting dangerously close to a circular argument.'

But the way he said it didn't sound sharp or hostile. I sensed that he was taking my theory at least half seriously. We sat in silence for a while. It was getting dark. He said he supposed we should be getting back, but made no move.

'Miss Bray...'

'Nell.'

'Nell, I know it's no use my telling you not to get involved. You are involved and that's all there is to it. But I'm sorry. Sorry for all of you.'

'It's worse for Alan. And for Imogen.'

He sighed and I thought I probably shouldn't have mentioned her. I couldn't help feeling a bit annoyed and this time I was the one who said we should be getting back. He stood up and held out a hand to help me. I ignored it, scrambled up in a hurry to make the point that I didn't need help, caught my boot in the torn hem of my dress and nearly pitched headfirst into the river. He grabbed my flailing hand just in time.

'Naturally if you prefer to drown, I'll respect your wishes and let go.'

He was laughing and far from being annoyed I found myself laughing too. 'I can swim, you know. I can swim quite well.'

'I'm sure you can.'

I hadn't pulled my hand away from him and he seemed in no hurry to let it go. I could make a lot of excuses for what happened next: that it had been a long day and we were all under strain, that grief and shock do odd things to people, that I was a little jealous of Imogen, that he made the first move. They'd all of them be true except the last one. I made the first move. I stepped towards him up the bank and kissed him, full on the mouth. When his face came back into focus, it looked surprised but I thought not unpleasantly so and I must have been right, because then he kissed me. After that he said 'Well.' I said nothing, wondering what had come over me and whether I'd behaved like a free and honest woman or a silly fool and if my kiss had tasted of mustard and if it mattered. We walked up to the field gate and along the track to the house, saying nothing and with a little space between us that somehow seemed to be humming like bees in the sun.

'Where have you been Nell?' Midge said, back in the lamp-lit kitchen. 'We were worried.'

Imogen just looked at me then at Meredith. Odd how some people guess.

Chapter Thirteen

The next day was a Saturday. The rest of the world left us alone over the weekend. In the normal course of country life I suppose there'd have been neighbours visiting, cards and letters commiserating, but the Old Man's death was as unconventional as his life. We all went about our tasks in a stunned way, not talking much about what had happened. It felt as if we were in a mountain village with a great rock slide poised above our heads that a loud noise or sudden movement might bring crashing down on us. So we kept quiet and moved carefully so as not to provoke it.

Luckily there were plenty of practical things to do. The Old Man's death had left a gap in the affairs of the household, especially the stables, that it took all of us to fill. Over the two days we managed to share out tasks. Alan and I, under Robin's instructions, helped with the horses. It seems odd to say instructions when he hardly said a word from morning till night but as long as we were around the fields or the stable yard he had a way of communicating what needed to be done that didn't need words. We filled mangers and water buckets for the mares that were kept in the stables, checked three times a day on the ones running free in the field and treated insect bites with some herbal concoction brewed by the Old Man and kept in a big green bottle. Sid was Robin's responsibility. Early in the morning and just before it got dark in the evening he'd go up to the top of the stallion's field just as the Old Man had done, sometimes with the Afghans running races round him, and stand with the horse under the trees. I imagined him crooning his soft Irish words to Sid but that was their time, his and the horse's, and none of us tried to intrude on it. Nathan and Meredith took over most of the odd jobs around the house, carrying in coal for the kitchen fire that had to be kept going for the oven even though the day temperature was now up in the eighties, bringing in buckets of water from the yard pump because the small pump over the kitchen sink was unreliable. Nathan tried to repair it, stripping it down and putting it together again, but it needed a new part that would have to be got from town. He was gloomy about that, his normal high spirits quite cast down.

As for Meredith, he and I sat at meals with the rest round the kitchen table or met on our errands about the house and yards and treated each other as if the evening by the river had never happened. That suited me. I didn't regret the kiss, not even slightly, but didn't want him to think I expected anything to follow from it. A kiss wasn't a brand of ownership.

The fact that we were all eating our meals together must have added a lot to Dulcie's work but she gave no sign of it and stayed in sole charge of the kitchen, though Midge and Imogen took over the hens and helped with the vegetables. They'd sit out in the yard, scrubbing carrots and peeling potatoes with straw hats keeping the sun off their faces. The heat inside the kitchen was the sensible reason for working in the yard but I knew there was another one – it meant Imogen didn't have to spend a lot of time in Dulcie's company. Midge and I didn't know why she wanted to avoid Dulcie as much as possible but we didn't want to add to the strain on Imogen by discussing it. And there was no doubt that the strain was affecting her worse than anybody else, even Alan. When their work allowed, the two of them would walk together slowly up and down the farm tracks and she'd come back more subdued than ever. Up in our loft at night she hardly seemed to sleep at all and there were deep violet shadows round her eyes. Kit seemed the least changed of us, but then he'd been downcast anyway. He did his best to help with the work and didn't complain about the pain from his arm, but it was clear that it was still giving him trouble. He spent a lot of time reading in the shade or walking on his own, carefully avoiding routes where he might come across Alan and Imogen.

On the Saturday afternoon the heat was bludgeoning. I'd offered to go and check the mares but had left my straw hat somewhere and needed it for shade. I went up to the loft in case I'd left it there and found Imogen sitting on her straw pallet, looking so dejected that I sat down and put my arms round her. She slumped against me and let her head fall on my shoulder. 'Oh Nell. Why did it all go wrong so quickly?'

'It hasn't gone wrong. You still love Alan, don't you, and he loves you?'

'Yes, yes, yes.'

'Well then.'

'It's as if all the old moralists were waiting to get us. Waiting behind the hedge for us.'

'What do you mean.'

'The night before last when Alan and I ... you know ... when we became lovers, I was so proud, Nell. Proud of us, proud of myself for not being a hypocrite and daring to say and do what I knew was right. Only it's all poisoned now with the thought that while we were ... while we were together, the Old Man was out there somewhere, the same night, doing that terrible thing to himself. It feels as if ... oh, I can't explain it, not even to myself ... as if somehow he were bringing death into what Alan and I were doing ... quite deliberately bringing death into it.'

She was shaking. I stroked her shoulder.

'The two things aren't connected. It was just a coincidence. You know that rationally only you're too tired and shaken to think clearly. Besides, I don't think the Old Man was like that. He loved life and he'd lived his own life to the full. If anything, he'd have approved of what you and Alan were doing.' Cheered them on, probably, but I didn't say that.

'No, you're wrong Nell. There was something sinister about him. Didn't you feel that from the start? After all, the first thing he did was shoot poor Kit.'

'He didn't mean to.'

'I hate him, Nell. I know I shouldn't say it because he's dead but I really hate him.'

'Why?'

'I'm sure he got Alan and the rest of us here quite deliberately to have an audience. He planned it all.'

'To kill himself, you mean?'

'Yes. He knew he'd got himself into trouble he couldn't get out of, and he wanted to go with as much drama as he could manage.'

I went on stroking her shoulder. After a while she stopped crying, got up and mopped her face with water from the washbasin.

'Sorry to be such a silly.'

'You're not.' I suppose I should have left it at that and it was tactless of me to say anything else. But I was used to Imogen as an intellectually robust person who'd discuss anything, so I misjudged her mood. 'Has Midge said anything to you about the way we found him?'

'What?' She had her face in a towel.

'Midge and I don't see how he could have tied himself on to the horse like that. If he really did kill himself, somebody must have helped him.'

'Nell.' It came out as a wail from under the towel. 'Don't make me think about it. I've been trying not to.'

'I'm sorry.'

The towel came down. She looked angry. 'This is exactly what he'd have wanted. Can't you just imagine him working out how to do it, laughing to himself about how it would puzzle everybody and the trouble it would cause?'

I couldn't, but I didn't want to start an argument so I suggested she should try to catch up on some sleep and went to look for my hat elsewhere.

By common consent we had our evening meal early, a high tea northern-style around six o'clock with cold meats, oatmeal bread and boiled eggs for those who wanted them. The hens seemed to be back in kelter again in spite of all the comings and goings. Afterwards we all went our separate ways and by the time it was getting dark Midge, Imogen and I were all up in our loft over the tack room. The men had suggested that they should clear a bedroom for us in the house – thinking, I suppose, of how the Old Man's body had been laid in the room just below us – but we were rational beings and anyway we'd come to like it there. We were all three desperately tired from the emotional strain and physical work and hoped we'd be able to sleep properly for once. I'd got undressed to my underwear when there was a high-pitched barking from outside. It sounded like the two Afghans and seemed to be coming from the small paddock in the angle between house and stable yard, where two cows grazed.

Imogen groaned, 'What's happening now?'

I started getting dressed again to go and look but before I'd finished we heard Robin down in the stable yard asking if anything was wrong.

Dulcie's voice answered him from the far side of the yard, 'Don't fash thissen. It's nobbut the dogs seen a hare.'

So we settled down again and for once I slept solidly until well past daybreak. In the morning, as we did our various jobs round the stable yard and paddocks, there were church bells ringing from the town. None of our party were regular church-goers and I couldn't picture the Old Man leading his little household into a pew. Still, I imagined congregations gathering outside churches and chapels, and the gossip there was bound to be about his death. In a small town like that, most people would be on speaking terms with at least one police officer, so the gossips probably knew more than we did about how the authorities regarded it. A bizarre suicide would fit the general view of the Old Man and perhaps everybody would be content with that. The one certainty was that there'd be more material for the gossips in the week ahead, with the opening of the inquest and probably a funeral as well.

Although I tried to sound confident with the others, I worried about having to give evidence at the inquest because I knew it might not be a simple matter of standing up and telling the truth. Not that I'd lie, of course, but there was the question of precisely how much truth to tell – as if it could be weighed out like sugar or dried peas in the shining scale pan on the grocer's counter. I'd found the Old Man. True. His hands and feet were tied. True. But then the weights started dipping. Could he have tied the knots himself? (I had an idea, from my tentative law studies, that they couldn't ask me that in a criminal case because it involved expressing an opinion. But inquests were different and coroners could probably ask pretty much what they pleased.) I didn't know – that was safe enough. What had happened to the knots after the bonds had been cut? I didn't know that either. I surely wasn't obliged to add that I'd thought of that, looked for them and not found them. Then there was the question of the Old Man's suicide attempt on the beach the day before he died. I hadn't told the police about that in my first statement, mostly from an instinct to keep things simple. But if I were asked at the inquest about his state of mind, surely I'd have to tell them. And that would make a suicide verdict more likely and leave everything as tidy as it was ever likely to be. But then just suppose that my Mawbray theory was right. In that case, by giving evidence to support a verdict of suicide, I'd be helping a callous killer get off scot-free. On the other hand, there'd be no point whatsoever of dropping a bombshell at the inquest by accusing a respected chairman of magistrates of murder unless I had strong evidence and I hadn't even a shred of it unless you counted a deep hoofprint in dry ground. My mind chewed away at it all that long hot day and got nowhere. I'd have liked to discuss it with Meredith. I nearly did that morning when I saw him walking back across the yard to the house in his shirtsleeves, his hair wet from washing under the pump, but then I thought he might think I was just making an excuse to be alone with him, so I let him walk on.

By mid afternoon, with heat haze trembling over the fields and the hens plumped down in the patches of shade cast by Dulcie's washing on the clothes line, I was so tired of going over the old facts that I decided I must have some new ones. There was nobody around, but a steady thumping sound from the open window of the kitchen meant that Dulcie was in there working as usual. I walked through the porch and into the kitchen. The fire had burned low and the windows were too narrow to let much sunlight in, so the room was shadowy and even seemed a little cooler than the yard outside. Flies circled lazily round a spiral of sticky paper hanging from a rafter that already held dozens of bodies of their predecessors. The Afghans were lying head to tail on the rug, the way they'd been on the first evening. At the big wooden table Dulcie, with her sleeves rolled up, was kneading a mass of oatbread dough, picking it up, turning it and thumping it rhythmically back down. She looked at me and gave her usual little smile and didn't seem at all put out that I was standing there watching. I said it was hot and she agreed. Talking to Dulcie was like hitting tennis balls into a feather bed. She absorbed what you said but nothing came back to you.

'You'll miss Mr Beston,' I said.

'Ah will that.' She picked up a metal canister from the table, dredged flour over the dough and thumped it again.

'How long have you been working for him?'

'More than a year since.'

'Is it right you were working for Major Mawbray before?'

Her face and the rhythm didn't change. She nodded.

'Did you like Major Mawbray?'

'He was a good enough man most ways.'

'But you left him and came to work for Mr Beston. Was Mr Mawbray annoyed about that?'

'He'd no cause to moan. He'd turned me off before the maister took me on.'

'Turned you off?'

'Didn't want any more of me, so I came up here and took work with the maister.'

She rubbed flour on her hands, tore off a piece of the dough and slapped it into a little flat cake. I watched, pleased to have got this much from her but wondering what it meant. Assuming that 'turned off' meant she'd been dismissed by Major Mawbray, that didn't go with the theory that the Old Man had stolen her from him but it would have been indelicate to enquire further in that direction.

'What about Robin? Was he already working for Mr Beston when you got here?'

Another nod. 'The maister found him at Appleby horse fair the year before. He'd come over with a lot from Ireland.'

This seemed to dispose of the idea that Robin might be her son. It was soothing in the kitchen. I stood watching as she transformed the whole mass of dough into little discs. Then she took a griddle pan out of the grate, floured her hand again and pressed down some of the little discs on it until they were flat pancakes.

'There's those fettled.'

She swept the trimmings from the table into the pig bucket and rubbed little slivers of dough off her fingers. It left her hands pink and very clean. Then she rolled down the sleeves of her blue cotton blouse and buttoned them at the cuffs. I'd got as much as I was going to get, so I said I'd see her later and walked out into the yard.

It was nearly time to check the water buckets for the mares in the loose boxes so I strolled through the arch and into the stable yard, with something nagging at my mind. It wasn't anything she'd said, it was something I'd seen, something out of place. And yet as far as I could remember the kitchen had been just as it usually was. I thought of her pink, capable little hands and saw them buttoning down the cuffs after a job well done. She'd roll up the sleeves, of course, so as not to get things on them when she was cooking – anybody would. Only she had got something on her cuff in spite of her care. I'd noticed it at the time but my mind hadn't registered it. I sat on the edge of the horse trough, closed my eyes and tried to call it back. Clean pink fingers, blue cotton cuff, something sparkling when a ray of sun from the window caught it. Not the button. That had been an ordinary bone button, no sparkle to it. Round, though, and much smaller than a button, two or three of them sparkling in the sun when she moved her wrist, like fish scales. Not even like – that was exactly what they were: fish scales. Nothing to get excited about then. Dulcie was the cook, after all, and even though she was careful, fish scales do stick to things. Only we hadn't eaten fish. We'd been there ten days or so and in all that time there'd not been as much as a whiff or a fin of a fish. Where would she have got fish anyway? Dulcie hadn't been down to the town since we'd been there and no fishmonger would make the journey out to Studholme Hall on the chance of selling a herring or two. I wondered if the scales might have been there from before we arrived but dismissed the idea. Dulcie might be casual in her clothing but she was quite cleanly. There were two or three of her blouses on the washing line in the yard. The thing worried me unreasonably all the rest of Sunday, but there was no point in talking about it because everybody would have thought me quite mad. Then on the Monday morning we had two visits that put it out of my head.

The first to arrive was a police constable in a gig soon after breakfast. He introduced himself as the coroner's officer, come to notify Alan that the inquest on his uncle would be opened at ten thirty the following morning. Only Alan would be needed as a witness on this occasion, to make formal identification of the body, then the inquest would be adjourned and re-opened later when the police had finished their inquiries. The policeman was unthreatening, even friendly, and offered Alan condolences on his sad loss but it brought the reality of the thing nearer.

The second visitor came at midday. The air around the house felt thick and heavy and I was taking a stroll up towards the road, so happened to be the first one to meet the lawyer. He didn't look like a lawyer and we hadn't been expecting one. I suppose it should have occurred to some-body that wills and lawyers come after deaths but we weren't experienced in these matters. Also the domestic arrangements of the Old Man had been so far from luxurious that we didn't think of him as a man of property. So when I saw a young, rather plump man freewheeling down the track towards me, bouncing in and out of potholes, I assumed he was a touring cyclist who'd lost his way. Just before he got to me he yanked on the brakes and jammed a booted foot down, nearly overbalancing.

'Excuse me, is this Studholme Hall? I've come to call on Mr Beston.' Then, hastily, 'Mr Alan Beston, that is.'

He looked hot enough to melt in his black suit, topped incongruously with a tweed cycling cap. A briefcase and bowler hat, very dusty from the journey, were tied on to a carrier behind the saddle. When I told him that Mr Beston was at home he propped the bicycle against the fence, untied the bowler and brushed it with his sleeve then substituted it for the cap.

'Good morning. I'm John Stone, solicitor to the late Mr James Beston. Come to offer my condolences and um…'

I introduced myself, adding that I was one of a party of friends staying at the house. John Stone seemed hardly of the age to be a fully fledged solicitor, only a few years older than I was, and very nervous. We walked together down to the house, he pushing the bicycle and apologising for arriving in such an unprofessional way, only his uncle had taken the gig to Workington.

'And he's very much the senior partner, you see, so he gets first use of it.'

'I don't suppose the old Mr Beston would have objected,' I said. 'From what I saw of him, he wasn't a conventional person.'

'I should say not.' His hot face glowed even redder. 'I've never met anyone like him. I must admit I liked the old boy, even when...'

'Even when people were saying he'd killed somebody?'

He nodded, professional discretion fighting a losing battle with good nature.

'He was my first client, to be honest. I think uncle gave him to me because he didn't want to offend his other clients by taking him on himself.'

'Did you know him well?'

'Only ever met him twice in my life, but he was the kind of man who made an impression, wasn't he? Even without all this.' He made a little flapping gesture towards the briefcase.

I said, 'I hope it's not more bad news for Alan.' Not nosey, I told myself, only wanting to soften things for him and even more for Imogen. Discretion won a partial victory.

'That depends on what he thinks of as bad news. Still, I suppose he knew what his great uncle was like.'

It didn't sound reassuring. There was nobody in the yard and I suggested that he should wait in the kitchen while I went to find Alan. Mrs Berryman would probably find him some ale or lemonade. He must have been as thirsty as a camel after that uphill ride from town, but he sounded alarmed at the idea.

'Oh no, don't bother Mrs Berryman yet. I'll wait out here.'

I found Alan in a shady corner of the stable yard with Imogen, Midge and Meredith. They'd brought out a table and chairs and a few books were scattered around, but they didn't look as if they'd been working hard. I told Alan, carefully not looking at Meredith, 'Your uncle's solicitor's here. He wants to speak to you.'

Alan stood up, looking bone-weary. I took him through to the other yard where John Stone was waiting and introduced them. It was difficult to tell which was the more nervous of the two. When they'd disappeared into the house I went back to join the others.

'Trouble?' Meredith asked, looking straight at me. How had he picked that up?

'I'm afraid it might be but I don't know what.'

'Isn't it just reading the will?' Midge said.

'If he asked for Alan, that must mean he's the heir.'

I took the seat Alan had left. Their pretence of reading Greek was given up and we talked about what had happened, going over and over the same things, not adding anything. Meredith said nothing about my investigations under the trees. After a while Kit and Nathan joined us. The angle of the shadow changed and we moved the chairs round. Somebody mentioned fetching water to drink. The pump was there but that would have meant fetching glasses from the kitchen and we were all avoiding the house, not wanting to interrupt whatever was going on inside. It was almost two hours before Alan came out. He was holding some papers rolled up in his hand and he was smiling, but not happily.

'Waiting for the next act in the drama? Well, gather round and curtain up.'

He swept some books aside and hitched his leg over the corner of the table, stagily deliberate. Imogen said warningly, 'Alan,' but for once he took no notice of her. He slapped the roll of papers against his thigh.

'I have here a copy of the duly witnessed and attested last will and testament of my great uncle, James Beston. I'll read it to you. It's not very long.'

Meredith said, 'Are you sure you want to?' but Alan ignored him as well.

He unrolled the papers and started reading in a clear, controlled voice:

This is the last Will and Testament of me James David Beston of Studholme Hall, Cumberland. Being of sounder mind than most people, I appoint my great nephew, Alan Charles Beston, to be the executor and trustee of this will.

To the said Alan Charles Beston I give and bequeath a.) my horses, my tack and all stable equipment and b.) the sum of five thousand pounds in the currency of the realm. I also request him to carry out my instructions for the disposal of my remains set out in the codicil below.

Imogen gasped, 'Five thousand pounds.'

That was enough for a house, enough to live on for years while they established themselves in professions. The Old Man, unknowingly, had given them their freedom to get married.

'Wait,' Alan said.

To Robin O'Kane, of Studholme Hall, I give and bequeath the sum of one hundred pounds and my silver-mounted hunting crop.

By the Old Man's standards that seemed fit and proper so far, but it didn't account for

Alan's expression or the tone of his voice.

To Mrs Mary Dulcie Berryman, of Studholme Hall, I give and bequeath my personal chattels and the remainder of my estate to be held in trust for her child...

'What?' Gasps from everybody. Alan disregarded them.

...to be held in trust for her child, fathered by me, until such time as the child attains the age of twenty-one. Until that time, I direct my trustee to invest the remainder of all monies in my personal estate, excluding the amounts bequeathed elsewhere, and to arrange that the aforesaid Mrs Mary Dulcie Berryman shall receive the dividends, interest and annual income thereof.

Alan added, into the breathless silence, 'It's dated June the nineteenth this year and witnessed by two clerks in the solicitor's office. All properly done, Mr Stone assures me.'

Then he waited, staring at the paper, while everybody talked round him.

'Can he do that?' Imogen.

'Fathered by him? Dulcie Berryman and him?' Kit.

'Where is the child? What's happened to it?' Midge.

'Is the rest of the estate substantial?' Meredith, sounding calmer than the rest.

'The solicitor says another five thousand at least, quite possibly more.'

Alan's reply was calm too, but only superficially. While we'd been talking he'd been biting his knuckle so hard I thought his teeth would crunch through to the bone. 'Then there's his codicil':

I direct that my great nephew, Alan Beston, shall arrange that my body is burnt on a pyre on the topmost field of my land without religious ceremony of any kind, as a beacon to cheer my friends and my enemies, and he shall light the torch for me.

Stunned silence. Then, as it sank in, Nathan gave a whistle of admiration.

'Well, the thorough-going old barbarian.'

Imogen laid her hand on Alan's arm. 'Nobody can expect you to do it. He just wasn't in his right mind.'

'That's why he said you'd got a good steady hand,' I said.

Alan swung round at me. 'What?'

'Just after we got here. He asked you to pour drinks and said you'd got a good steady hand and that's why he'd invited you.' I could see it so clearly, Alan pouring and the Old Man watching him in the lamplight. 'He planned it from the start, having you here to light his funeral pyre.'

'Which just proves it,' Imogen said. 'He'd planned to kill himself in the most melo-dramatic way possible, making as much trouble as he could for other people, and that's just what he's done. No court or inquest could possibly say he was sane.'

Meredith said quietly, 'If he wasn't in his right mind that would invalidate the whole will, the five thousand to Alan as well as everything else.'

'How could I take it anyway under those conditions?' Alan said.

'I don't see why not.' Kit's tone was harsh and bitter and he didn't look at Alan. 'We've all been discussing justice haven't we? Giving every man what's owing to him and so on? As far as I can see, everybody's getting what he wanted. The Old Man wanted to be dead and he's dead. Alan and Mrs Berryman get his money. And if he wants to be burned instead of buried I don't see that he's doing anybody any harm except cheating the worms out of a dinner.'

'Don't be so cold-blooded,' Midge pro-tested.

'I don't see the point of priding ourselves on our rationality and abandoning it as soon as anything happens.'

'He doesn't say whether the child's a son or daughter,' Nathan said. 'Are you assuming that—'

Midge shushed him and looked round the yard to see if Robin was within earshot but there was no sign of him.

'But I don't see how it happened,' Alan said. Then blushed. 'What I mean is, when did he have a child by Mrs Berryman? He's only been living in this part of the world for a few years and before that...'

He let it trail away unsaid, but I guessed what he was thinking. Until recently, according to local gossip, Dulcie Berryman had been Major Mawbray's more than housekeeper.

'Does Mrs Berryman know about the will?' Midge asked.

'The solicitor's in there telling her now – assuming that she didn't know anyway.'

I said, 'I wonder why he didn't name the child in the will.'

'I asked the solicitor about that. He said he suggested quite firmly to the Old Man that they should put a name in, but apparently he wouldn't have it. It creates what Mr Stone calls an ambiguous situation.'

Nathan said, 'You mean if she happened to have a child handy she could pass it off as his and claim the money for it?'

Alan nodded. I guessed like me that he was thinking of the anonymous note.

There was silence for a while, broken by Meredith. 'I don't know if you all realise that a consequence of this will is that we're

266

all guests of Mrs Berryman?' People made questioning or unbelieving noises. 'The remainder of the estate goes to her. I'm no lawyer, but I take that to include the tenancy of this place. Of course the will has to go for probate, but at present if anybody has the right to stay here, she does.'

Alan said, sounding dazed. 'I'm supposed to be executor, aren't I? Are you saying I should go and talk to her?'

'That's up to you.'

Another silence, then Alan stood up. The anger that had been there when he was reading the will had turned to bewilderment and he seemed hardly capable of walking until Meredith took his arm, turned him round and gave him a reassuring push towards the house. We all watched him go.

'I suppose he could just take the horses and go,' Nathan said. 'Shall we all take to the road as Scholar Gypsies?'

Kit growled at him not to be more of a silly ass than usual.

At any rate, Dulcie Berryman didn't turn us out. None of us knew what was said in the conversation between her and Alan (except possibly Imogen and she wasn't saying anything) but we all of us sat round the lamplit table in the big kitchen, Robin included, and ate ham and fried eggs almost as if nothing had happened. Nobody talked much, though. When we'd finished Robin went out to check the horses, Alan and Imogen disappeared somewhere and the rest of us stayed in the kitchen to help Dulcie Berryman clear up. She went about the business of collecting plates from the table, apparently calm and untroubled by either her scandalous past or her prosperous future. It struck me that in this respect Dulcie Berryman might be a better practical philosopher than any of us. Amused by this idea I looked up and saw her standing idle for a moment, watching Nathan as he worked the pump over the stone sink. She had a little smile on her face and was standing quite relaxed with her feet apart, a little flatfooted, with her stomach thrust forward and a hand supporting the small of her back, fingers spread.

At that moment, I recognised her from years back, from ten years back or more when I'd been a child in Manchester or Liverpool or maybe the East End of London. Then I knew I was a fool because I'd never seen Dulcie Berryman in my life before. It wasn't her I was remembering, but a way of standing. Goodness knows in what particular waiting-room at one of my father's many clinics I'd first been aware of women standing in that way and known why. Probably my mother or father, who unusually for their generation believed in telling children things, had explained it to me. But that stab of memory was quite unmistakable. Dulcie Berryman was expecting a baby. The child the Old Man had acknowledged by leaving a large part of his estate to wasn't Robin or any other child breathing or walking around. He or she was still waiting to be born. And at much the same moment another memory came to me, a much more recent one: the Old Man just after his stallion had mounted a mare, standing in the yard with his arm round Dulcie's haunches. And the words I'd overheard that had made Dulcie so anxious suddenly: 'You'd think he'd know when he'd done it, wouldn't you?' At the time, I could make no sense of them, but now it was all too clear. Dulcie had told the Old Man that the child she was expecting was his. He'd been pleased enough to make provision for it in his will then for some reason he'd come to doubt it. Dulcie saw me looking at her and smiled her slow, likeable smile.

'You all right, then?'

'Yes,' I said, 'and thank you for cooking the meal.' What else could I say?

Chapter Fourteen

I got up early next morning while the other two were still asleep and went down to the kitchen. Robin was sitting at the table, drinking tea. Judging by the straws on his jacket he'd already been at work. Dulcie was at the sink. She turned round when I came in, smiling as usual.

'Tea's in the pot. If it's stewed, I'll make you some fresh.'

Kind, smiling Dulcie, did you kill him because he was having doubts about who the father of the baby was? If the lawyer's right, your share of his property could come to even more than Alan's five thousand pounds, more than you could possibly earn in several hard-working lifetimes. Did you knock him on the back of the head when he was sitting at the table where I'm sitting, possibly with something like that old five-pound scale weight I see you use as a doorstop? Did you carry him out in those strong arms of yours that look so used to carrying things? He wouldn't be much heavier than a potato sack, I'm sure. Did you tie his feet to the stirrups and his wrists to a leather strap as calmly and neatly as you'd knot a pudding cloth?

'I like my tea strong,' I said, pouring. 'Don't brew fresh for me, thank you.'

Robin pushed the milk jug towards me, white china with broad blue stripes, chipped on the rim showing the yellowed clay under the glaze. He smiled too, more shyly than Dulcie, but not so scared as he'd looked when we first arrived. Working with the horses together had given us a kind of fellowship.

'The mare that was kicked's doing well,' he said. 'Will I put her out with the others?'

And you, Robin, with your soft voice and teeth as white as the milk I'm pouring into my tea. Did you fetch Sid from the field when she told you to, hold him still while she did it? You liked the Old Man, I believe it. So why would you do it? The baby must have a father after all, and if it wasn't the Old Man's there aren't many more men up here, miles from town. A hundred pounds is a lot of money for a lad too, more than you'd ever expect to hold. He was looking at me, waiting for an answer, and I felt my face going red and hot at what I was thinking.

'It's really for Alan to say,' I told him, 'but in your place I think yes, I'd put her out.'

I escaped from the kitchen as soon as I'd got the tea and a crust of bread down. We'd discussed the night before whether we should all go down to the town for the opening of the inquest and decided against it. Alan was the only one needed on this occasion and it would attract unwanted attention if we all turned up. Meredith, as usual, would go with him as moral support. I swept the stable yard while Robin took the mare down to the field and brought Bobbin back up, then helped get the wagonette ready for the trip to town. Alan climbed into the passenger seat, pale and serious in dark suit and dark blue tie. It should have been black, but naturally he hadn't packed a black tie to bring on holiday. He'd buy one down in the town if there was time. At least he had a black hat, a battered Homburg borrowed from the Old Man's wardrobe. Meredith got in beside him, picked up the reins and we watched until they were out of sight on the road.

After that we all went our separate ways. Midge suggested she should take Imogen's mind off things by teaching her some algebra in exchange for all that Greek so they took their books and papers off to some shady place. I didn't join them because I had my own plan for the day and was sure that Imogen wouldn't approve of it. Meredith probably wouldn't have approved either, which was why I hadn't discussed it with him. I didn't approve of it much myself, but it was the only thing I could think of that might help.

The fact was that the disclosure of the Old Man's will had come as a bad blow because now we had reason to suspect Dulcie and probably Robin as well. As I walked along the river checking the mares I wondered why that should matter so much. Less than two weeks ago we hadn't known either of them existed. I decided the Old Man would have had the answer. Bread and salt. The simplest of tribal laws from Homer to the Bedouin – if you ate a man's bread and salt there was a bond that couldn't be broken. His friends were your friends, his enemies your enemies. This was logical nonsense, of course, but it still had force. If you sat and ate with people it was almost impossible to think of them as murderers or do anything that would lead to their harm. If there was any possibility that they weren't guilty I wanted to follow it, which was why I'd made up my mind that before the day was over I was going to speak to Major Mawbray.

I waited until early afternoon, doing odd jobs around the place, then went up to our loft and made myself look as presentable as possible with the limited wardrobe I'd brought with me: navy skirt and jacket, blue blouse with ruffles at the neck, little navy straw hat with cornflowers on the brim that had miraculously survived in my pack no more than slightly squashed. It wasn't the most comfortable of outfits for walking in what felt like the hottest day of the summer so far and I was afraid Midge and Imogen would see me going up the track and want to know what I was doing.

I made it to the road unchallenged and consulted my map, trying to locate the house with the red roof I'd seen from up on the hill. As far as I could see it was Beck Hall, half a mile down the road as if going to the town, then left and another mile or so from there. The roads were narrow and shady, with no carts around to stir up dust so I enjoyed the walk in spite of the unsuitable clothes, not hurrying and trying to work out how I'd get him to talk to me. We hadn't been introduced, we had no friends in common and the only social contact between us had been two glares from him to me. Still, years of bargaining for cheap rooms in unfashionable hotels across Europe had given me a tolerably thick skin and an officer and gentleman could hardly have a lady thrown out on her ear, even if he were a murderer.

The road dipped down to a stone bridge over a stream. On the other side of the bridge was a drive entrance with a pair of white-painted wrought-iron gates closed across it and 'Beck Hall' carved on a slab of green slate, all very neat and orderly. I unlatched the gate and walked down the drive between tall dark hedges of rhododendron. After a bend in the drive the hedge on my right fell away and I was looking down on the side of the house and the stable yard. It was a substantial stable yard, almost as impressive as the Old Man's. Following the curve of the drive I came to a broad semicircle of gravel, a flight of steps and a front door flanked by red brick pillars curved like sticks of barley sugar. From the top of the steps there was a view down over the patch of woodland where Major Mawbray had been standing the morning we rode out with the Old Man and beyond it the mares' field.

I took a deep breath and tugged the black-lacquered knob labelled 'Bell' beside the right-hand barley sugar pillar. The door was opened almost immediately by a woman in her thirties, hair scraped back, and wearing a dark dress. She looked an achingly neat and respectable housekeeper, nothing like Dulcie. I asked if Major Mawbray were in.

'I'm sorry, miss, he's gone down to the town. Was he expecting you?'

I said no and don't worry I'd call some other time, angry with myself for feeling relieved. She asked if she should tell him who'd called. The response to that should have been to leave my card – but what student carries calling cards? I apologised again and heard the door close behind me as I walked down the steps.

After screwing up my courage to meet Major Mawbray, it would have been too much of an admission of defeat to walk straight back home. I went slowly back to the road junction and decided to stroll a little way towards the town on the chance of meeting Alan and Meredith coming back from the inquest. After a mile or so, with the temperature rising all the time and my best shoes pinching, I knew that was a bad idea and anyway they might have passed while I was at Beck Hall and be home already. So I turned back again but hadn't gone far up the road when I heard the sound of hooves behind me. Although they were coming from the town I knew from the light and sharp sound of the hooves that it couldn't be Bobbin and the wagonette. It was a smart little Stanhope gig with a bay going at a brisk hackney trot and the driver very correct and upright in black suit and bowler hat, holding a long driving whip. I stood aside to let it go past. The driver touched his whip to his hat brim, politely acknowledging me for giving way, and for the third time in a few days our eyes met. The gig's momentum took it past, then it came to a halt some way ahead of me and he turned round in his seat. I walked towards him, trying not to hurry, wishing my heart weren't thumping so much. He looked anything but pleased to see me.

'I've seen you before, haven't I?'

Not the most polite of starts, with him leaning down like squire to peasant, and yet I guessed he was a man who usually valued politeness. Sounding as cool and distant as I could with my face glowing from the sun, I introduced myself and explained that I was staying with his late neighbour, Mr Beston. He winced, but there was no telling if it was at the name or a twinge of pain in his stomach.

'Perhaps you'd care to accompany me some of the way back,' he said, very correct and formal.

'Thank you.'

He held out a yellow-gloved hand to help me as I put my foot on the step and swung into the seat beside him. We set off again at a trot, which in a two-wheeled vehicle on a rutted road doesn't make for conversation and he didn't try, just stared straight ahead. When we reached the point where the road turned off for Studholme Hall he brought the gig to a smart halt. This was where I should have thanked him and gone on my way. I was just nerving myself to say I wanted to talk to him when he got in first.

'Perhaps you'd care to come and have tea with me?' he said in that same weary voice that had sentenced the poachers. I stared.

'Won't you come into my parlour?' said the spider to the fly.

'Thank you. That's very kind.'

I smiled as well as I could manage and settled myself back in the seat. At a walk now, because the track was narrow, we turned right along the road then through the gateway and down the drive to his house. I noticed that the gates had been opened ready for him. There was more evidence of an efficiently run household when we turned into the stable yard and found a groom waiting to take the reins as soon as we came to a stop, touching his cap to the Major in a gesture like a salute. The groom was a strong-looking man, middle-aged with close-cropped hair, very much the ex-soldier. The Major and I walked round to the front of the house, our feet crunching on new yellow gravel.

'Was your groom with you in the army?' I asked.

He jumped, as if his thoughts had been a long way away and I suppose my question was impertinent, but I'd decided you didn't have to mind your manners too much in the spider's parlour.

'Oh yes. Sinclair's been with us a long time.'

No doubt he was strong, loyal, good with horses, used to taking orders and not asking questions. Useful, I thought, but didn't say it. The housekeeper must have heard us coming as well because she opened the front door as soon as we set foot in the porch. She looked surprised to see me again so soon, but said nothing.

'Tea in the front parlour please, Mrs Bell. I expect Miss Bray would like the chance to wash her hands.'

Mrs Bell showed me up a wide dark wood staircase, with rainbow colours spilling over it from stained-glass panels in the window on the landing. New, strident stained glass. The bathroom was the size of most people's sitting rooms, with mahogany fittings, modern plumbing and more stained glass in the window. I used the lavatory, washed my hands and smoothed down my hair with them (I'd lost my comb somewhere as usual) and inspected my sunburned nose in the mirror. Downstairs, the housekeeper was waiting to show me into the parlour.

'Major Mawbray will be with you in a minute. Do you take milk?'

She poured Earl Grey and left me to entertain myself with piles of sporting magazines or oil paintings of plain men with handsome horses. Neither appealed, so I wandered over to the grand piano. It was closed and looked as if nobody had opened it in a long time, with a fringed paisley shawl draped over it and family photographs in silver frames on top. There were several different portrait studies of the same person, a fair-haired woman with a soulful look, big dark eyes and a penchant for lacy shawls and collars. In one of the pictures a boy of about five years old was standing beside her in pale satin jacket and knickerbockers, glowering at the camera. He had his mother's fair hair and dark eyes, but there was nothing soulful about him. Major Mawbray came in and saw me looking at the picture.

'My wife Lilia. She died seven years ago.'

'And that's your son with her?'

He gave a nod. He didn't want to talk about him. He poured hot water into his teacup, took a small blue bottle out of his pocket, palmed a couple of pills and gulped them down.

'So you're a friend of Beston's nephew?'

'Yes. You probably saw us out riding on your land.'

There was no point in beating about the bush. I knew he hadn't invited me there for the pleasure of my conversation. In fact, it was hard to imagine him finding pleasure in anything. He was looking at me as he'd looked at the poachers in the dock and there was a tension about him, as if he didn't know what to do with me now he'd got me there. It would have been convenient to think it came from guilt, but I guessed there was another reason. Major Mawbray, protected first by military tradition then the life of a country squire, wouldn't have had any personal contact with what newspapers and magazines called The New Woman. He'd have read about her though and would know her habits, like appearing in public unchaperoned, wearing bloomers and having unconventional relationships with men. In his limited knowledge of me, I fitted the bill all too well. That question about being a friend of Beston's nephew possibly implied that I was Alan's lover but I could hardly say, 'No, that's my best friend'. I contemplated taking one of his cigars from the humidor on the table and sitting down to smoke it legs crossed, just to complete the picture for him, but I'd tried a cigar once and it had made me cough. Instead I settled demurely on an uncomfortable chair with a shiny and overstuffed seat. None of the parlour furniture seemed built for relaxing. He stayed on his feet.

'Old Beston never had any respect for anybody's property.'

Did that include Dulcie? I almost asked him. At least he wasn't pretending to be polite. It made things easier.

'Do you think Mr Beston killed your son?'

He looked at me steadily with eyes like wet pebbles. 'He admitted firing in the dark at where Arthur was. What am I expected to think?'

'But the police have never found your son's body.'

He shook his head and turned away to pour more hot water. While he was pouring he said almost casually, 'I've just got back from the inquest.'

That surprised me. I knew magistrates had no obligation to attend inquests.

'What happened?'

'They took evidence of identity and the doctor's evidence then adjourned until this time next week, pending further inquiries. The coroner released the body for burial.'

'Much as we expected,' I said.

'I gather you discovered his body, Miss Bray.'

'Did that come out at the inquest?'

'No.'

So the police had been talking. A magistrate would naturally hear the gossip. At least I knew now why he'd brought me there, so his next question didn't come as a surprise.

'How did he die?'

'On his horse, the stallion.'

'A fall?'

'No, but it looks as if the horse might have rolled on him and there was a bump on his head as if he'd hit it hard on something.'

He nodded. I suppose some of that might have come out in the doctor's evidence.

'I heard something about him having tied

himself on.'

Significant. It meant that either the police had no suspicion that anybody else was involved, or Major Mawbray was pretending they hadn't. It was an uneasy game I was playing, telling him just enough to see how he reacted without giving too much away.

'Yes.'

'Why would he do that?'

'I don't know.'

'Do you think he killed himself – remorse for what he did to Arthur?'

I turned the question back on him. 'Do you think so?'

'I don't think he was capable of it.'

'Remorse or killing himself?'

He didn't answer, apart from inviting me to help myself to more tea. I was thirsty so I did, taking a look round while I drank. The parlour obviously doubled as a library with several shelves of books that didn't look as if they'd been read for years, if ever, mostly campaign histories and manuals of estate management. But there was one section of poetry books, conventional enough in range – Keats, Tennyson, Browning, and Byron of course. The books were in a shelf by the window so I had to screw my eyes up against the sun, trying to see if the Byron might be out of alignment with the rest, as if somebody had been reading it recently. As far as I could see it wasn't. He saw where I was looking.

'Sun bothering you?' He made a move to pull the blind down.

'Are you fond of poetry?'

He blinked at this sudden dip into drawing-room conversation. 'Not much time for it. My wife liked it though.'

'Byron?'

'Mostly Browning, as far as I remember.'

That was as close as I wanted to get to *Mazeppa*. After the literary diversion there was more silence and I was on the point of saying I must be going when he spoke again.

'I suppose the nephew's the heir, takes on the horses and the lease and so on?'

From the hard edge to his voice and the way he'd turned away from me again this was an important question to him. It was certainly beyond the bounds of polite curiosity and I might have told him it was none of his business, except I'd got precious little for my trouble so far and was seized with an urge to experiment.

'His great nephew Alan gets the horses and quite a lot of money. The rest of his estate goes to Dulcie Berryman in trust for her child by him.'

'What?' An undisciplined yelp from a thoroughly disciplined man. 'What did you say?'

I repeated it. He looked at me for what seemed like minutes then sat down heavily on a couch.

'Can I get you anything?' I was alarmed at what I'd done. He'd looked ill before, but now he seemed to be struggling to sit upright. Luckily there was a knock on the door and the housekeeper looked in, probably to see if we needed more tea.

'Are you feeling bad, sir? Would you like me to fetch you your other medicine?'

He nodded, tight lipped. She was back soon with a spoon and medicine bottle on a tray. It gave him a chance to recover and me the excuse to go. I thanked him for the tea and the lift.

'Sinclair will drive you back if you like.'

But I preferred to walk, back up the drive to the crossroads, turn right for Studholme Hall. Why had the news about Dulcie done that to him? Simple jealousy? Men could be appallingly jealous in sexual matters. Midge, Imogen and I had discussed it sometimes in a mostly literary way, Othello and so on, and now we had the more immediate example of Kit, but I hadn't expected such an attack of it in the Major's case. Odd, too, how some women seemed to have a kind of gift for causing it. It was a relief to be out of the parlour and back in the sun. I strode along wondering what I'd got for my efforts and decided it didn't amount to much. I knew that the Major had a strong and efficient groom, but I could have guessed that. I knew the Major didn't writhe with guilt at the mention of poetry by Byron, but might have expected that too.

When I came to the gateway to Studholme Hall there was a vehicle ahead of me. It wasn't one I recognised – a rustic wagon with a black waterproof covering, drawn by a raw-boned dapple grey. It went very slowly, even allowing for the ruts in the track. It wasn't until I followed it down to the yard that I realised it had been bringing the Old Man's body home.

Chapter Fifteen

The men must have decided already to keep the women out of what followed. I suppose the Old Man would have approved of that, although I didn't. When I followed the cart into the yard I found all of them except Robin standing there. Alan said to me, 'Imogen and Midge are up in your room. They'll tell you what's happening.' His voice and face were so strained that I accepted he wanted me out of the way and didn't argue for once. I found them both sitting on their mattresses, making no pretence of reading or anything else. As soon as my head came up over the stairs from the tack room Imogen burst out, 'They're not really going to do it, are they Nell?'

'Do what?'

'Burn him.'

It was the problem of the codicil. They told me what I knew already – that the inquest had been adjourned and the body released to Alan as closest relative. He and Meredith had arrived home about an hour before, knowing that the body was following, and immediately gone into a conclave with the others in the parlour. Imogen was furious, not at being kept out of things but with the Old Man for imposing yet another burden on Alan.

'It's barbaric. I don't see how they can ever consider it.'

'If it's what he wanted, after all–' Midge started, but Imogen cut across her.

'What does it matter what he wanted? He was quite insane, the will shows it.'

In the silence that followed we heard wheels grinding away out of the yard, presumably the funeral cart starting its journey back to town. I wondered where the men had put the Old Man's body. Not in the tack room this time or we'd have heard. Although I didn't like to mention it to the other two, there must have been some urgency to the men's discussion. He'd been dead for four days and it had been unusually hot. As we waited the shadows stretched out over the room and we heard buckets clanking as Robin kept to his evening routine. Then there were quick footsteps and Meredith's voice asking Robin where they kept spades and shovels. Imogen drew a deep breath.

'At least it sounds as if its burying, not burning.'

Some time after that Alan called us from the stable yard and we went down to see what they'd decided.

'We're digging a grave for him up at the

top of the field near the woods. We're going to bury him at sunset.'

The Old Man had got half of what he wanted. There would be no funeral pyre but he would lie in the topmost field of his land and be buried without religious ceremony. Alan went back up to help with the grave digging.

'At least they haven't forbidden us to be there,' I said.

Imogen wasn't sure that she wanted to go, but Midge and I were determined to show that much respect for the Old Man at least, so she gave in. The clothes I had worn to visit Major Mawbray would have to serve as funeral wear as well, so I stayed as I was while the other two changed into the darkest things they had with them. We went downstairs, through the house yard and on to our familiar track to the top field. There was half an hour or so to sunset but we'd timed it right because the men were just ahead of us, silhouetted against the golden light, carrying the body on a makeshift bier, each to a corner. They'd put Kit on the right because of his injured left arm. We found out later that the bier was an old door. The shroud they'd wrapped the body in was a horse blanket – which seemed fair enough for the Centaur. There were two figures walking behind them, separate from each other, first Dulcie then Robin.

We fell in with the procession and went in silence through the gateway, up the cropped field, where the grass was beginning to grow again, past our abandoned college barn. They'd chosen a good place for the grave, at the very top point of the field, shaded by trees at the edge of the wood. The sun was almost down now, just showing over a low cloudbank the colour of purple grapes on the horizon of an inky sea. In the paddock just below and to the right Sid suddenly threw up his head, whinnied and cantered from one side of the field to the other, silver mane flying. It was wrong, I knew, to be superstitious about animals – he was probably just restless because nobody had been up to talk to him that evening – but the whinnying sent a chill down my spine and I could tell the others felt the same. The four men put down the door and we stood round the open rectangle gouged out of the grass.

Alan said, 'Well?' and looked at Meredith. Between them they gently lifted the blanket-wrapped figure and knelt to lower it, clumsily because the grave was deep. Although I wouldn't have wanted a conventional burial for the Old Man, I found myself wishing for the expertise of professional undertakers. But it was done. They straightened up and, with Nathan's help, started shovelling in the earth. Dulcie stood a little apart, face impassive. Robin had tears streaming down his cheeks and his lips were moving, probably in prayer whether the Old Man had wanted it or not. The first few dozen spadefuls were laid in carefully, as if the body in the blanket could feel hurt, but once it had disappeared from sight the earth rained in faster and by the time the sun had set and the edges of the cloud mass had turned red-gold from the afterglow, the job was done.

Perhaps it was that glow on the edge of the clouds that gave Midge the idea – Midge of all people, the practical mathematical one.

'I don't see why he shouldn't have a bonfire at least,' she said.

We all looked at her, surprised, but the suggestion chimed with the uneasiness I think we all felt. Death needs some ceremony after all and we knew we hadn't given the Old Man his beacon to cheer his friends and enemies. Without any more discussion we agreed that there should indeed be a bonfire and scattered in all directions to find things to burn. We had no more than half an hour of daylight left and must have needed some relief from the tension by then, because it turned into a wild hunt. Some people went back to the house, others through the fence into the wood. Still in our good clothes, we dragged and carried dead branches, bits of broken chicken coop, barrel staves, the remains of an old wheel-barrow. Even Robin joined in with the rest, bringing up sackfuls of old straw too musty for horse bedding. By the time the light was going we'd built up a good pile on a reasonably flat piece of ground, far enough from the grave for respect, high enough for the flames to be seen a long way away.

'Matches. Who's got matches?'

'Nathan's always got matches. Where is he?'

We shouted for Nathan, thinking he was still in the woods but his reply, breathless and fretful, came from lower down by the barn.

'I'm coming. Don't be impatient.'

When he appeared he was dragging the armchair he'd made so carefully.

Midge protested, 'Not that. It's nice.'

'It's meant to be a funeral pyre, isn't it? Besides, we won't be using it any more.'

Alan and Meredith helped him wedge it into the bottom of the bonfire. Robin and I pulled straw out of the sacks and pushed armfuls of it wherever there were gaps. A little breeze was ruffling the leaves in the wood. Alan straightened up and took the matches from Nathan.

'Are we ready then?'

'Here.' Kit stepped out of the shadows, holding a bundle of spruce and holly twigs. 'Might as well do it properly.'

He held out the bundle for Alan to light, waited until it flared up then passed it over.

'The bridal torch,' he said.

He and Alan stared at each other for a moment, the contours of their faces sharp in the light of the flames, then Alan made a lunge like a fencing movement and pushed the torch into the heart of the bonfire. The straw caught at once, then the dry branches and in moments the whole fire blazed up and ripped a hole in the dark sky that must have been visible for miles around. Down in the town people would see it from their back yards or doorsteps. The gossip about the will had probably got round by now and they would be sure it was the Old Man burning. Late walkers or shepherds would watch it from the hills on the Scottish side of the Solway, fishermen from the sea. Nearer at hand, Major Mawbray might be watching too, standing in his porch between his barley sugar brick pillars, and know it was a last defiance from his enemy. At least the Old Man hadn't been cheated of that. We stood round it, not saying anything. Once Alan had got the fire lit he'd stepped back alongside Imogen. They were shoulder to shoulder, hands probably touching. From where I was standing the rest were just dark shapes, with faces coming into view every now and then as the flames shifted. I thought about Kit and the bridal torch. Had he chosen that way of admitting defeat over Imogen? Quite possibly. There was a love of drama in both Alan and Kit.

The flames began to die down. Nathan's chair glowed red for a while, then flared and crumbled. We started patrolling the dry grass, stamping out bits of glowing ash. The fire drew in on itself until it was an untidy ball of burnt branches with a glowing heart. We drew in on it as well in an informal circle, kicking bits of smouldering wood back into the centre. As it happened, there was nobody close to me when my toe tangled in something that wasn't wood. I thought at first it must be a piece of tough bramble or bracken stem and knelt to pull it away before it could scorch my shoe but there was too much of it for that. My hands closed on something leathery, too straight-edged to be a plant stem. The burnt end broke and I was holding a length of it in my hand. Even then it took me a while to realise what it was. A leather thong. My heart jumped 'Not that,' even while my head was telling me there might easily be a leather thong on the bonfire, caught round some other piece of rubbish we'd burned. But a log at the heart of the fire gave a last little spurt of flame, just enough for me to see that the thing at my feet was a tangle of leather thongs and knots and string. My mind had hardly registered that before my foot was kicking it again and again, right into the heart of the fire. I felt my toes getting hot inside the shoe, heard Midge shouting to me to be careful. The tangle caught and hung on a red-black branch, flared and fell into glowing ashes. I'm sure none of the others noticed. Because of Midge's shout they were looking at me, not the fire.

'It's all right,' I told them.

The instinct not to talk about it came as suddenly as the one to kick. You couldn't call either of them decisions because that implies thought and I hadn't thought at all. I'd simply wanted the thongs and string not to be there and now they weren't. With the excitement of the fire gone the feeling of loss came back. Not simply the loss of the Old Man but of something in ourselves. It felt quite cold now after the heat of the flames and a tawny owl was calling in the wood. Somebody suggested going back to the house for tea and food if we could find any. I don't think many of us had eaten all day. We began to trail down the field in ones and twos, nobody talking. We'd closed the gate behind us and were on the track going down to the house when Midge said, 'Where's Nathan?' We called for him, but there was no answer.

'He's probably still up there mourning for his chair,' Kit said. 'He'll come in when he gets hungry.'

But when we'd finished the ham and oatbread and Dulcie – calm as ever – had brewed a third pot of tea, there was still no sign of Nathan. We had a half-hearted discussion about whether we should go up and look for him, but as Alan said he was adult and quite capable of finding his own way home, we stopped worrying about him and went to our beds.

Chapter Sixteen

The three of us went down to breakfast together the next morning. It was quite early, around seven, and there was nobody in the kitchen but Dulcie. She was stirring something in a saucepan and said would we take some poddish. It turned out to be a kind of porridge but Imogen said she didn't want any. Dulcie ladled poddish for Midge and me, poured tea and smiled her little smile as if nothing had happened and yet it must surely have been on her mind that she was a landed woman now. The roof we were sitting under and the table we were sitting at were hers as long as the lease lasted. The baby she was carrying would be born a wealthy child. But if she was thinking of that she gave no sign, her poise as perfect as ever. While we ate we could hear the men moving around and talking in the parlour next door. After a while, Alan and Kit came in and sat down at the table.

'Where's Nathan?' Midge asked.

Alan said quietly, 'I'm afraid he's gone.'

'Gone?' Midge dropped her spoon. 'Gone where?'

Alan looked uneasy. 'I'm afraid he just

didn't come in last night.'

'You mean he's still out there somewhere? Why on earth aren't you out looking for him?' Midge, usually so quiet, was practically screaming.

Kit said, 'It's not entirely accurate to say he didn't come in last night. He must have come back while the rest of us were up by the fire because he's taken his things with him – or most of them at any rate.'

'His pack's gone,' Alan added, 'and all of his clothes – not that he'd brought many. All he seems to have left here are some books he never read anyway and some tins of tobacco he must have forgotten he'd left on the mantelpiece.'

Imogen had grabbed Midge's hand under the table and was holding it tight.

'But Nathan's not the kind of man who goes off on his own,' she said. 'He likes being with people.'

Midge just nodded. She was trying hard not to burst into tears. I asked if Nathan had said anything to anybody. Alan shrugged.

'Not as far as we know.'

'Where's Meredith?'

'Out looking for him, in case he just took it into his head to go for a night hike.'

But we all knew that unnecessary hiking wasn't like Nathan, and it was no surprise when Meredith came in ten minutes or so later, shaking his head.

'I've been up as far as the woods and down to the crossroads. No sign of him.'

'But where's he *gone*?' Imogen insisted.

Alan said, 'Home, I suppose, or back to Oxford. He'd probably just had enough.'

'But he wouldn't do that without telling...' Imogen had obviously been going to say 'Midge' but made it more tactful '...without telling somebody.'

Midge said, her voice harsh from keeping the tears back, 'After it happened, he was trying to persuade all of us to go away with him.'

Alan was clearly hurt by the desertion too, but determined not to show it.

'It's not as if he could do anything, after all. Perhaps we'll get a polite note in a couple of days saying thank you for the hospitality.'

'It's simply not like him,' Imogen said. 'I've never known a man who'd do more for his friends than Nathan.'

All she got was another shrug from Alan.

For the rest of the day Midge kept glancing up the track from the road, hoping to see Nathan walking down it and thinking that Imogen and I weren't noticing. Towards the middle of the afternoon she decided she'd go up to the barn with a book and for once discouraged Imogen and me from coming with her. I went to look for Meredith and found him in the vegetable patch, weeding onions.

'Shouldn't you be working at the book?' I said.

He smiled. 'Most people get along without philosophy but we all need onions.' Then, more seriously, 'Yes, I know I should be but I can't concentrate.'

'Nathan?'

'Yes. It is very uncharacteristic.'

'What does uncharacteristic mean, after all? Only something that we didn't know about him so far.'

He pulled up a groundsel plant. 'That sounds bitter.'

'It is bitter. He's hurt Midge very badly.'

I knelt down and for a while we weeded companionably. When we got to the end of a row I made up my mind to tell him.

'Somebody put the knots on the fire last night.'

He stared. I told him what had happened and what I'd done, not trying to give explanations or excuses.

'Are you quite sure they were the same ones? After all, you only saw them for a moment in the firelight.'

'I'm sure. Leather thongs like the ones in the tack room and that thick string that went under the horse's belly.'

'We dragged a lot of things up for that bonfire. I suppose they could have caught on something without the person being aware of it.'

'Yes, but that would mean they'd been hidden somewhere for the past five days, wouldn't it? I've been looking on and off and haven't found them in any of the likely places.'

'You realise they're evidence – or would have been?'

'Yes. I can't justify it, but I think if I had it to do again, I'd make the same decision.'

'That's honest at any rate.' From his expression, he was seeing me in a new light. I was sorry about that. 'You must have had some reason.'

'At the time, no. At least I didn't think so. But I suppose I knew that if they'd been put on the fire deliberately, or hidden somewhere and put on accidentally, it had to be by somebody here.'

The kitchen door opened. Dulcie came out, threw a handful of crumbs to the hens, gave us one of her slow smiles and went back inside. We stopped talking until the door closed behind her.

'Where does this leave your hypothesis?' he said.

'Major Mawbray? It wrecks it, I admit that. He couldn't have hidden the leather thongs and string in the first place and he certainly couldn't have put them on the fire last night.'

And yet, stubbornly, I didn't want to give up my theory. I decided not to tell Meredith, for the meantime at least, about my tea with Major Mawbray and how he'd reacted to the news about Dulcie. I knew I'd given him more than enough to think about and quite probably wrecked my reputation in his eyes. I was comforted a little because he'd said I was honest – but he must have realised when he said it that what I was being honest about was dishonesty. He could even, if he wanted, go to the coroner and tell him Miss Bray had deliberately destroyed evidence. I didn't think he'd do that – at least not without telling me first.

I left Meredith in the vegetable patch and went through to the stable yard to wash the dirt off my hands in the drinking trough. Imogen was sitting on the edge of it, staring down into the water. She watched as I dabbled my hands.

'Weeding with Meredith,' I explained.

'Has he any more idea why Nathan's gone?'

'No.'

'Perhaps Alan's right after all. He's simply deserted us. Poor Midge is devastated.'

'I hadn't realised she felt quite like that about him. I knew they got on well but…'

'I don't think she'd realised either. It's funny how suddenly it can come to you. You think you know somebody as a friend, then…'

'Like you and Alan?'

'Yes.' She swung her foot in its white stocking and tennis shoe worn for coolness and stared at it. 'Alan and I have had an argument, Nell.'

'I shouldn't worry. Aren't lovers' tiffs considered a normal part of the process?'

'What's normal? I feel so bad about it now, making things even worse for him, but we had to talk about it.'

'What?'

'About that awful will. He says he's not going to accept the Old Man's legacy.'

'Five thousand pounds is a lot of money.'

'I know. Enough to start a school.'

That didn't come as a complete surprise. We'd all of us discussed educational reform, especially as a way of levelling inequality between classes and sexes. Still, I'd never thought of either Imogen or Alan as teachers.

'That's what you think he should do with it?'

'Yes. Not the usual sort of school. It's something we've talked about and he's discussed it with Meredith too. A new school for a new century with boys and girls being encouraged to ask questions, develop their minds, take nothing for granted. It would be quite small at first, but we'd write a book about what we were doing, perhaps train teachers to start other schools like it and...'

'I suppose you could still do that in time, even if he turns down the Old Man's money.'

'Time, time, time.' She flicked the surface of the water, ruffling it. 'If he's got no money he'll have to be an ordinary teacher in some awful boys' public school and all the ideas we have will get ground down to nothing or even if we believe in them still we shall get scared and conventional and not do anything because it might offend people. And in time we'll be a housemaster and his wife and have lots of ordinary children and go to chapel and die without doing anything with our lives. That's what time does.'

Perhaps she wanted me to argue, but the sheer bleakness of the picture and the anger in her voice took my breath away. She went on talking, looking down into the water.

'It's when you're young that you need to do things, when you still believe in them, but most people can't because they haven't got the money. Now it's happened and Alan wants to throw it away.'

'Has he told you why he doesn't want to accept the money?'

'Nothing that makes sense. There's this business of not burning the body as his uncle wanted...'

'But that was a codicil, not a condition of inheriting.'

'I know. So then he said he'd feel the

money was tainted.'

'You mean because of young Mawbray, or the way the Old Man died, or Dulcie?'

'I don't know. Alan won't talk about it. He just says it's his decision. He wants us to get engaged but keep it secret for a while, go back to Oxford and be patient.'

'And you don't agree?'

'It all seemed so clear a few days ago but so much has happened I don't know any more, except that I still love him. But I know it would be wrong to refuse the money.'

'I think I agree with you.'

'Good, because I want you to help me persuade him.'

'If he won't listen to you, I'm sure he won't listen to me.'

'You seem to be getting on well with Meredith. No, don't blush and look away from me. I saw your faces when you came in the other night. Will you talk to Meredith for me? If he tells Alan it's his moral duty, he might listen to him more than me.'

'I haven't got that sort of influence with Meredith. Anyway, I'm not sure he'd say it was a moral duty.'

'If money gives you power to do things, isn't it right that good men should have it rather than bad?'

'If good men can be guaranteed to stay good.'

'Nell, don't start a debate. Just help me.'
She leaned against me, heavy with the
accumulated weariness of the past few days.
I put an arm around her to stop her sliding
off the edge of the trough and into the
water. As far as their argument was
concerned I was on her side, but my mind
was full of another problem.

'Imogen, that night – the night he died.
Did you and Alan see or hear anything?'

She went tense. 'What do you mean?'

'The horse was still in the top paddock at
sunset and the tack's kept in the room under
our loft. Somebody had to do a lot of
coming and going in the dark, whether it
was the Old Man or somebody else. You and
Alan were out there until about one o'clock
so I wondered–'

'Nell, what is this?'

'Did you see anything?'

'No.'

'Hear anything?'

'No, no, no. And don't go asking Alan.
He's had enough from the police without
your interrogating him.'

'Am I interrogating?'

'Yes. For some reason you and Meredith
have got it into your heads to play detectives
and you're trying to impress him. I think it's
unforgivable to experiment with people's
feelings like that.'

She stood up, turned her back on me and

walked away towards the house. There was enough truth in what she'd said to leave me feeling sick and shaken. Perhaps because of my wandering life, the friendships I'd made in college meant a lot to me and now it looked as if I'd trampled on one of the closest of them.

The atmosphere in our loft that night was tense, with Imogen not speaking to me and Midge subdued. I guessed from the sighs and rustling of the hay mattresses that we were all sleeping badly but there were none of the whispered conversations we'd had on other nights. Long after midnight it was still oppressively hot. At Midge's suggestion we'd opened all the long windows over the stable yard before going to bed, but it didn't seem to make much difference, so I was at least half-awake when the shouting started. It came at first from the other yard near the house, a man's voice, shouting, 'Stop. You there, stop.' Then there was the sound of running feet, coming through the arch into the stable yard. All three of us were out of bed and at the open windows in the same instant. A figure came rushing out of the arch, on to the paving just below us. The moon was down and it was too dark to see more than a shape, except looking at it from above there was a glint of pale hair.

'Stop.' It was Kit's voice shouting, echoing

under the arch. The figure swerved, then ran diagonally across the yard making for the gateway that led towards the mares' paddock. Kit came into view, white shirt showing clearly, still shouting but running clumsily because of his arm. The figure got to the gate, vaulted over it and disappeared. I didn't see what happened next because the three of us were running down the stairs and out through the tack room. By the time we got into the yard only Kit was there by the gateway breathing heavily.

'This confounded arm. There's no point chasing him...'

'What's happening?'

The three of us must have looked a sight in nightdresses and bare feet, hair down. Kit wasn't much better with his shirt pulled out over his trousers, bare feet pushed into unlaced shoes.

'I was just going out to the–' Then the impropriety of what he was saying struck him. What he meant, obviously, was that he was on his way to the lavatory beside the cart house. 'Anyway, I'd been out in the yard and I was on my way back into the house. The kitchen window had been left open, because of the heat, I suppose, and I saw this man climbing in. I thought at first it might be Nathan coming back but he was the wrong shape so I yelled at him and he wriggled out and shot off.'

While he was explaining to us Alan and Meredith arrived in the yard, also in shirt and trousers. Robin came behind them carrying one of the big lamps from the kitchen. He was in his normal working wear of corduroy trousers, waistcoat and boots. When Kit asked if he'd seen anything, he shook his head.

'Did you get a proper look at him?' Meredith asked Kit.

'No. Medium height, I'd say, and he must be young from the way he ran.'

They discussed whether it was worth going after him and decided there was no chance of finding him in the fields in the dark. Alan suggested they should go back inside and check that he hadn't set fire to anything.

'Perhaps it's somebody who doesn't know the Old Man's dead, still trying to burn him out.'

'But everybody must know by now,' Imogen said. 'They've got nothing against any of us? How could they have?'

Nobody answered her. I left them to it and walked through the arch to the house, past caring about being in my nightdress, hard earth pleasantly cool to my bare feet. I was looking for the only person who hadn't appeared so far. Dulcie Berryman might be a sound sleeper in the big feather bed, but she could hardly have missed what was going on in the house and outside. The kitchen door had been left open when the men rushed out. I walked inside and there was nothing but the dark shapes of furniture and the smell of ham and cheese. Not a sound from Dulcie's room at the top of the stairs. I waited for a while in case she came down, then noticed something small and white under the windowsill. A piece of folded paper. I had to rustle around in the kitchen drawer for matches to read the writing on it. An educated person's writing, nothing like the scrawl of the other note. 'I must see you. Usual place on Saturday. Can you get some of the money now? Tell them you need it to pay bills. Ten pounds would do.' No signature. I put the matches back in the drawer and took the note with me. Imogen and Midge were both in the loft when I got back, but the men were still muttering below in the yard. It was beginning to get light.

'What's that in your hand, Nell?' Imogen said.

'Nothing important.'

I didn't want another argument.

Chapter Seventeen

I'd had enough. Enough of all of them, of worrying and quarrelling. The business of the resumed inquest next week and what I'd say was heavy on my mind, and there was nobody I could talk to. Not Alan or Imogen, obviously, and I'd never thought of Kit as a confidant and anyway he was too taken up with being jealous. Midge was normally a patient listener and a sensible adviser but she was too hurt over Nathan to be landed with my problems. As for Meredith, I could hardly bear to think about him let alone talk to him. What Imogen had said had struck home. In the sleepless times of the night I'd seen myself through her eyes – a besotted woman trying to impress. The blow to my pride was a bad one and I could only deal with it by walking away, not like Nathan had, turning my back on it altogether. As a witness I didn't have the choice – although I was sorely tempted. What I could do was what I'd promised myself in the train – go walking in the fells just for a day on my own. Since we'd got there so much had happened in the green Solway pastures and by the sea that the Lake District hills to the south of us might as well not have existed. Now I needed to run away to them like old friends.

At breakfast time I waited in the loft until Imogen had gone over to the house and told Midge I'd be back sometime in the evening. She didn't fuss and offered to bring me out some bread and cheese from the kitchen, sensing that I didn't want to talk to anybody. I put on my walking boots, washed my face at the pump in the yard and filled an old lemonade bottle with water then met Midge by the back door.

'It's that peculiar hard cheese. Hope it's enough.'

'Plenty thanks. Is Dulcie up?'

'Yes. They've just been telling her about the man last night.'

'What did she say?'

'That it was probably some thief who'd heard the Old Man was dead and thought the house would be empty.'

I stowed the food and water in my pack, waved to Midge and walked away up the track. Rather than having to pass the raw earth of the Old Man's grave and the bonfire ashes I decided to go across Sid's field to the open hillside. He was there as usual, grazing knee deep in buttercups. He raised his head and looked as if he might come towards me but I looked away and walked on as quickly as I could. I went round the edge of the wood and up to the high sheep pasture where I'd walked before, but didn't turn back this time to look at the Old Man's neat fences or the red roof of Major Mawbray's place or the sea in the distance.

For the first few miles uphill I walked too fast trying to get away from them, got hot and lost my temper in a maze of streams that formed the headwaters of our little river. The ground round them was boggy even in a dry summer like this one and the only way to negotiate it was by striding from one tuft of coarse grass to the next, risking ankle-wrenching slides into mud holes carpeted in bright green moss. Clouds of flies orbited my head. I took off the old squashy linen hat I'd worn as protection against the sun and flapped it at them but it only made them buzz louder. Disturbed grouse kept rocketing up with that cackling cry that sounds so much like a laugh when you're floundering in a bog.

The sun was high before I got to the road leading to Caldbeck, but at least this was the edge of the real Lakeland fells and the Old Man's territory was safely behind me. I crossed the road, followed a track up to Greenhead and once I was past the farm buildings sat down in a grassy place beside a stream for a drink of water and a look at the map. My plan for the day, as far as I had one, was to get to the summit of Skiddaw for the view southwards over the other Lakeland hills. It was an ambitious one even for a long summer day and when I checked the map I found I'd been over-optimistic in thinking it was a simple uphill hike from where I was. I'd have to climb another thousand feet or so up Great Sca, drop steeply down following a stream to join the path that ran over a pass from Bassenthwaite to Keswick, then a steep drag from the head of the pass up the eastern side of Skiddaw. Too ambitious almost certainly, but at least it gave me something else to think about. Meanwhile, it was restful here by the stream. A kestrel hovered overhead, the fanned-out feathers of its tail almost transparent against the sun. A sheep was bleating from the other side of a clump of bracken that closed in this little area of turf almost completely. A slab of slatey grey rock, turned sideways on by some convulsion of the earth millions of years ago, stood like a door in the bracken and completed the closed-in feeling. If I got benighted and had to sleep out on my way back, there'd be worse places than this to choose. Then I laughed because I realised the thought must have been put in my head by the signs that somebody else had done just that. I hadn't noticed at first because he – almost certainly he – had cleared up so carefully after him. If you looked closely there were cuts in the grass, marking out an area about two foot square divided into four, so that the sections of turf could be lifted up neatly without tearing them. There were some little fragments of charcoal and wood ash on the outside of the square, so small that you wouldn't have seen them unless you were looking. Somebody had neatly rolled the turf back and made his fire then just as neatly replaced it next morning when the ashes were cold, leaving no damage. Very few people would take that trouble. Almost everybody I knew would happily make his fire on the grass just as it was, leaving a burnt patch behind. Everybody I knew, in fact, with just one exception. And when I thought of that exception I was back at the Old Man's place as if I'd never gone to all this trouble to leave it. Back by our college barn, when we'd gone up to join the men for our first picnic there. I'd noticed then how carefully they'd made their fire, on a patch of bare earth with the turves taken away and rolled up by the barn wall where they'd keep cool and moist. Nathan had done that, as he did most of the practical things for us – neat, craftsmanlike, considerate Nathan. I told myself I was being stupid, making too much of a small thing. I remembered Imogen's bitter words and thought she was right. The place didn't seem so comfortable any more and I could hardly wait to refill my water bottle and get away from it.

I walked on, too fast again, but after a while the steady rhythm you need when you're walking uphill calmed me down. Nathan had probably got on a train and was hundreds of miles away by now. Hundreds, thousands of men would be just as careful making fires. Higher up, a little breeze blew from the west, scattering the flies and making walking a pleasure. The view from the top of Great Sca was like life opening out again, Bassenthwaite Lake two thousand feet below to the right with white sails of little boats moving slowly, nearer right the deep crease in the hills between the Uldale Fells and Skiddaw, with a well-marked track running along it that led to the pass. There was a group of hikers on it looking no bigger than tin soldiers, walking up from the Bassenthwaite side towards the waterfall. I'd forgotten about the waterfall until then but the name came back to me from when I was about twelve and my brother and I had first toiled up there with my father – Whitewater Dash. It was well named, a narrow but impetuous streak of water that looked near vertical from a distance, pinched at a few points between outcrops of rock. From up here it was a silver-white flourish on the hillside, like an Arab horse's tail. (No, don't think of that. It's just a waterfall with the sun on it.) I stayed where I was for a while, enjoying the height and the view then started scrambling down a little stream between Meal Fell and Frozen Fell that, according to the map, should join Dash Beck about a mile below the waterfall.

It wasn't an obvious route because most people didn't get to the waterfall from this side and there was no path, only sheep tracks that dwindled away into clumps of bracken or ended under stunted rowan trees where sun-sodden ewes dozed. So it was a surprise when I looked back and saw another walker coming down after me, about half a mile away. It was a man, walking quite strongly. I was amused at first, guessing that he'd got lost on the fells and was following me down. It became a game, whether I'd get to the path alongside Dash Beck before he caught up with me. I walk fast, but it's one of the little unfairnesses of life that trousers always go faster than skirts, especially when skirt hems are clotted with dried bog mud, bracken and wisps of sheep wool and keep snagging themselves on rocks and gorse bushes. When I next glanced back he was catching up with me fast, no more than a few hundred yards back. He was wearing a tweed jacket that flapped unbuttoned over his white shirt and he was hatless. Then I recognised him and my heart bounded and turned over. For a moment I had to fight an insane urge to run away from him, risking ankles and even neck on the steep ground. I stopped, turned away and took a couple of deep breaths, looked back towards him. He'd stopped too, just within speaking distance.

'Miss Bray ... Nell?'

His black squashy hat was in his hand, his face sweating and there was a scratch on his cheek, probably from a gorse bush. It was obvious he'd been walking long and fast to catch up with me, but now he'd managed it he seemed unusually at a loss for words.

'Well, Mr Meredith?'

It sounded as formal as Stanley to Livingstone and I meant it that way. I was rattled.

'Do you mind if I join you?'

'Do I have any choice?'

I'd intended that to sound just as formal, but I can't have managed it because he smiled and his voice when he answered was relieved, more like his usual self.

'If you tell me to climb back up there...' he jerked his chin towards the summit of Great Sca, 'then I'll do it, only it really is very hot so I hope you won't.'

'I was going to the waterfall,' I said. It seemed a more realistic choice than the top of Skiddaw, still a long way off. He seemed to take that as permission and came on down to where I was waiting, stepping more carefully now along the stream bank. I leaned against an outcrop of rock, aware of being tired and having come a long way.

'You set a fast pace, Nell.'

He propped a foot on the lower shelf of the same rock.

'How long have you been following me?'

'Midge said you'd gone for a walk on your own. I thought she meant just above the local wood. I went up there and saw you heading off into the distance as if John Peel and all his hounds were after you.'

'So you decided to join them.'

'Hunting you?'

'Or dogging me. Why?'

'What if I said I was concerned about you? Most women don't go off hiking on their own.'

'*Ergo* I'm not a woman?'

'A most erroneous conclusion. But I was concerned, yes. I thought you might have decided to leave us, like Nathan.'

Until he said that I'd forgotten about the little square of turf. He must have seen something in my face.

'I've offended you?'

'Not really, no. Only thinking about all that was something I wanted to get away from. I know I can't really, but for a day at least...'

'I'm sorry.' He genuinely looked and sounded it. 'Shall we walk?'

He let me lead the way. A little further

down our stream joined another one with a narrow path beside it. It led us to a bridge of stone slabs over the Dash Beck and on the far side of that the broad track to the pass that I'd been trying to reach most of the day. It was late afternoon by then, high time to turn back. If he'd pointed that out I'd have snubbed him because I was determined to get to the waterfall at least but he simply fell into step beside me when I turned uphill.

'The truth is,' he said, 'I wanted to talk to you, only I can see now that was selfish of me. I thought you were seeing all this as a kind of intellectual diversion...'

'Do I seem that cold-blooded?' Shades of Imogen again.

'Very far from it. I'm sorry, I know you're concerned for your friends. But the other evening when you were looking at the hoofprints I thought you were seeing it objectively as well...'

'I wonder if there's any such thing. So you came after me hoping for a nice objective discussion? I'm sorry if I'm disappointing you.'

'Are you still angry with me?'

'I'm angry with myself.'

'Why?'

There were several answers to that. Angry for being either too cold-blooded or not enough so. Angry because, in spite of everything, a part of my mind was turning somersaults with the delight of walking alongside this clever and good-looking man in the hills I loved better than almost anywhere in the world, finding that he seemed to care about what I said or did. The fly-away reckless feeling I'd had when I kissed him was fluttering inside my chest, threatening to take over again. So I said nothing and we walked along in silence for a while. There were shouts and laughter from up ahead of us. The hiking party I'd seen from up on the fell must have got to the waterfall. I wished we were just out for an uncomplicated walk like they were and must have sighed because his hand touched mine. It might have been accidental with our arms swinging so close together as we walked, but I knew it wasn't.

'You're sad, Nell?'

'I've quarrelled with Imogen.' It wasn't what I'd intended to say, it just came out. 'She accused me of playing detectives to impress you.'

'Ah.' The long sigh from him was almost a groan. 'What this is doing to all of us.'

The pain in his voice surprised me. In spite of what I felt for him he was still older, still a don and I hadn't guessed it affected him as badly as the rest of us.

'We're all coming apart,' I said. 'Imogen and I have quarrelled and Kit's hardly speaking to anybody because of Imogen, and Midge is hurt because of Nathan. You know, perhaps there's something to be said for convention after all. If we'd all gone our separate ways and not made such a point of coming away together, none of this would have happened.'

'You can't unpick the past like that. So why doesn't Imogen want you to play detective?'

'She's still convinced it was suicide. She thinks the Old Man was determined to kill himself in the most inconvenient way possible for everybody else.'

'Does she really?'

He said it in a different tone from the conversation so far, looking straight ahead. I started asking what he meant, then stopped. I didn't want to know because it was what I'd been walking away from all day. Imogen was intelligent so if she was holding to a theory against the available evidence, there must be a reason for it. I couldn't talk about it, not even to him. She was my friend. Desperate to change the subject, I pulled out of my pocket the note I'd found by the kitchen window. I'd kept it to show to him in any case but now I flapped it in front of him, stopping him in his tracks. He read it, frowning.

'What is it?'

'The man Kit chased last night dropped it in the kitchen. I think it must have been meant for Dulcie. Somebody's trying to blackmail her.'

He folded up the note and gave it back to me. We started walking again.

'It's an odd blackmail note, isn't it? No threats.'

'Perhaps he's already made the threats.'

'He?'

'It was definitely a man Kit chased. A man with fair hair. Major Mawbray's son has fair hair. There was a photograph of him on the piano.'

I'd forgotten that I hadn't told him about taking tea with the Major so I had to explain. The path had curved round, bringing the waterfall in sight. He listened, still frowning.

'So what's your theory?'

'It's nothing as clear as a theory, but you know I've thought all along that young Mawbray might not be dead. Then there was the way the Major reacted when I told him about the will and Dulcie and the Old Man's baby. And the other anonymous note on the wagonette.'

'Different paper and handwriting.'

'Completely, and quite probably a different person. But there's surely something there. If we could get a sample of young Mawbray's handwriting–'

His hand touched my wrist again, warningly this time. 'Nell, this is a tall tower of perhapses on a very shaky foundation. Are you even sure our burglar last night was fair-haired? It was dark, remember.'

'I had a good view of him from above. You can make out a white shirt in the dark, so why not fair hair?'

'Especially if fair hair is what you want to see.'

'So you're accusing me of making it up?'

'I'm not accusing you of anything. But even a good mind can play odd tricks.'

'Meaning my mind is playing odd tricks?'

'I'm sure it's trying very hard to put a fence round certain areas and not look over it. You said we're all coming apart. What did you mean by that?'

'That we've started quarrelling, people going off on their own, hiding things from each other. I've been doing it as much as anyone and I hate it. We started this holiday talking about truth and justice and now I'm honestly not sure what we mean by either.'

'You might say that's progress.'

'Except we both know that it isn't. What it's doing to us isn't progress at all.'

We walked on in silence for a while. The figures of the hiking party ahead of us appeared in silhouette then vanished over the brow of the hill. Long shadows were stretching out from the rocks over the heather and bilberry beside the track. Meredith broke the silence.

'Did you come out looking for Nathan?'

'No. But it was hard not to think about him. After all, he was always the one you could rely on to be cheerful whatever was happening, but he's been so quiet and odd since the Old Man died. He was totally loyal to his friends, but he's walked out on Alan when he's in trouble. Nathan's one of the kindest men I've ever met, but he's hurt Midge badly. Then there was something else.'

He gave me a questioning look.

'Then I found a place where somebody had made a fire. I've no proof of it but it was the way Nathan made fires. I think he's out here somewhere in the hills.'

'Do you remember, Nell, what I told you when all this started? You can't start a logical course of thought then stop because you don't like where it's taking you.'

'Why not? I might have been wrong about how the Old Man's hands and feet were tied. Midge might have been wrong too. We were hardly in a calm frame of mind. The coroner's jury would understand that, wouldn't they?'

'I'm sure they would. A country coroner and a jury of respectable middle-aged tradesmen faced with a good-looking and well-brought-up young woman who's been subjected to a terrible experience. They're certainly not going to be hard on you.'

'So all I'd have to do would be fluttery and

womanly and confused?'

'You'll probably be genuinely nervous in any case. Not many women like standing up and speaking in public.'

I could have got angry and pointed out that I'd lisped my first political speech (consisting of 'Vote for Papa') from a soapbox at the age of six. But I was too sad and this was too serious. Besides, he wasn't trying to be annoying. There was too much sympathy in his voice for that.

'Or on the other hand, you can go on thinking and asking questions and let the chips fall where they will.'

'That would be the right thing to do, wouldn't it?'

'I can't help you on that. I wish I could.'

His hand touched mine again. We were at the foot of the waterfall now and the noise of it almost drowned out our voices. Somehow that made it easier to tell him what had been on my mind since I'd noticed the cut turves, as if the water would wash it away.

'The trouble is, Nathan's such a practical joker and the Old Man would try anything. Supposing they were practising some silliness – like Nathan's knots that come apart when you pull them, only this time they didn't. Nathan would have meant no harm, only once it had happened he'd be too scared to say anything. Then those things on the bonfire... Do you remember how Nathan made a point of putting that chair on it? It could have been to stop us seeing something else, like a conjuror making you look in the wrong place.'

'All of us put things on that fire,' he said. 'It could have been anybody.'

'I know that, but Nathan's the one who went. And he went immediately after the bonfire.'

'Even if you were right, he must know he can't stay out on the hills all his life.'

'Perhaps he just wanted to get away. Or maybe he's just waiting until the inquest is over. Did you notice how nervous he was when the police were there?'

'If you were right – and it's just another hypothesis remember – wouldn't the proper course be to find Nathan and persuade him to talk to the police? It would have been an accident after all.'

'Yes, I suppose so, but...'

He raised his eyebrows. I remembered that I'd confessed to him already that I'd deliberately destroyed evidence and here I was, hesitating over a legal and proper action. I was thinking that even though it would have been an accident, having to stand up at an inquest or even in court and admit to it would blight the whole of Nathan's life.

'Shall we walk on?' I said.

We went on up the path to the right of the waterfall. I'd seen much bigger waterfalls but the narrowness and whiteness of this one gave it an especially headlong quality, as if the water were risking injury to itself in its hurry to get off the crags and down to the flat fields. Seen from close to it wasn't a completely vertical drop but three connected falls with little pools in between where the water swirled among grass and ferns before dashing on down again. At the middle pool, on the far side from us, a man was kneeling, bending down and cupping his hands to drink. At first I thought he must be one of the hiking party trailing behind the rest. The noise of the water would have prevented him from hearing our steps on the path opposite. He gulped, dipped his palms and gulped again, then looked up with water dripping from his beard – a bushy beard, ginger brown, worn with unfashionable sideburns that framed his face in a mass of hair. Plump round face and broad shoulders, glasses glittering as they caught the sun.

I shouted, 'Nathan.'

Perhaps if I'd thought about it I shouldn't have shouted. He saw us, started raising a hand in awkward greeting then thought better of it and hauled himself upright. He'd always reminded me of a big friendly bear but now he was an alarmed one. He turned away from the pool and started shambling across the rough grass. My only idea at first was to speak to him, see if he needed help, but the waterfall was between us and I'd have to cross the stream either above or below it. I decided on below and ran back down the path. At first I heard Meredith running behind me but when I got level with the bottom pool he wasn't there. It didn't worry me because my eyes were on Nathan on the hillside up above me, stumbling and making heavy going. Something fell out of his pocket. It caught the sun for a moment before rolling away down the hill and I realised it was a tin of tobacco. He must have felt it fall because he hesitated for a moment then blundered on. I was sure I could catch up with him once I was across the stream so I slid in and waded across, boots slipping on stones, cold water up above my knees. I pulled myself out on the opposite bank and started uphill.

'Nell, wait.'

Meredith's shout, not from close behind me as expected but at a lot higher up, just audible over the water. He was standing about forty feet above me, at one of the pinch points where the fall was at its most narrow between two large rocks, nearly on a level with Nathan but still on the wrong side. It struck me that he intended to jump across and I yelled to him not to, sure that the fall even at its narrowest point was too wide, the take off and landing too slippery. For a moment I thought he'd heard me and taken notice, then he was in the air, his foot touching down on the far side. There was a fraction of a second when it looked as if he'd managed it and he stood upright, then his foot slipped, his arms flailed in the air and quite suddenly he wasn't there any more. I don't know whether I screamed or not. I forgot about Nathan, who was still heading away and probably didn't know what had happened, and started climbing up beside the stream, slipping on wet moss, clawing at grass and ferns, with some mad idea of grabbing out for Meredith as he came down. He came too fast. The white water suddenly turned black from his shape in it then he was past me and it was white again. I'm sure I screamed then. I let myself slide down the grass on my side to the pool at the bottom and there he was floating in it, boot wedged between two rocks, a trail of blood spiralling out from his head into the water, like the red twirl in a child's glass marble. I went into the pool, waist deep, and hauled him upright. His eyes opened, looking hurt and puzzled as if somebody else had done this to him.

'Nell?' Then, more clearly, pulling his thoughts together by what seemed like a physical effort. 'I think my foot's caught.'

I was laughing from the sheer relief of finding him alive, but there was still a problem because I could only get his foot loose by letting the upper part of his body fall back in the water. I eased him down as gently as I could and dragged at the rocks. One of them was firmly set into the bank, but the other one moved an inch or two from my frantic pulling at it, just enough for his foot to come free. Somehow we got ourselves out on the bank, sodden and clinging together.

'Oh God, I'm sorry,' he kept saying. 'I'm sorry, I'm sorry.'

I think we probably lay there for a long time in a shivering mass, hardly knowing where one body ended and the other started. After a while as the warmth of the sun got to us we sat up and looked at each other and I found that I was furious with him.

'It was a totally insane thing to do.'

'I nearly managed it.' But he still sounded penitent.

'That's like nearly flying. Nearly's nowhere.'

'I thought we wanted to talk to him.'

'Of course we did, but it wasn't worth that. Anyway, I was catching up with him.'

'I suppose he's gone now.'

'I'm sure he has. I don't know what's possessed him – or you come to that.'

Then I felt sorry because he was shivering again. My clothes were wet but his were as soaked as it was possible to be, clinging to him. The gash above his right ear had stopped bleeding but the palms of his hands were raw and torn.

'I tried to grab for things as I went down. Odd how your mind goes on working – as if it's watching from somewhere quite calm, up above it all.'

'Can you walk, do you think? You need to get warm.'

He could, so we started walking down the path in the evening sun, trying to dry out and decide what to do next. We had no chance of getting home before dark even if we had been fit to walk that far. According to the map, the village of Bassenthwaite was three or four miles away down the path and I thought I remembered an inn there.

'They'll probably give us beds for the night, but there's no way of letting the others know.'

'They'll think we've deserted them too.' In spite of that he sounded more cheerful and was walking easily.

'We'll have to leave Nathan out here,' I said. 'We can't do anything else.'

'Suppose we stop thinking about him for a while. Do you happen to have any money with you?'

'Not a sou. I didn't think I'd need any.'

'Nor have I, as it happens. I was so eager to catch up with you I didn't bring my wallet and all my loose change seems to have gone as a tribute to the water gods.'

'So even if there is an inn, we can't afford it. We're rogues and vagabonds.'

For some reason this struck us as hilarious and we skipped along, laughing like children – reaction, I suppose. Then he stopped and looked at me, half seriously.

'Are you glad I didn't drown, Nell?'

'I suppose I had the choice. I could have left you there after all.'

He kissed me first this time, on the mouth, his tongue pushing in between my lips. When he put his arms round me the dampness of our clothes made it seem almost more intimate, like flesh to flesh. So it seemed a small step after all to lie down together on some soft grass behind a rock. He was tentative at first, tactful. I could have said no if I'd wanted to and when we got past the point of saying no I didn't want to in any case. Afterwards we stayed clinging together for warmth, because the sun was right down by then.

We were up and walking by first light, stiff and chilled, our clothes still damp and itchy with bits of grass and heather.

'Still glad, Nell?'

'Yes, I am.'

It was mid morning before we were looking down on the pastures and neat fences of Studholme Hall.

He sighed, 'I suppose we're going to have to tell them.' I looked at him.

'About Nathan, I mean.'

'Yes, I suppose we are.'

We went on down.

Chapter Eighteen

There would have been no question of slipping back quietly, even if we'd planned to, because nearly everybody was around the house and stable yard. Imogen and Midge were scattering food for the chickens, Dulcie sitting on a bench in the shade watching them, Kit reading at the other end of the bench. Midge saw us first and in her surprise threw a handful of feed so wide that the chickens cackled their annoyance and went sprinting after it, scrawny legs scissoring.

'Well, what have you two been doing?'

Then she went red, realising that the question implied a lot more than she'd intended. Meredith said he'd fallen in a stream and I'd pulled him out. It was less than a complete answer but at least it broke the awkward silence.

'Alan's out looking for you,' Imogen said, her voice carefully neutral. 'He's ridden the cob down to the town.'

Meredith sat down on the bench between Dulcie and Kit and started unlacing his boots. He was obviously waiting for me to break the news.

'We've seen Nathan,' I said.

'Where?' The question came explosively from Midge. More chicken feed went scattering.

'Up on the fells, on the way to Skiddaw.'

'Why didn't you bring him back with you? What did he say?'

'He didn't seem to want to talk to us,' Meredith said. 'In fact, he ran away.'

They were all staring now, even Dulcie.

'Are you sure it was Nathan?' Kit asked.

We both nodded. I felt desperately tired all of a sudden. The clothes I'd been wearing for twenty-four hours were itchy with sweat and bits of grass and heather. I told the others I was going to change and walked through the arch to the stable yard and upstairs to our loft. I wasn't surprised to find Midge following me.

'Nell, what really happened? He must have said something.'

I took off my boots, peeled off the clinging wool stockings. My feet were pale and wrinkled from being damp so long.

'No. He didn't want to talk to us. Meredith nearly killed himself trying to catch up with him.'

'But what's he doing? How's he living out there?'

'I think he's been building himself fires and he must have taken some food with him, or maybe he's been catching rabbits with snares. You know how practical Nathan is.'

Blouse and knickers joined the stockings in a pile on the floorboards. They'd have to be washed under the pump later. I stood in petticoat and chemise, poured water from the ewer into the basin and started sponging myself.

'So all the time we thought he'd gone off and left us, he was only a few miles away,' Midge said.

'Seven or eight miles perhaps. Not far, anyway.'

'Far enough. So that he could get here quickly if he wanted to, but we wouldn't know he was there. It all makes sense after all, doesn't it Nell?'

Midge's mind moved fast, not just in mathematics, but this surprised me. So did her calmness, if she'd been thinking along the same lines as I had.

'What exactly?'

'We were all surprised when he went off without saying a word to anybody. I admit it hurt me but he really had no choice. It meant if the police or somebody from the coroner came back to ask more questions, we could honestly say we didn't know where he'd gone.'

She sounded remarkably cheerful about it. Maybe we weren't thinking along the same lines.

'Why wouldn't he want to answer questions?'

'Surely you've worked it out, Nell. He was terribly nervous when the two policemen were here even though they didn't ask him anything. You must have noticed.'

'Yes.'

'And Nathan's no good at lying, is he? Can't act at all. So if they'd started asking him questions he'd have let out everything he knew and he simply couldn't let that happen.'

'Why not?' I stood, sponge in hand, terrified of what she was going to say.

'Please Nell, don't start another ethical discussion.'

'I wasn't...'

'That's the whole point, you see. Nathan's not a philosopher like the others. You said yourself, he's practical. He looks at some situation, works out what the results will be in real life and if he doesn't like the answer he does something about it. In this case, he doesn't want to see somebody he knows hanged for murder.'

She said it as calmly as if she'd worked out a mathematical equation. Suddenly, I dreaded what she was going to say because up to that point there had been something that I hadn't even let myself think about. In my mind I heard Meredith's voice saying 'Either don't start or go as far as it takes you.' I turned away, not letting her see my face and tried to keep my voice calm.

'You think the Old Man was murdered?'

'I'm as sure of it as you are, and the fact Nathan's gone off like that means he's sure of it too. He must have seen or heard something that night that he doesn't want the police to know about. So he'll probably stay out on the fells until the inquest is safely over and there's a verdict of suicide.'

'So you think he's shielding a murderer and you don't mind?'

'Oh, I'm sure we're all in favour of justice in the abstract. But it's a different matter, isn't it, when you think of a living, breathing human being you actually know being taken out one morning and ... oh, just think about it.'

'I am. But the Old Man was a living, breathing human being too.'

She touched my arm as if I needed consoling. 'Yes, I know. And somehow it makes it worse thinking of anybody doing it just for money. But I've been thinking about that. Perhaps when you've got somebody besides your self to worry about, you care about having enough money more than when it's just you.'

'You think that's how Nathan sees it?'

'I'm not sure he'll have thought about it even that much. But he's so loyal, you see. If he likes somebody, he has to protect them and that's all there is to it.'

I felt sick, my mind racing back over all the

things I should have noticed.

'So it's all right then,' I said. 'He stays out on the hills and next week I tell my story to the inquest about how the Old Man tried to kill himself, then we all go on as if nothing had happened.'

'Nell, please don't get angry with me. I hate the thought of that as much as you do. But think about what the Old Man would have wanted. He thought it was his baby, after all. Would he want her to give birth to it in a prison cell, then have it taken away from her so that they could hang her? How could that do him or anybody any good?'

I breathed, 'Dulcie Berryman.'

'Yes of course Dulcie Berryman. Isn't that what we're talking about? You must have suspected that before any of us.'

I said nothing, weak with relief, and let her go on talking.

'Only I don't think we should say anything to Imogen about this. She doesn't like Dulcie, does she?'

'No.'

She said she'd leave me to change and went clattering happily down the stairs, pausing only to ask if we shouldn't leave some food out where Nathan might find it. Better not, I said. Then I undressed completely, lay down on the hay pallet under a sheet and slept dreamlessly for the rest of the morning and most of the afternoon.

I woke around four o'clock feeling better. The panic that had come over me in the talk with Midge was because of reaction to all that had happened the day before. Her logical mind was on the right track and she'd got there even without knowing about the fish scales or the dropped note. But there was a thought I didn't want to come into my head again and the only way to keep it out was to find some certainties in this maze. One certainty at least was that Dulcie Berryman knew more than she was saying.

As I rummaged for clean clothes and got dressed I wondered whether to discuss what I was going to do with Meredith and decided against it. I was my own woman still and nothing that had happened the night before changed that. It was a relief to have got it over, after all the talking and reading and thinking, and to wake up in the same world as the same person. A little bit of my mind was appalled at what I'd done and expected retribution but that was primitive and superstitious and could be disregarded. On reflection I was still pleased with myself and perhaps that was why I now felt capable of tackling Dulcie. Brushing tangles out of my hair, I thought I should have done it before. There were excuses, of course – her own habit of silence for one thing, her age for another. From early twenties to mid or late thirties is a big gap and politeness to one's elders was something taken for granted, even in my unconventional up-bringing. But there'd been something else about Dulcie from the start that silenced us and I recognised at last what it was. As I pinned up my hair I said to myself, 'The sex question' and laughed to the empty loft. Dulcie had done it quite a lot and didn't regret it. Even before we knew about the baby it was there in the way she stood and looked, in the pad of her bare feet and the smell of her bed. It had disturbed all of us in our different ways, women and men. Well, since yesterday, I'd paid my entrance fee and joined that sisterhood. Somehow that made it easier to talk to Dulcie, even though it had nothing to do with what I needed to talk about.

I took the note out of yesterday's skirt and went downstairs, through the arch and across the yard to the kitchen, meeting nobody on the way. Even the hens were dozing in the heat. The porch was full of the usual clutter of tack, with the carriage whip where I'd left it and a pair of the Old Man's riding boots still there, as if he'd walk out any moment and put them on. The door to the kitchen was half open. Inside a few slow-moving flies circled in a shaft of sunlight and under them Dulcie sat at the kitchen table scraping carrots. That should have been somebody else's job under our new arrangements but she didn't seem to mind. She had an enamel bowl of earthy water in front of her, a pile of carrots and a tin colander beside her.

'Dulcie, may I talk to you?'

She nodded and went on scraping. The blade of her knife was worn to a crescent with years of use and re-sharpening. I drew out a chair and sat facing her.

'There's something I want to know. I'm not going to the police with it and it's done now in any case, but if we don't know what really happened we're going to go on wondering for the rest of our lives.'

The knife made a little rasping sound, whittling the dirty brown of the wet carrot into glowing orange. Her big amber-brown eyes were fixed on me, her hands so well accustomed to what they were doing that she didn't need to look at them.

'I wish now that I'd never known about it,' I said, 'but you can't unthink things, you have to go on.'

She dropped the scraped carrot into the colander and dunked another one in the bowl. I took the note out of my pocket and smoothed it out on the table.

'This was meant for you, wasn't it?'

She read without touching it, head tilted sideways, muddy water drops from the carrot falling on the table, spreading into wood made soft-grained by scrubbing. After a long time she looked up at me, raised and lowered her head.

'Where d'you find it?'

'He dropped it climbing in. He wasn't a burglar, was he?'

Another nod. It was all so much easier than I'd expected that I felt off balance, like pushing on a door that opens too easily.

'Arthur Mawbray?'

'Did he tell you?'

'I've never met him, apart from seeing him in the stable yard. It was Arthur Mawbray?'

Another nod. She started rasping the carrot, but slowly now, looking down at her hands.

'And he's the baby's father, isn't he?'

Her head came up, frowning now. 'Who says that?'

'Somebody was writing anonymous notes to the Old Man about it.'

'You allus get blatherskites. He didn't believe them.'

'He wasn't sure. I think the Old Man tried hard to believe it was his because he wanted it to be, but he knew in his heart it wasn't.'

'It made him happy. Is there awt wrong in that? Anyway, nobody can prove or disprove who the father of a baby is. Not all the slape and slippery lawyers in the world can prove that.' She was beginning to get angry.

'No, and the Old Man acknowledged the

child in his will. Did he tell you he was going to do that?'

Another nod.

'And Arthur Mawbray knew that too?'

'I told him.'

'And now he's asking for money from you. Why?'

'Because he needs it, I suppose.'

'Did he suggest killing the Old Man before he could change his will?'

'What?' The carrot thumped on to the table and her mouth fell open. 'What are you talking about?'

'There's a lot of money involved, thousands of pounds. Perhaps Arthur Mawbray decided that since the Old Man had tried to kill him it was fair enough to return the compliment.'

'Compliment? I don't understand a word you're saying. He never killed anybody. Nobody killed anybody.'

'The Old Man didn't do that to himself. He couldn't have.'

'He could do anything once he'd set his mind to it. Nearly anything.'

She stared down at the carrot then up at me, as if she couldn't make sense of either of us any more.

'You going to talk to the lawyers about this?'

'No, but on one condition.'

I was surprised at my own brutality. I'd no

intention of saying anything to any lawyer but was ready to use the threat of it, desperate that my idea of Arthur Mawbray should become reality.

'What's that?'

'I want to talk to Arthur Mawbray.'

'I don't know where he is.'

'No, but you know where he'll be on Saturday, that's tomorrow. The usual place, he says in his note. He was here last Saturday too, wasn't he, when the dogs were barking?'

'Yes.'

'Take me with you when you go to meet him. I promise not to say anything to anybody else until I've talked to him.'

She sat with her hands on the table. They were neat pink hands with shiny little fingernails like sea shells, amazingly unroughened by her hard work. I felt touched by them, almost ashamed of myself.

'All right. Tomorrow night, when it's getting dark. But he never killed anybody. He'll tell you himself.'

It was rabbit stew again for dinner, with plenty of carrots. Dulcie behaved just as she always did, apart from not looking at me.

Not much happened on the Saturday. It was thundery, headachy weather and Imogen, Midge and I spent some of it attending to our clothes, washing blouses and underthings in buckets in the yard with cold water and hard soap, then rigging up our own washing line to dry them. Usually this would have been a splashy, girlish time with gigglings and harmless banter. Now Imogen and I were treating each other with careful politeness and Midge hardly said a word. I noticed her glancing up to the fells now and again and guessed she was thinking about Nathan. When we needed to borrow soap or clothes pegs from the kitchen I let Midge do it. I was in no hurry to face Dulcie again before the rendezvous in the evening. I'd told nobody about that, not even Meredith. I'd been tempted, but I'd made a promise to Dulcie. Besides, he might have turned anxious and protective and that was the last thing I wanted from him. When we met going about the yard or at mealtimes we behaved normally to each other I think. Or perhaps we didn't. It was like one of those terrible opening scenes in an amateur drama when the producer appeals to the bit-part players, 'Just behave normally', so of course they do anything but.

It was a relief when the evening meal was over – cold ham, hot potatoes and cabbage – and everybody went their various ways, Alan and Robin to see to the horses, Imogen and Midge to the loft with armfuls of dried clothes, Meredith and Kit strolling up the drive in the last of the sun. I offered to help

Dulcie with the clearing up as an excuse to stay with her in the kitchen when everybody else left. We worked in silence, she swirling plates and cups in a bowl of greyish water, I stacking them on a rickety wooden rack to dry. The light went from the kitchen early because of the walls round the yard so it was dusk by the time we'd finished but we didn't bother to light the lamps. She dunked the last cup, emptied out the water and dried her hands on the whitish apron she was wearing.

'Are we ready then?'

I nodded. She took off the apron and arranged it over the back of a chair to dry.

'Have a look and see if anybody's around.'

I looked out into the yard and up the drive and came back to report that nobody was about. Dulcie licked her lips and smoothed a hand over her hair. She was nervous, Dulcie of the creamy calm.

'Better be going, then.'

Outside it was still more light than dark, with some clouds in the west. We went quickly through the arch into the stable yard, across it to the gateway on the far side. It creaked when we opened it and Dulcie caught her breath, but nobody came.

She said, 'He won't like me bringing you.'

'Tell him you had no choice.'

We went side by side down a little track to the paddock at the back of the house where the two cows grazed. They raised their heads and ambled up to Dulcie. She pushed them gently away. We walked on across the paddock, Dulcie looking over her shoulder sometimes. As we got near an unkempt hedge on the far side a dark figure came out from under the trees.

'I'll tell him first,' Dulcie said and broke into a run, stumbling on the cow-trampled earth. I kept striding close behind her, not wanting to give them time to work out a plan of action. I heard her say. 'There's somebody with me. She's one of the people staying. She made me bring her.'

'Hello Mr Mawbray,' I said. 'My name's Nell Bray. I picked up the note you dropped the other night.'

My voice sounded a lot more confident than I felt. He made a sound something between a snort and a nervous giggle and took a step towards me. Even in the half-light his hair was as yellow as straw. It wasn't a bad-looking face, a little weak about the chin and the eyes narrow, though that might have been with the effort of getting a good look at the stranger in the dusk. The broad forehead was very like his father's.

'Moy name ain't Mawbray. Oi'm Diggory, Dick Diggory. What be you wanting with me?' The rustic accent wouldn't have fooled a baby.

'If you go on trying to talk like that, you'll

get very tired of it. I know you're Arthur Mawbray because Dulcie told me. I'd guessed in any case.'

'Oh.'

The look he gave Dulcie was bewildered rather than reproachful. He was off balance and I had to keep it that way.

'I told Dulcie I had to speak to you because you're both in very serious trouble. It's up to you what you do about it, but people have guessed and you haven't got much time.'

I said 'people' because I wasn't fool enough to let him know that I was the only one. My idea was that they'd probably run away together and I shouldn't try to stop them. It wasn't a carefully worked out ethical position, just revulsion at the idea of Dulcie's pink hands with their sea-shell nails being strapped behind her one morning in a cold shed after a walk across a prison yard.

'It was a joke. We didn't mean any harm.' He looked about my own age but he sounded like a schoolboy.

'Joke!'

'Well, he had tried to kill us, after all. He deserved worrying a bit. Anyway, we wouldn't have let them hang him or anything. If the police had arrested him Dulcie would have got word to me and I'd have popped up right as ninepence, wouldn't I, Dulcie?'

'So all the time he thought he'd killed you, you were hiding?'

'Yes. When he started letting off that bloody ... excuse me, that shotgun in the dark, me and my mates naturally hit the deck. We crawled away and somebody said it would have served the old b... the Old Man right if he really had killed somebody. Well, I knew I'd be in a bit of trouble with my father anyway if it all got out so I thought I'd make myself scarce and my mates put the word round that he'd shot me. We didn't mean any harm by it.'

'And you didn't mean any harm deceiving him about Dulcie and the baby?'

A long silence. He'd been standing his ground up to then and sounding confident. Now he took a step back into the shadows and his voice went hurt and gruff.

'Why did you want to tell her about that, Dulcie?'

'She didn't need to,' I said. 'The gossip's all round the town. I suppose the idea was once the Old Man was dead and the baby born, you'd share the money.'

'It'd be the baby's money, wouldn't it?'

'So you knew about it, then?'

'He told Dulcie what he'd put in his will, and she told me.'

'Because it was your baby?'

Another silence then, 'Yes.'

'But you were quite prepared to let him

351

think it was his?'

Dulcie said, 'He was that pleased about it. His merry-begot, he called it.'

'Merry-begot?'

'That's what we say round here for the wrong side of the sheets. He was as happy as when one of his mares falls pregnant. And we'd been sleeping in the big bed together and ... and cuddling up and he was a lish enough man considering his age so...'

The picture came into my mind of Dulcie and the Old Man in the big four-poster.

'Then he started getting anonymous letters saying the baby was somebody else's. Did he discuss them with you?'

'No, he didn't.'

'But you could tell he was having doubts. Even I could tell that.'

'The day with the mare?'

'Yes. So you and Mr Mawbray decided you had to do something about it before he found out the truth?'

'It wouldn't have mattered once he'd acknowledged it,' Arthur Mawbray said. 'Once he'd held it in his arms and acknowledged it, it would have been his. That's the law.'

And he a magistrate's son. Yet he'd brought out this piece of rural primitivism with what sounded like total conviction.

Dulcie backed him up. 'Arthur was away anyway. It was just a case of him staying away a few months more until the child was born and the Old Man had got him in his arms and everything would have been all right.'

'You weren't far away, were you Mr Mawbray? You were seeing Dulcie regularly.'

'Not regularly, just sometimes.'

'Often enough to come up with a plan at any rate. Once he started thinking the child might not be his you had to do something quickly before he changed his will. Dulcie knew the Old Man was walking round outside most nights, guarding his horses...'

'We never meant any harm to the horses!'

'...so while she was keeping an eye on him it would be an easy enough matter for you to catch the horse and get his tack. It must have been you I heard down in the tack room. I think you waited with the horse just on the far side of the gate to your father's land. He'd see the horse, come through to take it back, then you hit him on the head and tied him into the saddle. Whether he was already dead by then...'

While I'd been talking, he was trying to stop me, inarticulate sounds at first then 'no' repeated louder and louder. Now his hand closed round my arm in a crushing grip and started pumping it up and down.

'No, no, no. What are you talking about? You're mad.'

Dulcie called to him to stop, but he got his

other hand on my shoulder and twisted me round so that he was shouting into my face.

'You're calling me a murderer? You're saying I did that to him?'

'Yes, and the police know it too.'

Not true, but all I could think of to protect myself. As the shock of it hit him his grip went slack and I managed to pull away from him. I took a few steps back, expecting him to come at me again, but he suddenly sank down into a sitting position on the ground, head on his knees and arms clasped round them, rocking backwards and forwards, keening 'no, no, no'. His collapse horrified me more than the attack. Surely this wasn't the way murderers were supposed to behave.

Dulcie moved first. She came forward and put both hands on his shoulders, staring at me over his bent head.

'If the police think they know it, they're wrong. He couldn't have done it. He wasn't here.'

If she'd sounded angry it would have been less convincing. She just stated it as a fact, her fingers kneading the sides of his neck like a mother with a fretful child. Arthur stopped keening but his head stayed bent.

'He'll tell you himself in a while. You can't expect him to be thinking straight after what you said to him.'

After a few minutes he got himself

clumsily upright but stayed in contact with her, arm against arm.

'I didn't even know it had happened until two days afterwards.' He sounded sulky now rather than fearful. 'I got back here and met Dulcie by the gate as usual and she told me.'

'Where had you been?'

'Out in the boat.'

'What boat?'

'The *Eastern Light*, fishing boat out of Maryport.'

'What were you doing there?'

He stared. 'Fishing.'

Dulcie explained, 'It's what he likes doing, only his father won't let him.'

'He wanted me to go into the army like he did. I wouldn't have minded the fighting but then there was all the rest of it, shouting orders and standing in line and so on. I ran away once, only he brought me back. He said he'd disinherit me. Never mind the inheritance, I told him, just set me up with a nice little fishing boat and I won't bother you again. That was fair enough, wasn't it?'

He looked at me as if the answer to that was as important as whether he'd killed a man or not. Now I'd got him, I felt a deep disappointment in him. The belief that young Mawbray was still alive had created a picture of him in my mind: ruthless, intelligent and sinister. One thing I could certainly rule out now was intelligence.

Stupidity is one of the most difficult things for a clever person to act convincingly and every tone of his voice and movement of his body told me I was face to face with the real thing. But stupidity can be dangerous too.

'So you needed money?'

'Doesn't everybody?'

'Enough to kill for it?'

'I expect a lot of people would if they thought they could get away with it. Only I didn't. I've told you, I wasn't here.'

'Maryport isn't far away.'

He stared, 'Do you know anything about tides?'

'Only that they go in and out.'

'You ever tried to row a boat in from a long way out at sea against the tide?'

'No.'

'Well, take it from me it's true what Dulcie told you. What day of the week did the Old Man die?'

I told him it was the night of Thursday the twelfth. He wrinkled his broad forehead, working it out.

'All right, that was the night before that we took the *Eastern Light* out on the night tide. We stayed out all night and came in with nets pretty full when the tide turned in the morning. Even if I'd taken the tender, I couldn't have gone out in the boat and rowed myself back and got here before daylight, could I?'

When he talked about boats there was a confidence and maturity in his voice that wasn't there otherwise. Dulcie gave me one of her sweet smiles as if that cleared up everything.

'If you really went out that night,' I said.

'I've told you.'

'You're sure it was that night? It took you a while to remember.'

'You don't go by clocks and calendars if you work at sea. It's tides and winds and when it gets light or dark, the things that matter.'

'So you can't be sure what night it was you went out?'

He ran a hand through his hair and looked appealingly towards Dulcie, waiting for her to rescue him.

'Mr Morrisey would know what night you were out,' she said.

He picked up the cue. 'Mr Morrisey, of course he would. You ask Mr Morrisey. He'll tell you.'

'Who's Mr Morrisey?'

'My skipper. He owns the *Eastern Light.*'

'Where can I find him?'

'You go down to Maryport and ask the first person you meet. Everybody knows Mr Morrisey.'

A local character, I supposed, or as otherwise expressed, local rogue. Either Arthur had come equipped with an alibi or Dulcie

357

was in the process of making one for him, as calmly and efficiently as she jointed rabbits for stewing.

'I'll speak to him, then.'

'You do that, and when you have you go and tell the police what he told you.'

He sounded confident now, almost happy. I wasn't, because I had a problem. If they hadn't already stewed up his alibi – and it was possible that they hadn't – I needed to get to the obliging Mr Morrisey before they did. But Maryport was about fifteen miles away and it was already nearly dark. Even if I ran all the way down to the town and managed to catch a late train to the coast, assuming there was one, I wouldn't get there before most people had gone to bed.

'So that's all right then,' he said. The tone was dismissive, almost cocky.

Short of making a citizen's arrest on suspicion of murder, which wasn't worth even considering, there was nothing I could do.

'Goodnight,' I said. And had to bite my tongue to stop myself adding something bitter and useless. The fact was that they'd won and though I'd never wanted to hang them I was furious for being so much at a loss. As I went back up the field I thought I heard Dulcie's soft laugh from the darkness behind me, but it might have been one of the cows snuffling. I sat on a bench outside the house and about half an hour later she came back, walking heavily as if tired, and let herself in at the kitchen door. If she saw me there she gave no sign of it.

Chapter Nineteen

I heard Imogen and Midge talking softly to each other as I went up the stairs to our loft but they said nothing when I came in. I expect they thought I'd been with Meredith. When I got up and dressed before it was light they probably thought that I was going to him again and in this case they'd have been right, only it wasn't intentional. I'd planned to leave him a note. I'd scribbled it by the light of a candle stub downstairs in the tack room: *Gone to Maryport. Back this evening. Will explain then.* I folded it and wrote his name on the outside and thought I'd fix it on a nail on the back of the porch door. I walked as softly as I could through the arch and into the yard, not wanting to wake anybody, but when I came to the porch there was somebody standing outside. Although he was no more than a shape in the half-light I knew instantly that it was Meredith. He was facing the east, where the curve of the hill was just becoming visible against a sky of the taut blue-black that comes just before dawn in summer. He heard my step and turned, cigarette butt glowing.

'Nell.' A statement not a question.

'I was coming to leave a note for you.'

'Are you going away?'

'Only for the day. I've got to go to Mary-port.'

We were talking in whispers. He touched my hand and indicated that we should walk up the track. There was such pleasure in walking beside him before the rest of the world was awake that I wished I didn't have urgent things to tell him.

'Young Mawbray's alive. I've talked to him.'

I told him everything that had happened the night before, including my strong suspicion that Dulcie had suggested an alibi to him while we were talking.

'I don't think he's very clever but he can't have missed what she meant. I'm sure he went straight down to Maryport last night and agreed the story with some crony of his. I was tempted to try to get there first, but he knows the country better so I'd have had no chance.'

'I'm glad you had that amount of sense. If you think he's a murderer, didn't it occur to you that you were taking an unjustifiable risk seeing him at all?'

'Not until he caught hold of me. Until then I'd just been excited about being able to prove I was right.'

I'd been angry when Imogen accused me of playing detective to impress Meredith, but had to admit to myself that I enjoyed having him listen to me so intently.

'Pointless if you'd managed to prove it by being murdered as well.'

'Dulcie stopped him. It's funny, I think I was relying on her to protect me.'

'In spite of being a conspirator with him in killing the Old Man?'

'More than a conspirator, I think she planned it. She's a lot cleverer than he is. We've all been underrating her because she keeps quiet and does the cooking.'

'So what's your next step? That is if you intend to take me into your confidence this time.'

'I'm going to walk to the station and take the first train down to Maryport. He said anybody there would know Mr Morrisey. I'd guess the man's a notorious local smuggler or some such.'

'If young Mawbray's been down ahead of you and fixed up his alibi, what's the point of talking to him?'

'To get some impression of what the man's like. Liars usually give something away, or embroider too much, don't you think?'

'Bad liars do. Though logically, I suppose, you could argue that there is no such thing as a bad liar because against his will a bad liar reveals the truth therefore is not lying at all. On the other hand, a good liar–'

'Are you trying to distract me by any chance?'

'A good liar makes us believe he is telling the truth. Therefore the only good liar is a man to whom we can never logically give the name of liar because once we arrive at the conclusion he is not telling the truth he becomes a bad liar...'

'Goodbye. I'll see you this evening probably.'

'...and as we have agreed, a man who could be described as a bad liar is not, properly speaking, a liar at all. So... Where do you think you're going?'

I was walking away fast up the track. I called over my shoulder, 'I told you, Maryport.'

'Wait for me. I'll come with you.'

'But you think there's no point in going.'

'Just wait while I go back for my wallet. I'm not making that mistake again.'

So I waited while he went back, impatient to be going but with a warm laughing feeling inside at having won. He came running up the track to join me and we walked fast down the lanes and roads to the town with the colour coming back into the sky and fields as we went, not talking much except for something he said that sounded like an apology.

'I'm sorry, perhaps I was trying to stop you. I've been worrying more than you know, hoping that we could leave things as they were, I suppose.'

'Only they weren't, were they?'

Which was hardly a logical contribution from me, but he didn't pick me up on it. We arrived at the station with half an hour to wait for the first train. This early on a Sunday morning it was practically empty when it came. He asked if I minded being in the same compartment and volunteered not to smoke if it bothered me. Not at all, I said, amused at his formality. It was almost as if our time by the waterfall hadn't existed, but the consciousness of it was there under everything we said or did. We had the compartment to ourselves and as we passed the coalmines at Aspatria, with the coast and Maryport not far away, we started talking about Mawbray again.

'You were determined he should exist, weren't you?'

'Because he was the only possible explanation.'

'Logically there are limitless explanations.'

'I'm not talking logic, I'm talking facts. Once you accept that the Old Man was deliberately killed, and I've been sure of that almost from the start, there has to be a reason. Dulcie and Arthur Mawbray had a very good one.'

'So how do you propose to set about breaking this alibi if we find the obliging Mr Morrisey?'

'I'm not sure that we can – not to the

satisfaction of the police or a lawyer at any rate. I just want to see and hear him and be quite certain in my own mind that he's lying.'

'But if your certainty isn't the police or lawyers' certainty, what's the point?'

'They don't come into it at all. Once I know for certain, we can put the whole thing to rest.'

He frowned. I'd surprised him, perhaps even shocked him.

'By not telling anybody?'

'Probably not. What do you think?'

But he just went on looking at me in that disconcerting way. I found myself tripping over my words, trying to convince him.

'There's the inquest next week. I'll probably be lying to it – not in words but by implication – nudging it towards a suicide verdict. That's the case, isn't it?'

'It's your decision.'

'But I know it's the decision everybody else wants me to make. It might even be the right one. Please don't ask me what I mean by right in this context, because I don't know myself. But I can't imagine giving evidence that would help them hang Dulcie.'

'Even though you think she planned it?'

'She must have known his heart was weak, living so close to him. Perhaps she guessed he wanted to die. And she had the baby to think of.'

'So that makes it all right?'

'No, of course it doesn't. But she's not ... well, not somebody with a strong moral sense. It would be like ... like a fox say, not so much wanting to kill the goose as having to eat.'

'In that case, you'd pardon most of the murderers who ever existed or will exist.'

'No. Anyway, it's not all murderers I'm talking about. It's Dulcie.'

'And young Mawbray?'

'He's like a spoilt child. I don't think he understands even now what he's done.'

'Not responsible for his actions?'

'Not quite. But not ... not living up to them, or perhaps I mean down to them. The dreadful thing about murder is it's an extraordinary crime done by ordinary people. The world's made all wrong. It shouldn't be so easy to take somebody's life.'

He took his cigarette case out of his pocket and a cigarette out of the case, still keeping his eyes on me.

'So you're saying you want to find out for certain then forgive them?'

'Not forgive, no. Just find out and decide to leave it there.'

He lit his cigarette, drew on it and blew out a cloud of smoke, wafting it away from me.

'And you'll find out from Mr Morrisey?'

'Yes. I'm expecting him to be a bad liar

366

who, by your definition, isn't a liar at all.'

'So in spite of himself, your slippery Mr Morrisey tells us the truth – that young Mawbray cobbled together his alibi last night?'

'I think so. If he does, I'll let it drop. I'll say as little as I can at the inquest and get away from here as soon as it's over.'

'Where?'

'Greece perhaps.'

He raised his eyebrows and wafted another smoke cloud. The train started slowing down for Maryport.

Still early on a Sunday morning, the town was more than half asleep as we crossed the bridge over the River Allen on our way from the station. It was a bigger town than I'd expected, with warehouses and factories off to the left, but the narrow streets of terraced houses were quiet. Only an occasional cat loped across the pavement and an old man shuffled bent-backed down a side street with a newspaper-wrapped parcel under his arm. We followed the smell of fish up Senhouse Street and found ourselves looking down on the harbour. It looked as sleepy as the rest of the town with fishing boats tied up and nets piled on the decks, no putting to sea on a Sunday. We went on down to the quay, passing at least four public houses on the way. Their doors were closed and barred but the smell of stale beer crept out, mingling with the fishy odour.

'We might as well have a look at the *Eastern Light*,' I said.

I expected it to be some rickety old tub, on the grounds that anything connected with Arthur Mawbray's alibi wasn't likely to be watertight, and was surprised when Meredith called, 'Here it is.' He was standing by a boat that stood out from the rest because it was so trim and bright, newly painted in dark blue and white, deck scrubbed and ropes coiled with naval exactness. No sign of life apart from a herring gull screaming at us from the bows. There was a line of fishermen's huts at the seaward end of the harbour wall. We walked along them hoping to find somebody to ask where to find the *Eastern Light*'s skipper, but the doors were shut and padlocked. I suggested we should go back towards the town but Meredith stopped and sniffed the air.

'Fire somewhere.'

We rounded the corner to another smaller harbour and there was a cluster of more dilapidated huts at the top of a slipway. Outside one of them a white-haired man in seaman's boots and canvas tunic was bending over a bucket on an open fire. The fire was crackling with the blue salty flames of driftwood, the bucket propped on a tripod of rocks. When he straightened up we saw he had a pointed stick in one hand and a mug in the other. Without meaning to I sighed, 'Tea.' We'd had nothing to eat or drink and I felt as if my throat were covered in fish scales.

'Want some?' said Meredith, starting to walk towards him.

'We can't just go up and ask.'

'Why not?'

I hung back and let him do the talking. I didn't hear what he said but the man laughed and Meredith laughed too and beckoned to me. By the time I got there the man had disappeared inside his hut.

'He says we're welcome but he's got no cups and saucers for a lady.'

'I'd drink it out of a bucket if necessary. What were you laughing at?'

'He asked if we were waiting to be ferried over the Solway. He thought we might be eloping to Gretna Green.'

For a mad moment I looked out to sea and wished we were.

'Like the ballad,' I said. *'A chieftain to the Highlands bound cries "Boatman, do not tarry!"'*

'Don't know that one.'

'It doesn't end happily. *"The waters wild went o'er his child and he was left lamenting."'*

The man came out of the hut grinning, a steaming mug in each hand. The tea was as dark as teak and tasted of tar and fish but I drank half the mugful in a few unladylike gulps. Meredith had moved over to the bucket.

'Good catch?'

'Good enough, sir.'

I looked and saw a forest of open claws sticking out of the bubbling water. The man was boiling crabs.

'About done they are, sir. Would you and the lady like one?'

Meredith said yes please, so the man speared a specimen the size of a dinner plate out of the bucket and cracked open body and claws with a few deft hammer blows. Meredith and I sat on the slipway outside the hut and shared the sweet warm meat with the man's black and white cat winding itself in and out between us, cadging scraps. By the time we'd finished there were a few more people walking by the harbour, a church bell was ringing a monotonous summoning note and there was a feeling of the town waking up. Meredith felt in his pocket and passed the man some coins while I fed the last of the crab to the cat.

'Do you happen to know where Mr Morrisey lives?'

'Joshua Morrisey? Along there in King Street, sir. But you wouldn't want to call on him this time of a Sunday morning.'

'Wouldn't we?'

Flat out drunk, I wondered. It was clear

from the way the man was looking at us that Joshua Morrisey had a local reputation.

'No sir. He'll be getting ready for chapel.'

Meredith raised his eyebrows and I tried not to laugh. So he was probably a hypocrite too, our Mr Morrisey.

'The methodist chapel, that is. Service starts ten o'clock. If you go there, you can't miss Joshua Morrisey.'

So we walked around the harbour and along the seafront and just before ten o'clock found our way to the methodist chapel. The entrance to it was crowded with men, women and children in their Sunday best. I went up to a friendly looking woman and asked if she could kindly point out Mr Morrisey. She gave me an odd look. 'He'll be inside already.' So there was nothing for it but to go in and find a space at the end of a pew near the back. I was conscious that we were getting some stares from the congregation, probably because our dress wasn't up to standard. At least I was wearing a hat but we were both gloveless and our boots and hiking tweeds made us look like country bumpkins.

It was some time since I'd been inside a church and I resigned myself to a long dull service but was pleasantly surprised. The congregation sang the hymns tunefully and with an enthusiasm that seemed fit to blast them through the chapel walls and out to sea. The sermon – on the parable of the workers in the vineyard – was given by a lay preacher with a round suntanned face. He spoke with a Cumberland accent and with unusual sense and practicality about men's and women's work in the world. Still, I have to admit my attention wandered because I was looking round the congregation, as unobtrusively as I could, trying to spot a likely candidate for Mr Morrisey. The favourite was a wizened-looking man in his forties or fifties with sparse grey hair sitting at the end of a pew two rows in front of us. He was on his own, fidgeted a lot and had a shifty air. A plump man sitting near the door with a boil on the back of his neck and his collar coming loose from its stud was another possibility.

The sermon ended, we knelt for prayers, stood for a final rousing hymn, and then everybody started filing slowly out into the sunlight. I worried that Mr Morrisey might have escaped by the time we got out and tried to keep the wizened man in sight. On the street outside the preacher was surrounded by people who wanted to talk to him. There was a plump smiling woman with three children standing beside him. I touched the arm of a woman at the back of the group.

'Excuse me, I wonder if you could point out Mr Joshua Morrisey.'

She stared at me as if I were crazy. 'That's Mr Morrisey.'

She was indicating with her head not the wizened man or the man with the boil but the lay preacher.

'Mr Morrisey, skipper of the *Eastern Light?*'

'That's his boat, yes.'

Most of the hope went out of me then. Still, we pressed on. Meredith and I waited until most of the group round the preacher had melted away, then went up and introduced ourselves to him.

'I think you know an acquaintance of mine,' I said. 'Arthur Mawbray.'

A look of concern came over his face. 'Young Arthur, yes. I hope there's nothing wrong with him.'

'No. But did he happen to come and see you last night?'

He was honestly puzzled. Much though I'd have liked to interpret his expression in any other way, there was no getting away from it.

'No, but I wasn't expecting him. He knows we never take the boat out on a Saturday night.'

'Do you happen to remember if he was out with you on Thursday the week before last?'

He pushed his glasses up on his forehead. 'I'm nearly sure he was, but may I ask why you want to know?'

'Something happened that night, near where his father lives. Arthur Mawbray says it was nothing to do with him because he was out fishing with you.'

'I don't want to seem at all rude, but may I ask why you're concerned with it?'

'The thing that happened involved a friend of mine.'

'And it's a case of give a dog a bad name, I suppose. I'm not blaming you and I know there's a wild side to young Mawbray, but I can only speak as I find. He works hard on the boat, he's never been anything other than polite and honest with me and the other fishermen like him.'

I thought it was just as well that gossip about young Mawbray and Dulcie hadn't travelled as far as the coast.

'And you're almost sure he was out with you that night?'

'If you'd care to walk home with us, we can make quite sure. We live just along the street here.'

We fell into a procession, Joshua Morrisey and his wife first, then Meredith and me, then the children. Our progress was slow because we kept meeting people who wanted to talk to the preacher but at last we got as far as the front parlour of his little house. It was a neat and comfortable room, with a potted fern on a bamboo table, shelves of books with the emphasis on travel and missionaries, two chintz armchairs facing an empty fireplace with a pink paper fan in it. There were framed religious texts on the walls but at least they were of the more cheerful kind. He invited us to sit down and his wife brought in tea and home-made biscuits.

'Now, if you'll excuse me for a moment, I'll fetch something that will answer your question.'

When we were left alone Meredith grinned at me and said, 'Not what we expected.'

At least he said 'we', not triumphing that I was wrong. I was grateful to him as well for leaving the questioning to me. Joshua Morrisey came back into the room with a long black-covered book under his arm.

'The *Eastern Light*'s log and account book. I write it up every time we're out.'

He moved the fern aside and opened it on the bamboo table. We stood, looking over his shoulder. 'That's the night you're interested in, isn't it? You can see Arthur Mawbray was there. We went out on the night tide and came back in the next morning. There's the weight of fish we caught in that column, total value of the catch and Arthur's share of it. Does that answer your question?'

I said it did and thanked him. We finished our tea, thanked him again and he shook hands with us on the front step.

'Please give my regards to Arthur if you see him. There's a lot of good in that young man.'

Meredith and I walked slowly down the street to the station.

'Do we ask ourselves if he's a good or bad liar, Nell?'

'He's not a liar at all. You're as sure of that as I am. Would a man with family, prosperity and public respect risk it all through telling lies for a young man like Mawbray?'

'Some people might, but Mr Morrisey didn't strike me as one of them.'

The heavy feeling that had come over me when I realised who Mr Morrisey was had spread to everything, draining the colour out of the sky. He sensed it.

'I'm sorry you were wrong, Nell. It seemed a reasonable theory.'

I felt sorry too, but it was something worse than hurt pride.

There were other people in our train compartment going back so we didn't have a chance to talk until we were walking uphill from our local station to Studholme Hall. There was a smell of grass baking in the heat and a thundery feel to the air. By then I'd done a lot of thinking.

'Dulcie could still have done it, even if

young Mawbray wasn't there to help her.'

From the look on his face, he felt as weary of it all as I did. His voice was tired too.

'On her own?'

'No, she'd have needed help. She might have persuaded Robin, especially if she knew about his hundred pounds in the will and had told him.'

'You really believe that?'

'No, I don't. I think he respected the Old Man too much, loved him even. I could imagine Robin helping him commit suicide if that was what he wanted, but not help kill him.'

'Imagining is not proof. Still, I agree with you for what that's worth.'

'When I guessed about her and Mawbray, it seemed such a neat motive – killing the Old Man before he found out the child wasn't his. But it's quite the reverse. They needed him to be alive when it was born.'

'This business of acknowledging it?'

'Yes. They'd managed to convince themselves that once he'd taken it in his arms, he'd accepted it as his. The odd thing is, I don't think they were far wrong. When the child was born I think he would have acknowledged it – if only to annoy the gossips in town. After all, he had a great admiration for ... for fertility.' (I felt myself blushing but pressed on.) 'And he'd like to think of himself as a father, at his age.'

I had a mental picture of them going in procession through the town, Dulcie pushing a perambulator, the Old Man riding in front of her on Sid, then Robin with all the mares in tow. I laughed and so did he, though neither of us very heartily.

'You're right about the admiration for fertility. It was the core of him.' It occurred to me then that practically all Meredith had been doing on our walk so far was to echo what I was saying and agree. This was so uncharacteristic that it scared me.

'You haven't told me yet how stupid I've been.'

'That's the last thing I'm thinking.'

'I have been though. I was so determined it should be Arthur Mawbray I practically conjured him up from nothing.' From a few fish scales on a cuff, a glimpse of pale hair in the dark. 'Then when I did conjure him up, he wouldn't oblige me by being a murderer.'

'What about his father?'

'That won't work either, will it? The main motive for killing the Old Man would have been avenging his son. I think Major Mawbray had at least a suspicion all along that the prodigal was still alive. That was why he didn't press the police to arrest the Old Man.'

We were near the turning that led to Major Mawbray's house. In half an hour or so we'd be back with the others. Goodness knows what they'd make of our crack-of-dawn departure together but I was past caring about that now.

'So,' he said, 'where does that leave us?'

'With a resumed inquest in less than forty-eight hours' time and Nathan living as an outlaw on the fells.'

'Um, Nathan.'

'Midge is quite convinced that he's taken himself out of the way because he knows something that would convict Dulcie. She thinks he'll come back once there's a verdict of suicide.'

'You didn't tell her your theory about the practical joke that went wrong?'

'No, I couldn't. I'm pretty sure she's in love with him.'

'Another one!' His sigh was exasperated, almost explosive. I couldn't take it as a compliment.

'Yes, another poor fool. And it is only another theory, after all. You remember how we discussed it when we were walking up to the waterfall?'

He nodded. It was difficult to think about the waterfall and everything that happened there and keep my voice level, but I tried hard. I remembered what he'd said in the train on our journey from Oxford about love being an illness, a madness.

'I should have asked you a question then, shouldn't I? After all, the four of you slept in the same barn. Nathan would have had to be gone quite a long time.'

'And your question?'

'You know very well. Was Nathan away for long enough to have tied the Old Man on the horse?'

'To the best of my knowledge, no.' But it had taken him some time to answer, several steps.

'Why was that so difficult?'

'We were all waking and sleeping. We'd go out at various times to ... answer calls of nature.'

'Alan went out for longer than that, didn't he? To meet Imogen.'

That was hardly a secret after all. He nodded.

'Would it be possible for Nathan to be out long enough and you and the others not notice?'

'In theory, I suppose so. But Nathan snores.' He said it so seriously that I almost laughed, wondering if I should warn Midge.

'Loudly?'

'Yes. There was a certain amount of ribaldry about it. We persuaded him to move his pallet further away from the rest of us.'

'Meaning he could have got out more easily without your noticing?'

'The reverse. Even sleeping further away, he was very audible. If you happened to wake up during the night, you'd be very conscious of Nathan still with you.'

'So you heard him snoring all night?'

'I can't say that. All I can say is that on the occasions when I was awake, I was very conscious of Nathan snoring.'

We'd got to the gate at the top of the drive by then. We paused, leaning on it.

'So that's another hypothesis of mine collapsed,' I said. 'You might have told me that back at the waterfall.'

'I did have other things on my mind.'

He smiled at me, looking so vulnerable suddenly that I touched his hand that was resting on the top bar of the gate. His hand grabbed mine, as fiercely as if I were pulling him out of the pool all over again, and his head came down on my shoulder.

'Nell, I'm so sorry.'

Then his head came up again, his hand released mine and we were walking down the track side by side. I was sorry too, but I wasn't sure whether for the same thing.

Chapter Twenty

The others hardly asked us any questions. For a party of talkative people it was amazing how quiet we'd become. Dulcie was owed something and I managed to get a moment on my own with her in the kitchen.

'We've seen Mr Morrisey. Arthur Mawbray was with him that night.'

There was no surprise or relief on her face. She just gave me her usual smile and nodded as if some minor problem had been sorted out. When I left the house I found Alan sitting on an old barrel in the yard, a panama hat tipped down over his eyes for shade. He looked tired and his face had gone pink from the sun. It turned out that he'd been waiting for me.

'Meredith said you might have something to tell me.'

That came as no surprise. The news was hardly my private property after all and he had a right to know if anyone did. He suggested we should go somewhere we could talk without being interrupted, so we went up the track to the barn field and found a shady place on a bank under some hawthorn trees. I guessed he might have been there before with Imogen.

'Your great uncle didn't kill anybody,' I said. 'Arthur Mawbray's alive and well.'

He listened, sucking on a grass stem, while I told him about young Mawbray and Dulcie.

'And he has an alibi for that night?'

'As solid as taking tea with the Queen at Balmoral. Probably more so, as far as people round here are concerned.'

He threw his grass stem away, pulled another one.

'Odd, isn't it? A fortnight ago if you'd told me the Old Man wasn't a murderer, I'd have felt as if every care I had in the world had been lifted from my shoulders.'

'And now?'

'What do you think? Have you decided what you're going to say at the inquest?'

He'd turned away from me when he said it, but the grass stem was trembling in his hand. Then he noticed the tremble and clenched his fist on it.

'Sooner or later the police will have to know that young Mawbray's alive – if they haven't guessed already,' I said. 'But I don't think that's relevant to the inquest.'

'No, it would only complicate matters and we don't want them complicated any more than they are already, do we?' Then more urgently, when I didn't answer at once, 'Well, do we?'

'No.'

'I'm afraid Imogen's got it into her head that you are trying to complicate things.'

'I know she has. I'm sorry.'

'I thought what we wanted was a verdict that he killed himself while the balance of his mind was disturbed. Then we can all go away and get on with our lives.'

'Yes.'

'Has Imogen told you that she and I had an argument over his money?'

'She said you thought you couldn't take it because it was tainted. What did you mean by that?'

'I'm not even sure. But I have this strong feeling that it would be cheating him. I didn't do anything to help him and he's left me a small fortune.'

'You came here. He wanted that. He'd almost certainly decided to kill himself while you were here. I think Imogen's right about that.'

'I really thought he'd killed the Mawbray fellow. Now we know he didn't, it's too late.'

'Wouldn't you be untainting the money if you did something good and useful with it?'

'I'm not sure I trust myself as much as I did.'

'If you turn it down, I suppose it will all go to Dulcie Berryman.'

'Let it. I don't care.'

'That wasn't the way you felt the day the

will was read. You seemed angry.'

'It caught me off balance, finding out all the things I hadn't been told. I really don't mind about Mrs Berryman. All I want is to get away from this nightmare as soon as I can and have a life with Imogen.'

'I'm sure that's what she wants too.'

'Then we must make sure she gets it. On Tuesday, you stick to the story about the Old Man trying to kill himself on the beach the day before...'

'He really did. I'm sure of that.'

'Yes, but the coroner might take some convincing. Still, you can be very persuasive when you want to be.'

'Thank you.'

He missed the sarcasm. 'And I can tell them how depressed he was about this Mafeking business, probably without bringing young Mawbray into it.'

'I'm not sure depressed is quite the word. Embattled, more like.'

'Nell, this is an inquest, not a *viva voce* for finals. I don't think we need to be too critical about the exact word.'

'What a waste, after all that Plato.'

This time he did notice the edge to my voice. His tone changed and he stretched out his hand to me on the grass, almost touching mine.

'All right, I know you hate the idea of it. So do I. For two pins I'd follow Nathan's example and do a bunk until it's all blown over.'

'You think that's all it is with Nathan?'

'I'm sure of it. He's a cheerful sort of creature, just not made for unpleasantness. Anyway, we can't do a bunk, you and I. All we can do is wait for Tuesday morning and put as good a front on it as we can.'

'Only I want to know,' I said. 'Yes, I'll play my part at the inquest if that's what's best for everybody. But I want to know what happened.'

'Perhaps there are simply some things we shouldn't know.'

'That's a new doctrine for us, isn't it? Weren't we all meant to be fearless seekers after truth? Away with lies and hypocrisy and pretending not to see things that don't suit us.'

'Of course. Nothing that's happened changes that.'

I was angry already and the way he said that, humouring me, made it worse.

'So nothing's changed? In spite of hiding things from each other and lying to each other?'

'Who's lied?'

'We all have, by implication at any rate. I'm as guilty of it as anybody.'

'I haven't lied.'

'Perhaps it's because nobody's asked you the right questions yet. Like what happened with you and Imogen on the night he died.'

He went red, 'Nell, you can't expect me to–'

'I'm not talking about that. There was something you heard or saw, the two of you. I asked Imogen and she was angry with me. Whatever it was, it was serious enough for you to leave her and let her walk back on her own – on that night of all nights.'

'You've got no right to ask.'

'Haven't I? If you're expecting me to help mislead an inquest, I think I've got every right to ask.'

'It's got nothing to do with what happened to the Old Man.'

'How do you know? Whatever happened to him happened in those few hours between sunset when Robin saw him with Sid in the paddock and just after sunrise when I was out and about. That's no more than six or seven hours and for some of that time you two were out here in the fields. Anything you saw or heard matters.'

He said nothing for a while then sighed. 'If I tell you, will you promise me that it goes no further?'

'If it's really got nothing to do with this, yes.'

'It hasn't, but it is embarrassing. To all three of us.'

'Three?'

'Imogen and me and Kit. You know that

Imogen and I had an arrangement to meet that night?'

'Yes.'

'We were sitting on the bank in this field, but further up under that maple there.'

I looked where he was pointing, to an old hedge maple with a knobbly trunk throwing a fan of shade over the field.

'That's not very far from where Robin last saw the Old Man, in the paddock just the other side of the track.'

'Nell, I told you, this is nothing to do with the Old Man. We didn't hear him or see him or even think about him. Do get that clear.'

'All right.'

'So Imogen and I were sitting under that maple in the moonlight – it was just a day after full moon – watching a hare in the field. And I remember thinking that I'd never felt as entirely happy as I did then, as if my whole life had been leading up to that moment, sitting there with the woman I loved, watching a hare in the moonlight. Can you understand that?'

'Yes.'

'The hare heard something first. She went bounding away and Imogen said maybe she'd smelled a fox and she thought she'd heard something moving in the hedge behind us. So we turned round to look and there was Kit, standing there on the other side of the hedge, quite still. The first thing

I saw was his white sling, then his face. I've never seen anything so ... so concentrated. I think he might have been watching us for a long time.'

'What did you do?'

'Jumped up and asked Kit what he thought he was doing. Then I pushed through to his side of the hedge and asked him again. He started talking Greek. Do you know that amazing passage from the *Symposium* where—'

'People cut in half and looking for their other half?'

'Yes. I kept telling him to go away, but he wouldn't. He started saying things, really wild things, that I didn't want Imogen to have to hear. I ... I suppose I made a grab for him, just wanting to stop him, and I got his hurt arm by mistake. He drew in his breath and said, "Go on. Do what you like. You can't hurt me any worse." Imogen was scared by then, begging us to stop, so I told her to go back to you and Midge and I'd deal with it. She didn't want to, but her being there only made things worse.'

'What happened after she left?'

'We ... we went on arguing. But I was afraid if I stayed I might hurt him again. So I just left him there and went back to the others in the barn.'

'Was Nathan snoring?'

'What?' He'd been staring out over the hay

meadow, as if still seeing the hare in the moonlight.

'When you got back to the barn, was Nathan snoring?'

'What's that got to do with anything? I suppose so. Nathan was always snoring.'

'When did you get back?'

'Some time after one o'clock, probably. I didn't look at my watch.'

We were both silent for a while. Alan had relaxed a little now the story was told but there was a feeling of sadness about him that I thought I understood. He and Kit had been friends from schooldays after all.

'Poor Kit,' I said. 'It must be awful to feel so jealous of somebody.'

'I suppose so.' But he said it off-handedly, like a man who'd never needed to feel jealous of anybody.

'He's obsessed with that passage about the bodies finding each other,' I said. 'He quoted it in the letter to Imogen as well.'

'What letter?' He was suddenly tense again and staring at me. 'What letter was that?'

Until that moment it hadn't occurred to me that Imogen wouldn't have told him about her letter from Kit. She'd shown it to me after all. I realised I'd blundered and accidentally betrayed a confidence. Still, I couldn't see why Alan was looking so thunderstruck. He was the man who'd won. I stammered out something about Kit writing Imogen a letter begging her to think again – but it hadn't impressed her and to forget I'd said anything.

'A love letter? Kit wrote Imogen a *love* letter?'

'A plea more than a love letter. I think he already knew he'd lost her. There's no harm done to you. I'm sorry I mentioned it.'

But the man who, just a couple of minutes ago, had sounded as if jealousy didn't exist for him, was looking like Othello presented with the handkerchief. He seemed beyond speech and just went on staring at me.

'I don't know why that's so surprising,' I said. 'Surely you knew how he felt about her.'

He just shook his head.

'It was obvious. You only had to look at his face when the two of you were together. You really didn't notice?'

Perhaps he and Imogen had been so absorbed in each other that he hadn't. I hoped he'd let the matter of the letter drop, but he went on worrying away at it.

'Did he give it to her? Post it to her?'

'If it matters, he just left it in her copy of the *Republic*.'

For some reason, it did seem to matter to him. 'What did he call her? Dear Imogen? My dearest? My darling?'

This was approaching the romantic-morbid. 'None of those. As far as I remember he just launched straight into it. And please don't go and quarrel with Imogen. I promise you she wasn't impressed by it. Horrified, more like.'

There was nothing else I could think of to put right my mistake, beyond admitting it to Imogen and warning her. It annoyed me, though, to have to add this little worry to the rest of them. Why in the world couldn't you love somebody and still be rational? Like, for instance … well, like a lot of people. People you could drink tarry tea with on a harbour wall and not think about Gretna Green and eloping Highland chieftains – except in jest of course.

I found Imogen in our loft. She'd folded her mattress in two and was sitting on it like a cushion with her back against the wall, reading.

'I've got something to confess,' I said.

She looked downright scared at that, so I explained my clumsiness over the letter. Considering that we'd managed to get ourselves on bad terms already, I expected her to be angry with me. She took it better than I expected.

'Should I have told him?'

'I don't know. It seemed to surprise him. Shock him, almost.'

'I suppose that's why I didn't tell him. I knew he'd be angry.'

'And they'd have had their argument earlier than they did.'

She let the book fall to the floor. 'Did Alan tell you about that?'

'Yes. I'd guessed something happened and you wouldn't tell me, so I asked him.'

Again I was expecting her to flare up, but she didn't. She seemed exhausted, the skin on her forehead pale to the point of transparency.

'I didn't want to talk about it – to you or anyone else. I felt so ... so ashamed for Kit, I suppose.'

'For loving you?'

'Guilty too. I know it isn't my fault, but I still felt guilty.'

I said I'd leave her to her reading and bent to pick the book up from the floor. Plato's *Republic* again. It had splayed open and I looked round for something to mark her place. The margins were crammed with sprawling pencilled notes.

'That's not your writing, is it?'

'No, it's Alan's. I lent my copy to Midge so he gave me his.'

I went down the stairs, my brain worrying away at what had happened that night. There had been four hours, probably less than that, between the time that Alan got back to the barn and I went out for my early morning swim, and at around one o'clock Nathan was still snoring – or rather, Alan supposed he was. But would Alan have noticed either way? That night he'd become Imogen's lover and quarrelled with his best friend, more than enough to drive a mundane matter like snoring out of his mind. The same applied to Kit after the quarrel. I supposed I should find him and ask him but that would mean admitting that I knew what had happened between them.

I walked away from the house, back up the track towards the barn field but kept on the outside of the hedge. Alan had gone from the place under the hawthorn bushes. I went on towards the maple tree and stood under its branches. The argument between Kit and Alan had happened there, after Alan had pushed through the hedge. Alan had actually struck him. 'Do what you like. You can't hurt me any worse.' I didn't know why I'd needed to come to the place where the words had been said but there was a terrible fascination about them, something humbling and terrifying about that naked need. No wonder Imogen had been horrified that this was happening because of her. The whole sex business simply wasn't fair. I thought about that, wandering a little way up the track. My feet scuffed dead and dry hazel leaves, un-expected in full summer until I remembered why they were there. There'd been so much else to think about that I'd forgotten finding the Old Man's carriage whip but it had been stuffed into the hedge, just a few steps up from where Alan and Kit had their argument. I stared at the hedge and the rabbit holes in the bank underneath it, feeling things moving round in my mind like uprooted trees in a hurricane. A letter. A book. *Oh my dear, the other and better half of me.*

I said to the hedge, 'Surely he must have known. He must have known all the time.'

The rabbit holes and the hedge still looked the same as a few seconds ago but the rest of the world had gone spinning round them and changed beyond recognition.

Chapter Twenty-one

I left the house, knowing it was for the last time, in the early hours of Monday morning while it was still dark. As I went down the stairs Midge woke up and asked sleepily where I was going. I didn't answer. I was sure Imogen was awake, but she said nothing. There was no moon but the sky was full of stars. This time there was nobody standing outside the house but I walked fast up the track to the road just in case. At the crossroads I headed away from the town and took the Caldbeck road, walking more slowly now I knew nobody was following me. I had hours of time, eight hours at least before the public houses would be open for hikers and farmworkers with midday thirsts. Or, in Nathan's case, a midday craving for tobacco. I'd been going over in my mind that evening when he ran away from us and dropped one of his precious tobacco tins. Nathan living as a wild man on the fells without company was almost unthinkable – without the sweet clouds from his pipe unthinkable altogether. In a numb way, I was pleased that my mind was still working well on details like that. In fact, it was working all too well, fitting things together, throwing up scenes from the past few months with the vividness of magic lantern slides on a white wall. The one that kept coming back was the evening of the play, the white moths in the candlelight, the two swans and the men with their eyes on Imogen. That and Meredith in the train corridor, looking out at the fells and wondering how we managed to convince ourselves that being in love was an enviable state.

When it was light enough I stopped, drank water from a little beck and looked at the map. The area of the fells where we'd seen Nathan was sparsely populated even by Cumberland standards, but I remembered a remote little inn at a crossroads a long way from anywhere else. I walked on, passed only by the occasional farm wagon, and long before midday I had it in sight. It was a white-painted house in a cluster of outbuildings. There were only two or three other houses in sight and it was hard to see where it would get its customers. Perhaps it had been built to serve cattle drovers and shepherds or even travelling tinkers. Today there was nobody, only a sheepdog sleeping in the sun, stretched out across the front door. I turned off the road before I came to the inn, climbed a little way up the hill and found a shady place to sit in the bracken where I could watch for people coming and going. As the sun rose higher the white walls shimmered in the heat haze and the dog got up, stretched itself and limped into the shade of an outhouse wall. A woman in an apron came out and brushed the step, then went in again. When the sun was directly overhead and flies were buzzing round the bracken, drunk with heat, two men who looked like farm labourers appeared on the road from the Caldbeck direction. I watched them from about half a mile off as they closed slowly on the inn, like snails to a lettuce leaf. They went inside. The dog got up, turned round, went back to sleep again. I was beginning to think I'd been wrong about Nathan. There was no point in going to look for him in the lonely fells behind me. It could take days to find him again and I didn't have days, less than one day now. A small cart drawn by a grey cob with half a dozen barrels on it came slowly along the road from the same direction as the two men and turned into the forecourt of the inn. The driver got down and a plump man who was probably the landlord came out from the porch. Together they started unloading the barrels while the cob stamped and twitched against the flies. I got up, brushed bracken off my skirt and walked down the slope to the inn yard. No question of going inside of course. Respectable women didn't do that and the landlord, whether I liked it or not, would rate me as respectable. I waited until the last barrel had been rolled into the porch and the driver was back on his seat turning the cart round before introducing myself.

'Good morning. I wonder if you happen to have seen a friend of mine.'

Until then the landlord had been intent on the barrels and hadn't seen me. He whirled round, looking alarmed at an alien voice and probably wondering where I'd sprung from. He relaxed a little when he saw my hiking boots and pack.

'You lost, miss?'

'No, but I was hoping to meet my friend here. Big tall man with a beard.'

His face cleared, he even laughed. 'Would that be the artist, miss?'

'Yes. Yes, I'm sure it would.'

'He usually comes in about now for a pipe and a pint. Look, there he is.'

He pointed up the slope. A battered panama hat, moving fast downhill, was just visible above the bracken. As it came lower I saw the red face beneath it and the familiar tangle of beard and sideburns. He was concentrating on where he was stepping, not looking at us. When he got clear of the bracken on to the open grass just above the inn I saw that his clothes were more than usually unkempt, one boot sole gaping so that a naked big toe was visible poking through a hole in his sock. But in spite of that there was as always something so amiable, so reassuring about the sight of Nathan that even now I had to fight a mad impulse to rush up the slope towards him and hug him like a brother.

'That your friend, miss?'

'Yes.'

He didn't see me until he came right down to the yard. When he did it looked for a moment as if he was going to flee straight back up the hill.

'Hello Nathan,' I said. 'Please don't run away again. I've got to talk to you.'

The landlord looked from Nathan to me and back again. I could see he was registering possible trouble, of the emotional kind.

'Bring your beer and tobacco out here if you like, sir. And a lemonade for the lady?'

There was a bench in the angle between the house and porch. Nathan sat down heavily on it, his legs stuck out in front of him, and sighed.

'How's Midge?'

'She's all right, or as all right as anybody can be in the circumstances. You know the inquest is tomorrow?'

He nodded. The landlord came out with a pint of beer, a glass of cloudy home-made lemonade and a stone tobacco jar. Nathan took his pipe out of his pocket and filled it, making the process last until the landlord had gone in.

'Of course, you knew that the day you went away,' I said. 'You decided you'd stay out here until the inquest was over and there was a suicide verdict. Was that your own idea or did somebody else suggest it?'

He took matches out of his pocket and went through the usual long pantomime of getting the tobacco to light. I was fuming long before the pipe was.

'Nathan, I'm not going to the police with this. I've already worked out most of what happened but I need to know for sure. It's nothing to do with the inquest. It's for us – all of us.'

Clouds of blue smoke wafted round us. It didn't smell as sweet as Nathan's usual tobacco, but at least it kept the flies away.

'I've been hoping against hope that all this had nothing to do with us,' I said. 'I was so sure that it was young Mawbray, or his father, or Dulcie even. We were the innocent ones, the unlucky ones who just happened to be here. Only that's not true and you've known it for a lot longer than I have.'

He moved his big paw of a hand, wafting some of the smoke away from us, trying to waft a lot of other things as well.

'All of you've known, you four men. There I was, thinking you were all together in the barn the night the Old Man died but that just wasn't true. Alan was out with Imogen and Kit was out quarrelling with Alan. You knew that.'

He looked at me through the two veils of beard and smoke, eyes big and pleading.

'Nell, this isn't going to do anybody any good. Just leave it while you can.'

'I can't leave it. Imogen's in love with Alan. She wants to spend the rest of her life with him. She's my friend. Can I just stand back and let it happen while there's any doubt at all?'

His eyes turned pained and troubled. He looked away from me.

'Nell, I can promise you it wasn't Alan. Can we leave it at that now?'

'No. I wish we could, but we can't.'

'Don't you believe me?'

'At the moment I don't believe anybody. That night, Alan went out to meet Imogen.'

'A lady's reputation–'

'Bother a lady's reputation. Midge and I were in the same room with her. We know she went out and I know she and Alan met. She was back with us around one o'clock and by then Alan and Kit had met and quarrelled very badly. What time did the two of them get back?'

'I'm not sure. I was asleep.'

'I don't think you were. I don't think any of you slept much. You must have had an idea what was happening between Kit and

Alan. So when did Alan get back?'

'Around one o'clock.'

'Did he say anything?'

He looked at me pleadingly. I'd have given almost anything to do what he wanted – to say 'Don't worry, it isn't important. Drink your beer and smoke your pipe and be the Nathan we all know and love.' Instead I just kept looking at him and he shook his head, like a tired horse trying to get rid of a fly that's sucking its blood.

'Not to me. He and Meredith were talking. My bed was a bit away from the others because of–'

'Your snoring. Yes I know. Alan thought you were snoring when he came in.'

'I was pretending. I didn't want to hear what they were saying. I knew ... I knew this thing with Alan and Kit was coming to a head. I just didn't want to know about it. And none of us wanted you or Midge or Imogen to know.'

'Very protective of you. So Alan got back to the barn about one o'clock?'

'Yes, and he stayed there for the rest of the night. Nell, I promise you you don't have to worry about Imogen. She's not marrying a...'

'A murderer?'

He nodded.

'And Kit? What time did Kit get back?'

'Nell, how could Kit have done it? He can

403

only use one arm remember, and he's scared of horses. He wasn't pretending. He can hardly go near the beasts.'

'I know. We all know. So what time did Kit get back?'

'Later. A lot later. He didn't come in. He just called from outside the barn.'

'Called what? What did he call?'

Nathan clapped his head between his big paws like a hurt animal at bay.

'It was a name, wasn't it? He was calling somebody.' He looked at me, hands still over his ears. I mouthed the name at him. Then he closed his eyes, but not before I'd seen my answer in them.

Chapter Twenty-two

The coroner had a bald head and a little snub nose that gave him an oddly cheerful air, in spite of the dark suit and serious expression. When a police officer had shown me into the witnesses' waiting room he'd reassured me, 'Don't you worry, miss. Our coroner's a kindly man.' He was right, because when it was my turn to give evidence he'd made it as easy for me as a conscientious man could do, putting his questions in an unaggressive way, assuring me several times that he knew how difficult this must be for me. Now he was summing up in a calm, almost monotonous voice for the benefit of the jury – ten respectable tradesman types almost melting from the heat in their best suits.

'You have heard from Dr Morris that the immediate cause of Mr Beston's death was a blow to the back of the head, fracturing the skull. It is his opinion that the injury could have been caused by sharp contact with a branch or post. He considers it possible, though less likely, that it might have been caused if the deceased had struck his head on hard earth. There is evidence of broken ribs and damage to the deceased's internal organs, strongly suggesting that a horse might have rolled on him. You have also heard from the doctor that Mr Beston had been suffering for some time from a heart weakness which might have proved fatal at any time, although that was not the cause of his death.'

After I'd given my evidence I'd been shown to a seat at the end of the front row. Alan had given evidence before me and was sitting at the other end of the row. Glancing over my shoulder among a mostly male audience I saw Midge, Imogen and Meredith sitting together eyes fixed on the coroner.

'You have heard from his great nephew, Alan Beston, that Mr Beston had seemed anxious and nervous in the days preceding his death, because of real or imagined hostility from some of his neighbours owing to certain of his political opinions. I must emphasise very strongly to you that it is not your duty to determine whether the hostility was real or imagined or to pass judgment on events which might have led to it. The only question we are concerned with is whether the belief that it existed affected Mr Beston's mental state.'

From the far end of the row Alan caught my eye and gave a little grimace that might have been apologetic. He'd been furious with me when we met on the pavement outside the coroner's court about ten minutes before the inquest was due to start.

'Nell, where in the world have you been? We've been desperate about you.'

'Desperate about me, or desperate in case I wasn't here to give evidence?'

He'd looked at me as if I'd slapped him, but I was in no mood to reassure him. All the time I'd been giving evidence I'd been aware of his eyes on me, willing me to say what he wanted. I said it, but not for his sake.

'You also heard from Miss Bray, a house-guest of Mr Beston in the days before his death. She is of the firm opinion that she witnessed an attempt made by Mr Beston to take his own life by throwing himself off a galloping horse the day before he died. She also told us of his devotion to what you may regard as a somewhat barbarous piece of literature about a man who was sentenced to death by being tied to the back of a wild horse.

A grunt of agreement from one of the jurors to that. There'd been a palpable wave of shock in the room when I told the jury about *Mazeppa*. Some of them, I could tell, felt that it wasn't the kind of thing a well-brought-up young woman should be talking about.

'Miss Bray, as it happens, also had the

407

misfortune to be the person who discovered Mr Beston dead. I know you will want me to offer her your sympathy for what must have been a most distressing experience for a young woman, and the courage and self-possession she has shown in giving her evidence.'

Both the jury and audience gave a murmur of agreement. I'd gone down well, I knew that. Lots of training from childhood in amateur theatricals. I hated myself.

'She has told you that Mr Beston's hands and feet were bound to a strap round the horse's neck and to the stirrups. Whether Mr Beston could have done that himself, whether it could have been done by some other person or whether it could have been the result of some grotesque accident are questions which the police have found it impossible to resolve. Miss Bray was naturally too distressed to be expected to make observations of that kind...'

(He'd assumed that, luckily, and not asked me direct questions.)

'...and the rest of his household, also quite naturally, would be concerned to get him off the horse, to the exclusion of other considerations.'

I looked at Alan. He was nodding his head, a few nods too many, at a danger point almost passed.

'You have heard Mr Alan Beston's opinion

that his great uncle was a man of considerable determination and force of character in spite of his age. You may ask yourselves, if he were determined to take his own life, whether he might have chosen to do it in such an unusual and one may say...'

(You could tell he wanted to use the word 'grotesque' again, but was hesitating out of consideration for our feelings.)

'...such a flamboyant way. I will sum up. If you consider that the medical evidence, combined with the evidence you have heard on Mr Beston's state of mind, point to the conclusion that the deceased took his own life, then your verdict must be suicide. If you form that opinion and also think that he was not capable at the time of taking a considered judgment of what he was about to do, you may add "while the balance of his mind was disturbed".'

A couple of jurors nodded at that. Most of the neighbourhood thought the Old Man was mad in any case.

'The other verdicts available to you are that he died as a result of an accident, that he was unlawfully killed or that there is not enough evidence to show how he died. Given there is evidence that Mr Beston was actually tied on to the horse, it would be difficult if not impossible to envisage circumstances in which this might have happened accidentally. As for unlawful killing, no evidence has been brought before this court which would lead to that conclusion. You may be aware of reports that Mr Beston had made enemies in recent months but you must put those out of your minds. Even if the reports are true, they are not in themselves enough to lead to such a verdict. If in spite of all you have heard you feel you cannot come to any conclusion then you must bring in an open verdict, but I would suggest that you don't resort to that without a very thorough discussion of the alternatives. Now gentlemen, have you any questions before you retire to consider your verdict?'

They hadn't. As they walked out a buzz of talking started and Imogen swooped down beside me. She looked terrified.

'Nell, where were you last night?'

'The temperance hotel by the cattle market.'

It was a grim place, with beds as thin and hard as ship's biscuits. They'd been reluctant to take me in – a woman travelling on her own – but they couldn't pretend not to have rooms free and I'd scraped together the few shillings needed.

'Something else has happened. This morning. It's–'

Midge came pushing past people and caught her by the arm. 'Not now. Not in here. Afterwards.'

Midge was nearly in as bad a state as Imogen. Her eyes were puffy, the hand on Imogen's arm was trembling.

'What's happened now?'

Midge gave me a look, begging me not to ask. I saw Alan was walking towards us. Whatever else had happened, it looked as if he hadn't been told about it because the two of them went quiet.

I said to Midge, to try and calm her, 'Nathan's all right. He sends you his very best wishes and hopes he'll be seeing you soon.'

He'd sent more than best wishes. He'd been practically incoherent with concern for her when we parted in the yard of the inn, I making for the town, he for what he hoped would be his last night out on the fells. 'Look after her, Nell. Tell her I hated leaving her. Tell her ... oh, you know what I want to tell her.'

A few days ago this would have delighted Midge but now she just nodded, biting her lip. Alan had drawn Imogen aside and was talking to her. Meredith hadn't left his seat and was sitting several rows back, head down, an island of silence in a roomful of chattering people.

'I'm going to get Imogen outside, Nell. She needs air.'

Midge grabbed her by the elbow and practically dragged her outside, leaving Alan open-mouthed.

'What's happening, Nell?'

I didn't know, but there'd been so much kept from me that I hardly cared about this latest example of it. He saw from my expression that he wasn't going to get an answer and went back to his seat. Midge and Imogen came back to their seats just before the jury filed in. They were clinging together and crying. A murmur of sympathy went round the room, dying away as the coroner took his place. He asked the foreman if the jury had reached their verdict.

'Suicide while the balance of his mind was disturbed.'

Outside the sun was shining, a cart of vegetables was grinding past, and people were coming and going with shopping baskets. I was one of the first out because of sitting at the end of a row and started walking away, not caring where I was going.

'Nell.'

Running footsteps behind me, people turning to look.

'Nell, Miss Bray, please wait.'

Meredith. He must have pushed past everybody to get out so quickly. He looked desperate enough for anything, hatless with tie and hair flying. I waited, in the middle of a square by some statue or fountain, I don't remember what. He caught up with me and stood, trying to get his breath.

'You knew all the time,' I said. 'He came to you for help.'

'Yes. There's something you should–'

'And you did help him. You remembered what I'd told you about *Mazeppa* and helped tie his body on the horse.'

'Yes. But you've got to know–'

'And it's all right now. You've got a suicide verdict so the police will lose interest and he can just go away and get on with–'

'No!'

Then somebody behind us shouted, 'Meredith' and Alan came rushing across the cobbles, weaving around strollers and shoppers. He practically barged into us.

'Meredith, what's happened? Imogen can't tell me. She's practically collapsed. What is it?'

Meredith looked at Alan then at me, his eyes more miserable than anything I've ever seen.

'Kit's shot himself.'

Chapter Twenty-three

Imogen, Midge and I found ourselves stowed in the small parlour of a commercial travellers' hotel while Meredith and Alan went to report another death to the police. I don't remember how we got there. I had no more to do with it than a portmanteau or carpet bag has to do with where it's put. All I remember are armchairs in red plush, an aspidistra in a bronze bowl with dragons writhing round it and a marble-framed clock on the mantelpiece ticking out the minutes with a noise like a hammer hitting tin tacks. A tray of tea was brought in.

Imogen said, 'Did Kit kill him, Nell?'

'Yes.'

'Did Alan know?'

'You'll have to ask him.'

Maybe he'd be able to explain, and she understand, how you can both know and not know something at the same time if you try hard enough. The tea got cold. Alan and Meredith came back, faces still blank with shock. We got ourselves to the public house yard where the wagonette was waiting. Meredith stood at Bobbin's head and held the reins while Midge, Imogen and Alan got in. Imogen and Alan were holding hands so tightly that I wondered whether they'd ever get their fingers unlocked. Meredith looked at me, waiting for me to climb in too. I shook my head.

'Where are you going then?'

'Anywhere.'

'Wait for me here. Let me explain.'

'I know what happened. I've known since yesterday. Not quite as long as you have of course.'

'Nell, please wait. Give me a few hours at least.'

I said nothing. He looked at me, then swung himself into the driving seat and they went.

I'd made no promise. I could have gone to the station and taken the next train to Carlisle, then southwards, but I didn't even have the energy to make that decision. It was market day. I left my pack somewhere or other and strolled among the stalls, trugs of eggs pillowed on straw, zinc buckets, rope halters and scrubbing brushes, a willow basket full of greengages with a silver bloom on them like a dusting of frost. By late afternoon most of the things had been sold and the stallholders were folding their tablecloths and sunshades and loading what was left into handcarts and pony carts. I was staring at a coop of black-feathered hens, listening to the owner and a customer trying to strike a last-minute bargain over them, when I felt his presence behind me. He didn't have to touch me or say anything. I knew he was there.

'Thank you for waiting.'

I didn't say I hadn't intended to, because I knew now that I had. In my wanderings I'd found a little park not far from the market square, shaded with horse chestnuts so we headed there. At this time of the afternoon, with most people going home for tea, we had it to ourselves.

'Why did he do it? He must have known we'd have got a suicide verdict on the Old Man in a few hours – just as you planned it.'

We were walking side by side under the shade of the trees.

If anybody had been watching they might have thought it a nice place and time of day for sweethearts.

'I think that was why.' His voice was tired, less confident than I'd ever heard it. 'I think in his heart he hadn't expected to get away with it. This morning it finally occurred to him that he might – and he knew he didn't want to.'

'Justice?'

He shook his head. It looked like helplessness rather than denial.

'What happened?'

'Alan decided this morning that he

wanted to walk part of the way into town, to steady his nerves before giving evidence. He was worried because he thought you wouldn't be there. So we arranged that he should go on ahead and we'd follow in the wagonette and pick him up. We'd already decided that Kit wouldn't come with us. We all went out to wave Alan off and Kit said goodbye to him and thanked him.'

'As if he intended–'

'No. No indication at all. So Alan went and the rest of us started getting ready. I was in the parlour when I heard the sound of a shotgun. It sounded as if it came from the stable yard. I went running through and Robin joined me. We found him in the yard by the water trough, with the Old Man's shot gun beside him. He'd left a note in the tack room, pinned up under that picture of the horses.'

'What did it say?'

'It was in Greek, about the Eumenides, the avengers. Then one in English addressed to the coroner saying he was of sound mind and he intended to kill himself. Nothing more.'

'So all your efforts were wasted?'

'Yes.'

If he'd wanted, he could use words to defend himself more expertly than anybody I knew. He didn't even try. If anything, it made me even more angry.

'Even the lengths you went to to deceive me. I suppose that was a great intellectual diversion for you, watching me get things wrong, encouraging me to chase down all those blind alleys.'

'No. Not that.'

'Did you and Kit laugh about it together?'

'No!' He was angry now. 'That was the last thing we'd have done.'

'Just another nice little intellectual experiment for you, then. What did you learn from this one?'

For a few paces he didn't say anything but he must have come to a decision, because he started talking.

'It wasn't an experiment. Perhaps at the very start of it I saw myself as an observer, perhaps a guide even. If that was arrogance, I've been well punished for it.'

'A guide for all of us?'

'Mostly for Kit and Alan.'

'So you knew?'

'I knew they had a deep friendship. I delighted in it. It was something Plato would have understood – two talented and clear-minded young men, with such a lot to contribute to the world. I thought they'd do great things, both of them. Particularly Kit. I've never in my life had a better pupil and I shan't now.'

'You loved Kit?'

'Yes. More than he ever guessed, thank the

418

gods. I wanted, quite fiercely, to protect him from what I guessed was going to happen. I knew what he felt about Alan and that Alan simply didn't feel the same way. Best friend, old school friend – that's what it was for Alan.'

'So you came with us to protect Kit from Imogen?'

'Yes, I suppose in all honesty that was what it amounted to. I was worried back in Oxford when Alan informed me he was going to invite you all to go away together. I knew he was very much attracted to Imogen. Kit was obviously in for a bad few weeks and I thought I should be there to try to prevent him from doing something regrettable.'

'Only regrettable?'

'Nell, I'm talking to you the way I'd talk to no other woman, probably no other man either. If Kit ... if he had made a fool of himself somehow and gossip got around it would have stuck to him for the rest of his life. He'd probably have had to leave Oxford and all that intelligence and promise would have turned to bitterness and cynicism or worse. I thought at least if I were here for him to talk to – to rave like a fool if he wanted to without anybody else knowing – it would all be over safely in the end. He could leave the bitterness here, somewhere he'd never set foot again, even never speak to me again if he wanted to forget it altogether and get on with the rest of his life.'

We'd reached the end of the path. We turned, walked back. I didn't feel angry any more, just loaded down with his regret and weariness.

'But it didn't work.'

'No. There were forces I simply hadn't given enough weight to.'

'Like Imogen falling in love with Alan?'

'Yes. I simply hadn't allowed for her being so...'

'Passionate? You know it was the Old Man who brought that to a head – firing at them?'

'Yes. He was a force of nature, wasn't he? I hadn't allowed for that either.'

'I can see now that it drove Kit practically mad. He told you about that love letter?'

'Yes.'

'Once I'd realised that it was meant for Alan, not Imogen, I began to see what might have happened. Then the horsewhip...'

'Yes. The Old Man must have been mad too, that night.'

'Or very angry.'

'It comes to much the same thing. As far as he was concerned, Kit had just been blaspheming the god he worshipped.'

'God?'

'Fertility. The Old Man knew he hadn't got long to live. He didn't care about that but there were two things he hoped would survive of him – the baby Mrs Berryman was carrying and his own bloodline in Alan. In his heart he must have had doubts about the baby, so the Alan bloodline mattered more. Then he overheard what poor Kit was saying to Alan. You guessed that?'

'Yes.'

'Alan left Kit standing there, practically ran away from him, Kit says. Then the Old Man appeared suddenly out of the hedge and started raving at Kit, calling him an offence against nature and – well, you can imagine the rest perhaps. Then he started laying about Kit with the horsewhip he was carrying. Kit says he tried not to retaliate at first but the whip got him on his hurt arm. He pushed the Old Man. He fell and cracked his head against the tree.'

'Then it was an accident. Manslaughter at worst.'

Meredith shook his head. 'Kit was always intellectually honest. He said in that moment he wanted him to be dead. I suppose he was a symbol of all the hurt and loss.'

'And Kit ran to the barn and called to you to help.'

'Yes, and that's where I'm most to blame. If I'd told Kit there and then that he must go and confess, he'd have done it. But I thought I was the cool-headed one. I should have stopped you all being there at all, so it was my responsibility. Why should a few

421

seconds of grief and anger ruin his whole life? The Old Man had wanted to die after all.'

'If it happened the way he told you, couldn't he have admitted it and pleaded self-defence?'

'So he goes to the police and pleads self-defence. How does he explain why the Old Man's out there in the dead of night, horse-whipping him?'

We took a few more steps. 'I see.'

'Yes. Even at best, he'd have had to give evidence to an inquest. If the reason for the quarrel came out, any chance that Kit might have had of doing anything in the world would have been destroyed. The same would probably have applied to Alan. Could I let their lives go to waste like that without trying to do something?'

'So that justifies everything?'

'I'm not claiming it justifies anything. I'm just trying to make you understand what I was thinking, out there in the dark with a dead body, a young man too shocked to think for himself and only a couple of hours until daylight.'

We walked on in silence for a while. Two wood pigeons pecking in the dust flew up with a clattering of wings.

'If you're thinking it all sounds cold and rational,' he said, 'I can promise you that wasn't how it felt there and then, getting the horse to stand still, practically hypnotising Kit into helping.'

'He couldn't have been much help.'

'He wasn't much. That was one of the reasons I did it that way. Everybody knew Kit was scared of horses. With that and only one useful arm, he'd be the last suspect even if the police were suspicious.'

'What would you have done if anybody else had been accused of killing him?'

'Told the police. There wouldn't have been a moment's doubt about it for either of us. But I believed it wouldn't come to that.'

My mind was making a lot of connections, all of them bitter ones.

'That's why you came with me to Maryport, isn't it, to make sure that Arthur Mawbray's alibi was a good one?'

'Partly that, yes.'

'And that's why you persuaded Nathan to go away until the inquest was over. He'd heard Kit calling to you.'

'No, I didn't persuade him. It was his own decision to go away but...'

He stopped walking and looked at me. I stopped too.

'But what?' Then, as it struck me, 'Oh no.'

'I'm afraid so. I'm sorry.'

'You didn't fall into that waterfall – you jumped. I was nearly catching up with Nathan and you wanted to distract me because you knew I'd get him to tell me.'

He nodded and put out a hand to me. I turned and started walking fast away from him to the other side of the park, practically running. I turned at the wall and there he was behind me.

'Nell, Miss Bray ... please listen.'

'And what about the rest of it as well? Was that just to distract me? Another heroic sacrifice for Kit and Alan?'

He shook his head. He was crying openly, tears running down his face. 'If I've made you think that, then I've done even more harm than I've imagined. Please, if you never believe anything else I say, believe that's not true.'

'How can I?'

I think by then I was crying too, turning away from him and trying to hide it. His hand came round my wrist as urgently as if I were the one in danger of drowning this time.

'Look at me. Listen. Some of this has been wanting to know how much you were finding out. But that's only part of it. As soon as we talked in the train, I felt there was a kind of courage and certainty about you that I respected. More than respected, wanted. And the more we were together ... I'm not saying love because I'm not sure what people mean by it...'

'Nor am I.'

'Liking, respecting, believe that at least.

And wanting. Will you believe that?'

I think I must have nodded because the grip on my wrist relaxed enough for our hands to slide together, palm to palm.

'Thank you. Oh, thank you.' It was more of a groan from him than words.

After a while I asked him what he was going to do now.

'I must go back. The police will be there again. Or did you mean in the longer term?'

'No.'

'I shan't go back to Oxford. I'm exiling myself.'

'I'll go back, I think.'

'Yes.' The grip on my hand turned urgent again. 'Nell, do something with your life, you hear me? Whatever happens, don't let this wreck you. Do something.'

I told him yes, I heard. The light was getting low and golden and even if I couldn't get far away that evening I wanted to make Carlisle at least. I disentangled my fingers from his and turned away.

'Nell.'

I'd only taken a few steps.

'Nell, there's something you should know. Something silly perhaps. You remember that morning on the harbour at Maryport?'

Tar-tasting tea and a cat taking bits of warm crab from our fingers. I nodded.

'The old fisherman joked about were we eloping and you quoted the ballad?'

425

'I remember.'

'For a moment I wished – more than wished, I suddenly quite desperately wanted – to be doing just that. To be getting into a boat and sailing away with you. Absurd, but I wanted to tell you.'

'Absurd, yes. But thank you anyway.'

I think, I hope, I might even have managed to smile at him. Then I turned away and kept on walking.

Epilogue

I'd have tried to do something with my life in any case. Whatever I've done, it wasn't because of what he said or did. If anything influenced me from that summer it was what the Old Man said, not Meredith.

As for Kit, the verdict was suicide. In spite of what he'd written in his note to the coroner, the jury again insisted on padding the hard fact with 'whilst the balance of his mind was disturbed'. I wasn't there at the inquest and heard about it afterwards from Alan. Meredith had to give evidence and whatever he was feeling at the time he must have been as convincing as usual. A brilliant student, he said, probably the most brilliant he'd ever taught. The implication that brilliance may tip over into temporary madness probably wasn't lost on the jury. He hinted, delicately, at an unhappy love affair, pointed out that Kit had been in great pain from an arm injury and had naturally been distressed at the death of his host just eleven days before he took his own life.

After that, Meredith disappeared. He kept to his decision, resigned his fellowship and didn't go back to Oxford. It caused some comment in the first few weeks of the new term but not a lot of surprise. Meredith had always been regarded as a wild man and university affairs jogged on much more smoothly without him. Later – many years later after a lot of things had happened – I met him again unexpectedly and heard what he'd been doing, but that doesn't belong with this story.

The rest of us, Alan, Nathan, Imogen, Midge and I, went back to our colleges in October and although some rumours must have circulated the policy seemed to be the less said, the better. Cumberland was a long way from Oxford, after all, and it had been such an unusually hot bright summer that – once the autumn mists had set in – it all seemed as far away as an ancient Greek myth. So we were allowed to stay and take our final exams. Midge and I managed to persuade Imogen not to give up her course to marry Alan at once. I think, secretly, she was more ready to listen to us than she admitted at first. We all needed time to recover. As it happened, the three of us did as well or better than Alan and a lot better than Nathan, who scraped a cheerful third. Alan and Nathan took their degrees. Women weren't allowed to, of course, but at the time it worried us less than it should have done.

Imogen and Alan married in his college chapel two weeks after their finals. By then he'd been persuaded to accept the Old Man's money so that they could set up their experimental school together. It went well. If you're interested in advanced theories of education, you'll have heard of it and probably read their book. But we lost touch, Imogen and I. Things were never the same between us again.

Midge and Nathan, on the other hand, are in touch all the time. I am honorary aunt to their children. So far the tally is three, plus two influential books on mathematics by Midge and a large number of beautiful and rather expensive pieces of furniture by Nathan.

After a while, when some of the rawness had worn off, I was curious enough to get news from Cumberland and found that Arthur Mawbray and Dulcie Berryman had got married and moved to Maryport with the baby. She was at least ten years older than he was and what with that and her reputation his father disowned him, but that didn't matter because he had what he wanted at last. They used the interest from the Old Man's money to buy Arthur his own fishing boat and named it *The Prodigal Son*. I'm sure the name's considered highly appropriate at the methodist chapel where, I'm told, Mr and Mrs Arthur Mawbray and their four children are now frequent attenders.

What the Old Man would have thought of that I can't imagine. But he should have been pleased by a generous act on the part of his great nephew. Alan went to the solicitor and had Sid, Bobbin, all the mares and the two Afghan hounds made over to Robin, properly done by a deed of gift with a red seal so that nobody could accuse the Gypsy boy of stealing them. Robin sold the mares – probably for a very good price – but kept Sid at stud. I'm told that in Cumberland they still speak of Sid's prowess as a stallion with great respect, and his progeny are galloping over green fields, winning awards and carrying on the bloodline all over the north of England and across in Ireland as far down as County Cork. If he'd wanted a memorial, I'm sure that would have pleased the Old Man more than anything.

This Large Print Book, for people
who cannot read normal print,
is published under the auspices of

THE ULVERSCROFT FOUNDATION